Killing
The Girl

Elizabeth Hill

ISBN: 978-1-0931-2373-9

Acknowledgements

A novel is rarely written in isolation, and there are many people to thank for their support.

Lisa Hofmann, Trudi Clarke and Liz Hedgecock, the 'first' readers who pointed out the anomalies and helped shape the early drafts.

My family and friends for their support, especially Lee Beal and Christine Stephenson, and also all those whose encouragement was invaluable and are too many to name.

Please find details of my work on my website:

wickedwritersite.wordpress.com

Part 1

Prologue

Perry Cutler and I buried Frankie Dewberry in the orchard. He lies close to the garden wall, under the shade of the apple trees. Over the last forty-odd years, I've spent many hours sitting on the wooden bench we placed next to his grave. It's a peaceful spot near the boundary wall running to the south-west of my estate. Sitting near him comforts me. I tell Frankie how restricted my life has been since his death. I tell him how sorry I am that our daughter, Francine, died so young. Although I loved him, I never tell him I'm sorry he's dead.

Outside my study window, the trees and bushes sway stiffly in the winter breeze; their shifting branches stripped bare in the cold air. January is my least favourite month, with its grey, joyless days and cruelty towards my garden.

On my desk, my notebook lies waiting for my reluctant attention. The sick feeling I've had this last month stirs as I touch it. It lists the many tasks I have to complete; inventories to write and documents to sign. Chilly air surrounds me as Frankie's spirit enters the room. Shivering in his ghostly presence, I reread the newspaper article. My house is to be demolished to make way for a ring road. They will find Frankie's resting place when they cut into the soil protecting my lover, my darling man. Police will ask questions. Strangers, who know nothing about me or my

1

pain, will look at me in disgust.

After they have finished with his skeleton, we can arrange his funeral so they can lay him to rest in consecrated ground. We will say prayers and sanction his long-awaited trip to heaven, although when I killed him, I was sure that he went straight to hell.

Chapter 1

Now - January

There's not been a schedule requiring my strict adherence since the birth of Francine and motherhood duties. Now the number of things to do enabling me to leave my home overwhelms me. Doing nothing is preferable. No one will die if I stay in bed and read; inactivity tempers the crushing sensation that my life is out of my control. But dread edges closer, carrying with it the knowledge that I have to act, do, process, move. Those verbs build into a crescendo, threatening to stifle me. I pull the sheets over my head and, to distract myself, ponder that I hate verbs. But now my feet itch with frustration at my inability to step up to the tasks required to secure my future, and I should get out of bed to calm them.

I'm moving into Perry's house until a new replica of my home, Oaktree House, is built using many of the bricks, tiles, fixtures and fittings of the original. We will be kind to the environment as we churn up the green belt and replace it with tarmac. We will build my new home on the other side of Perry's farmhouse, in one of my fields. There will be a house, a copse and an orchard in the new setting. It will be exactly the same. But Frankie will not be resting close by. I will miss him. It will be the first time we have been apart in over forty years.

They leave my post in a letterbox next to the locked gate at the end of the lane adjoining the main road. This is where the new road will carve through my land as it progresses along its destructive route. Leaving my home once a day to collect it is a must, as failure to collect it will cause alarm to the post-person, who may call the police. A police presence upon the land concealing my dead boyfriend is not conducive to a quiet life. That thought spurs me on as I shower, dress and eat breakfast.

Wearing my heavy coat and wellington boots, I hesitate on the threshold. One day, I chide myself, I will leave the confines of my home without giving it a second thought. Gathering my nerves, I step out as though into the unknown, instead of into an area secured by walls and locked gates. The twelve-bore and air rifle sit in the hallway cupboard. On days when I need extra support, I rest one of them over my arm. Why an empty gun that I've no intention of using calms me defies explanation; I suppose the weight comforts, and the menace any trespasser might imagine when confronted, boosts my confidence. There's no intention to kill anyone else. I'm not a killer. I'm someone who makes bad choices.

In front of me, in a circle of grass, is a magnificent oak tree. It has a twin growing behind the house, in Dawnview Wood, on the path leading down the hillside to the rabbit warren of council streets below. That other tree has distressing memories surrounding each branch and leaf. Guilt and damnation ooze from its core like poison gas. That tree will remain untouched by the coming destruction–an act of God, or whoever decides I need reminding of the frailty of human nature. It will remain to symbolise what happens when you mistakenly place faith and trust in the wrong person. My new house will be further away from it, so that is some consolation.

My driveway is large and circles the tree. Making my way across it, I try not to think about a time when all this will disappear, but to, as one of my counsellors puts it, 'live in the moment as it is now, not the future, nor the past'. Nevertheless, I cannot shut out the imagined noise of future traffic screeching along. Or the disturbance to nesting birds and scurrying voles, field mice, foxes and arguing magpies as they live, die, and kill, unaware that their time is running out. There's a wish on my breath for strength as I suck the atmosphere in and commit it to memory. More sadness to add to the depressiveness of life. Reaching the lane, I hang on to a fence post and breathe and count and breathe and count.

The lane runs through a wooded area that conceals my house from the road. No one can come along here, as the gate by the road is padlocked, except Perry. Perry has keys to every lock on my estate and in my home. Not that he would enter my home, but he has them anyway. He will only venture into the orangery adjoining the kitchen. There's a reason he won't. I shall explain in my confession.

There's time for me to write down the reasons why I became a killer, and it's better to do so and be judged on the truth than be unable to explain my actions under the duress of police questioning. Perry will be horrified if he knew I was doing this, even though it will help us.

My fingers press my forehead above my left eye, and I worry at an imagined dent in my skull. Aged seven, I knocked myself unconscious when falling from the gate between Dawnview Field and Dawnview Lane. Thoughts of Perry always incite this automatic response of fingers to my forehead, as the injury happened the day I first met him.

My father had died suddenly from a heart attack, leaving me distraught. The sense of loss was so overpowering that I feared to leave my bed. My mum was losing patience with repeatedly assuring me he was safe in heaven. Two weeks later a storm raged, rousing me from my bed to watch as lightning sparked above the hills behind our council house. The hills that are now my home. I realised as I watched that the lightning was showing me a path to heaven, a path leading to my dad. If I ran as fast as I could, I would find him, and he would kiss and reassure me, and maybe let me stay with him.

Leaving my bed in the middle of the night, I'd run the gauntlet of rain and wind to take myself up above the city, to the top of the world. Climbing the gate leading to Dawnview Lane, I'd balanced on the slippery rails. For a moment time seemed to stop, the wind calmed, and the icy rain no longer cooled my body.

Then gravity won and zapped me like a puppet, slapping me down onto the gritty edge of the lane.

Waking, I'd stumbled on, concussion interfering with my consciousness. Up ahead, the cows were making their way to milking. Wavering amongst them, they greeted me; their swollen sides brushed my hands, their snorts deafened, and their size engulfed. They filed past, surrounding me with heat and the smell of grass and earth. Joyfully I shouted into the heaving mass, 'Daddy, I'm here.'

The strong arms of Perry's father, Mr Cutler, saved me from being crushed to death. He took me to Cleave Farm, where Mrs Cutler put me to bed in their dead son's bedroom. As my world shifted in and out of focus, Perry came into the room. An unsettling awareness of fear came with him. There was no reason for my skin to prickle cold under the blanket that had once covered Perry's dead brother Simon. Perry didn't touch me or abuse me or shout at me. But something about the way he watched me as I lay helpless and alone in that bed stirred anxiety. From then on, he seemed infatuated with me. He knew I disliked him, and he suffered silently. Until the day I killed Frankie. That day he gained the upper hand. Unfortunately for the pair of us, our financial security depended, and still depends, upon our mutual respect. We have respected each other ever since, and dance a strange waltz around each other, both grateful for the other's strengths and weaknesses.

Perry's home, Cleave Farm, lies to the south of mine and adjoins my land. Perry rents many of my fields for his organic farm and lavender crop. Oaktree Cleave Village lies ahead to the west, and the main road cuts up through the Cleave, separating my house from the church and village. That road will branch across and destroy everything I'd salvaged after Frankie's and Francine's death.

There is a letter in the post-box along with flyers for pizza and gutter cleaning. It's from Lily, my solicitor's legal executive. She deals with the day-to-day running of my affairs. She does not like females addressed with a prefix, so instead I am 'Carol Cage' and have lost the 'Miss'. The heavy vellum envelope is stamped 'Thwaite & Hamilton', and although Thwaite 'Junior' died a few years ago, his name was of significance in the city, and the associated celebrity was highly regarded, so the name remains. I pocket this and make my way back. Today I will begin the long process of transcribing each moment that led to me destroying Frankie's life. Kicking at the gravel, I drag my feet back home, determined to find the strength to commit this painful recall to paper. Whether it will do me any good, only time will tell. But as my dad used to say, 'If you don't try, then you don't know.'

Chapter 2

Saturday, 6 September 1969

The orchard at Honeydew Farm was three miles away, southeast and over the hills surrounding the southern edge of the city. Sarah Burcher and I made our way there to scrump apples. We wore gym shoes that made our feet sweat, with shorts and blouses of thin cotton and cardigans tied around our waists.

Sarah pulled her hair tighter through its elastic band. She eyed the air rifle I had taken from the Cutlers' house, Cleave Farm. She expected it to discharge of its own accord, so stayed away from it.

'Did Perry see you?' she asked.

'No.' Perry Cutler was probably following us, I thought, dipping in and out of the field alongside us, like the pervert he was. Hard to believe he was sixteen. He was such a child. Best that Sarah didn't know.

'Why get the air rifle, Carol? We're in trouble.' She fidgeted, picked a nail and shuffled her feet in the dusty grit at the edge of the lane.

'No one's gonna know. Need to practise. Gotta wipe that smirk off Denny's face. He's not beating me again. I can shoot better than him. Stop worrying.'

'I'll get a pellet in my eye just because you won't let your brother win.' She scuffed her foot, and I contemplated that she would tell on me. She was becoming contrary, cantankerous, and getting podgy. 'Filling out', my mother said, as she looked at my athletic body with disappointment. I didn't want to be like Sarah; her ability to climb fences had lessened as her thighs had widened. 'You're not gonna tell are you, Sarah?'

''Course not!' However, her look was fragile, like ice in the melting sun, and the feeling that we were growing apart assaulted me again. That she would betray me wouldn't have crossed my mind in the past, but the tide of hormones seeped in relentlessly, already altering my skin, bones and brain. Too much was changing. Leaving school or not leaving school. Boys. Clothes. Boys. Make-up. Boys. Virginity. Boys. Why were we talking about these things?

Footsteps crept behind us, making Sarah jump.

'Oh, it's you,' she said, and moved to me to shield the air rifle.

'Don't be afraid of him, Sarah. He's harmless. You haven't grown up yet, have you, Perry? Still a little boy. Try standing in some fertiliser. Might help you grow up a bit. You short squirt.'

Grabbing Sarah's arm, I pulled her along. Taking the rifle had been easy, as Perry was well aware. The front door of Cleave Farmhouse was always open, and the gun cupboard was in the hallway, with the key on top. Mrs Cutler had been in the kitchen, and Mr Cutler had been working on the tractor in the backyard.

'Give me the rifle. Carol! Stop where you are right now. Or I'll, I'll…' Perry strode after us.

'You'll what? Fetch your Dad? Go on then. I don't care. I'll tell him you got the rifle for me; that you're showing off. Trying to make me your girlfriend.'

'You wouldn't dare, you little cow. Sarah will back me up, won't you, Sarah? She won't lie in case something happens to her.' He stared at her left arm. She'd broken it, aged nine, when Perry had pushed her over. Her parents blamed her for playing with the boys when she should have been helping her mum with the cooking.

Sarah put a restraining hand on my arm. Pushing her off, I snapped the rifle shut and drew it to my shoulder. Anger slipped through my finger, and I pulled the trigger. The pellet scooted past Perry's foot with a mechanical crack, sending up puffs of dirt. Sarah squealed and jumped.

'You stupid cow. You hit me, you bitch.' He sat on the dusty lane and examined his daps.

'Stop being a baby. I missed. But I won't next time if you don't piss off.'

'No, you didn't. Look at my dap. A hole straight through it.' He held it out to me.

'There's no way from this angle…' But inquisitively, I placed the rifle down and went to him. 'Where?'

'Here.' He lunged at me, grabbing my shoulders and pushing me back onto the lane. As I fell off balance, I flailed and tensed my neck to stop my head from hitting the floor. He was on top of me. His sweat-gleaming skin slid over mine as I frantically pushed at him, scrabbling for leverage. 'Get off, you creep.'

'Got you.' His arm swept up across my neck, pinning me down, as his other hand grabbed my breast. Sickening heat squeezed into my flesh. His pimpled face hovered over mine as I inhaled his breath into my lungs. Before he could bring his lips down, I pulled my knees up, dug my heels in, thrust my body up in an arch and rolled left.

'Piss off, you pervert.' Scrabbling up, I ran forward and punched his nose before grabbing the rifle. 'Run, Sarah. Now!'

We took off up the lane, leaving Perry to cover his bloody nose with a handkerchief. He wouldn't be happy. A frisson of nervous tension fired through me.

Chapter 3

Saturday, 20 December 1969

P erry's auntie Thora wanted to learn how to bake and had recruited Sarah and me to teach her. In return, Thora helped us with our homework. She was an excellent teacher, explaining difficult subjects calmly and logically. Much better than the ones we had at school. Except she wasn't a teacher but a psychiatrist, Doctor Thora Kent. She had just retired from the psychiatric hospital, Maytree, known by us kids as the 'nut house'.

Thora first invited us into her home, Oaktree House, the day Perry attacked me. We came upon her as she sat alone and crying in her broken-down car. We abandoned our apple scrumping mission until the next day and try to help her. Luckily my brothers had taught me everything about cars, including how to drive, and with a mixture of rallying and turning the engine over in first gear, we got her home.

When Thora invited us back that day, I fell in love with Oaktree House. The children on the council estate had always called it 'the witch's house' because trees surrounded it and someone had said that children disappeared if they entered the grounds. All a load of nonsense, but Sarah found it hard to relax whenever she visited.

Now it is my home and I remember first walking along the beautiful floors and a feeling of déjà vu nestling in my bones. Oaktree House reminded me of another home, my grandparents' home, the home my dad rejected so that he could marry my mum. His parents didn't approve of her.

There are two front rooms, one on each side of the hallway, furnished with sofas. One has several floor-to-ceiling bookcases, and a piano with a stool. There's a dining room with a massive table. And a kitchen three times the size of what was then my home, with easy chairs by the range. The place is big yet homely. Back then it was a place to dream about living in.

When Sarah and I first arrived, we waited by the front door while Thora fetched us some water. There was a hall-stand at the bottom of the staircase, with a telephone on it. I'd flipped through a pile of letters, guilt-tripping through my fingers, compelled to find out more about Thora and this house. Some had the address of her old workplace, Maytree Hospital. The city hospital headed another, and then the words 'oncology department'. But there was another, more interesting letter, handwritten with blue ink on thick cream vellum. The heading was 'Blanchard Place', and seemed to inform of something interesting, a secret accidentally revealed.

On the Saturday before Christmas, we were in Thora's kitchen teaching her to make a Christmas cake. She smiled with pride as she hovered near the oven, itching to take it out.

'Don't open the door,' I warned. 'It needs three hours, or it'll sink in the middle.'

She sat next to Sarah. 'Can't believe I've done this! My mother never cooked and I don't have a clue. We had a housekeeper. I've lived on hospital food most of my life; it's a wonder I survived.' She smiled, and her features softened. A beautiful woman shone through as years melted from her face.

'Let's do this washing-up and then we can have a piece of your birthday cake, Sarah. And let's have coffee instead of tea.'

Sarah went to the sink. 'I'll wash. I'm fed up with writing. Wish I was smart like Carol.' She picked up the washing-up liquid. Sarah had turned sixteen the previous Thursday, and the Victoria sponge cake she'd made sat waiting on the table, its sixteen candles in pink icing a confusing mix of little-girl and grown-up girl.

'Carol is smart because her father left her the gift of books when he died, and she made good use of them.' Thora smiled at me. 'He ensured she enjoyed what he enjoyed – books and learning.'

It had appalled Thora that I had lost my dad, and at every opportunity she brought him into our conversations. I'd told her that his books and encyclopaedias took pride of place in my bedroom bookcase.

'Is that why she gets all A's and knows big words?' Sarah said as she sloshed water.

A knock at the door startled us. This house is in the middle of nowhere and did not have secure fencing and locked gates around it as it does now.

'I'll go.' I made my way along the hall, brushing at my hair to get rid of any stray flour.

Dull afternoon light spooked the hallway. A figure darkened the leaded light glass panels surrounding the door. The body shifted; fluid movement; male, maybe. I opened the door and caught my breath. Standing outside was a gorgeous young man. I closed my mouth, conscious that I was gawping at him.

'Who is it?' Thora stepped forward. 'Oh.'

My face heated at my inability to say anything. Thora had noticed the change in my demeanour and bristled with irritation at it.

'Hi, Auntie.' He smiled; he was an absolute dream.

'Frankie.' Thora stepped to the door. 'What brings you here?'

'Thought I'd see how you are.' He shrugged. 'Are you going to leave me on the doorstep? I've been driving for hours.'

He winked at me. His strong shoulders, clearly defined under his open jacket, caused a thrill through me and I crossed my fingers and prayed, 'Let him in, let him in, let him in.' He was at least six foot tall, with shoulder-length hair dropping in soft rats' tails from a jagged parting. Tensing to stop my quaking nerves, I'd let my breath out softly through open lips as Thora spoke.

'Come in if you must. This is Carol.' Thora turned and walked back to the kitchen.

Frankie stepped in front of me. 'Well, hello, Carol.' Heat rippled between us, causing my blood to flow quickly through every part of me.

'Hi.' My voice caught as he turned away.

'Don't try flirting with her; she's too smart for you.' Thora sounded irritated: his arrival unwanted.

'I'm sure she is.' He turned towards me and whispered. 'Doesn't suffer fools gladly, my Auntie.' He smelt of musk and something else intoxicating that I breathed in deeply.

'I know,' I said, embarrassed at my agreement.

We followed Thora into the kitchen. Sarah packed her homework into her satchel. Frankie flopped down into the chair opposite.

'This is Sarah,' Thora told him as she picked up the kettle.

'Hello, Sarah.' Sarah blushed and nodded at him, fussing inside her bag before dropping it and kicking it out of sight. I watched him look at her. Did he like her? His jaw was square with soft stubble. His high cheekbones thinned out his cheeks. As he turned, his face, although angular, had a soft covering of flesh stopping him from looking gaunt.

'Bloody hell, that's a drive.' He looked around, noting and appraising things. 'Those roads out of London are getting worse.'

'You should've phoned. A lot easier.' Thora was not happy, and I wanted to distract her from her negativity towards this dream of a man.

'What car have you got?' I asked.

'MGB,' he said with a note of arrogance that should have made him sound offensive, but it thrilled me.

'MGB! Can I see it?'

He followed me out of the house. The blue car sat on the drive emitting soft ticking noises as the engine cooled. Walking around it, I ran my fingers along the wings and wished for the clouds to clear for better light.

'Wow, it's new.' The car was amazing.

'Yes.' He grinned at my delight and tilted his head as he looked at my hair.

'Can I have the keys?' A surge of desperation to get inside it pushed aside my shyness.

'The keys? You look all of thirteen, so, no.' He pulled the keys out of his pocket and gripped them tightly as though to keep them safe.

'Why not? I can drive.' I reached for his hand, holding his gaze. His fingers unfurled as a glint of devilment crossed his eyes. He wanted to see what would happen if he surrendered them to me. I knew at once that he liked the thrill of the unknown. His hand was smooth, and he registered surprise as I took them from him saying, 'I've got three older brothers. They've taught me about cars. And how to drive.'

That should reassure him, I thought as I got in and moved the seat forward. The engine throttled into life with a deep-throated rhythmic vibration. 'Get in, or I'll go on my own.'

He slid in, stretching his legs out and relaxing back into the seat saying, 'Sorry, no petrol. And I'm broke,' with a wicked grin kissing his lips.

'How are you getting back to London?' The irresponsibility of his situation evaded me as the thought that he'd have to stay caused my heart to race.

'Not sure.' He ran his fingers along his jaw and looked towards the house. Thora would have to bail him out, obviously. She was annoyed, so maybe she wouldn't give him money. Then he would stay. Excellent.

'I'll just go around the driveway. It's big enough.'

He laughed as I pulled away. 'So you *can* drive.' His thigh was close to mine.

'Course I can. Why lie about being able to drive?' I steered around the oak tree that stood in the centre, exactly where it is now.

'You don't look old enough to have a licence.' He looked at

my legs; my short skirt had ridden up, and I didn't feel an urge to pull it back down.

'I haven't. I only drive up here, in the countryside. Sometimes round the estate – mostly vans, Transits, tractors, whatever my brothers are fixing. They've got a garage in the village. Needs pulling down but they like it.'

'So how old are you?' There was a note of expectation; of wanting me to give an age older than my fifteen years. I couldn't do that.

'Tell me how old you think I am, Frankie.' I spoke his name, and the sound of it softened my tongue.

'Well, you look thirteen and act thirty.'

'Thirty? That's ancient!'

He laughed and shook his head as I parked.

***

On the walk back home with Sarah, Frankie consumed my every thought. As we reached Dawnview Wood, where the other oak tree grew, I tripped and crashed to the ground. Perry's laughter boomed out. Scrambling up, I turned to find a makeshift loop of metal sticking out across the path.

'Are you okay?' Sarah placed a hand on my shoulder. I shrugged her off and headed for Perry.

'What do you think you're doing? You could have killed me.'

He jumped down from the oak tree and walked towards us. 'Stop fussing. You're fine. You weren't looking where you're going. Something distracting you, maybe?'

'What d'you mean, you idiot?'

'I saw you driving that dickhead's car. What a slapper you are. Did you give him one?'

He turned and let out a shriek as I raced towards him, fists clenched. He weaved through the copse and headed across Dawnview Field to the lane. For a moment I gained on him, but then he vaulted the gate and sprinted away.

'Let him go, Carol. He'll hit you.' Sarah paced by the trees, rubbing her left arm. 'We shouldn't be here. It's dangerous up here on our own.'

'For God's sake, Sarah. We can do what we want.' She looked away. 'We can come up here if we want to. Take no notice of your dad. My dad said I was better than my brothers at everything. Girls can do what boys do, remember. We can even beat them at some things.'

I took her hand, and she smiled. 'I'd like to beat Perry.'

'And me. He's a wanker. I'll smash his face in next time.'

She flushed and giggled as I looped my arm through hers and turned us towards home. My dad had always told me I was as strong as any boy, but he didn't say that one day I'd meet a boy who I didn't want to be stronger than.

'D'you like Frankie?' I asked, although I didn't care what she thought.

''S all right. Do you like him? He's old.'

'No, he's not.' The world turned out of step as I scraped my foot along the ground.

'Bet he's got a girlfriend in London. Bet she likes long, girly hair. We don't like boys with girly hair, do we?'

I jogged ahead, not wanting to listen to her. 'I've got to get back. Sammy and Valerie are coming over with Julie. She's pregnant again already.' My middle brother, Sammy, wanted to father a football team, but his first child was female. Valerie seemed happy to let him have his way.

'Slow down. Can I come 'round to see Julie?' Sarah was already talking about having a baby, yet failed to note that she needed a boyfriend first.

'Yeah, of course.' Letting Sarah play with Julie would save me from having to coo at the milky little sick-bag.

The hill sloped down, as it does now, at a low gradient for a quarter of a mile before meeting the estate. Sarah caught up as I stopped to take in the view of the city below. The familiar landmarks and buildings shimmered in a pale-yellow glow from the low winter sun. Looking towards my home with its familiar surroundings, I'd felt a shift of perception towards an unknown kingdom. There was a king, with silky, shoulder-length hair, a shirt rippling across tight muscles, and an upper lip carrying the honey-coloured sheen of a moustache. His kingdom was seductive and made me question where my home was.

But I knew where my heart was.

Frankie had my heart.

Chapter 4

Friday, 13 March 1970

The back of Erik Schmidt's car smelt of toffee and earth but mainly of mildew. He'd said he'd be late, and told me to make sure that no one saw me get in, and to cover myself with the rug – the usual warnings. The staff car park was empty, but I was wary of teachers making their way home. Josephine Francis seemed to have the hots for Schmidt. She flounced over whenever she could, her perfume so strong that it seeped into the car. Someone needed to tell her that being a drama teacher didn't mean that you had to ham it up all the time. One day she would force her way into the passenger seat and get a massive shock to find me hiding in the back.

Another person to worry about catching me there was Sally Major, my nemesis. She wasn't happy that I'd smashed her head against the wall the day before. She'd seemed to think I'd hand her my dry socks because hers got wet. Some kids thought others were around simply to do their bidding. Not me. If she had a problem, I'd set my brother Denny on her.

The wind was getting up, and the chill hit my bare legs below my short skirt. Mum had promised to buy me a coat that weekend; I couldn't do mine up. My brothers gave me money if I babysit or something. It was a Friday: the day Mum went out with her workmates. She'd been going out a lot.

Erik Schmidt had approached me the first week of the new term. He wasn't one of my teachers, but he'd raved about my published poetry in the Christmas edition of the school magazine. Said that I must go to university. I had talent, and he would ensure that I'd not be like other girls, abandoned to fall into marriage and children, wasted on servitude and reproduction. I was special and must fulfil my potential. When I'd said that I

19

wanted to paint in oils, not write poetry, he said that was just as good.

Each Friday evening and Sunday afternoon I'd work at his house under his supervision to complete a portfolio of artwork. Sarah didn't know. She didn't like that I was better at Art than she was. That I was better at everything. Sarah needed to study more, but she'd already given up. I'd had a weird dream that her new curves would expand until she spewed out half a dozen babies, all snot-covered and wearing acid nappies.

Schmidt insisted we drove even though he lived a short walk away. The novelty was getting tiresome. It was ridiculous. I would not hide in his car again. He would not dictate to me. I was fifteen, not five.

*****

The car stopped, and he got out. The garage door swung up with a grating creak. I froze, hidden under the blanket, as the usual chorus of children's voices shouted, 'Hello, sir,' as they gathered around him.

Schmidt said, 'Hello, boys. Are you going somewhere nice?'

'Up Oaktree Cleave, sir. Do you want to come, sir?'

'No, thank you. It's too cold for me. Anyway, I've homework to mark.' He got back into the car and drove it into the garage and got out.

'Have you got any spare change you can give us, sir?'

'Oh, Samantha. I didn't see you there.' He seemed flustered, and I wondered why she had asked for money. 'Not today. Now run along and have a good time and don't forget to tell your parents. And don't talk to strangers or get into strange cars.'

'We won't, sir. We're not daft. We know what perv's look like.'

I got out as soon as the garage door rattled back into place, determined to tackle him about having to hide in the back.

'I hope you don't mind, sir – Erik – but I don't want to hide in the car anymore.'

He walked away. 'Let's put the kettle on to make some of your nice English tea.'

The house is still there on the posh estate where people buy, not rent, the houses. The kitchen was also a dining room and was tiny. It had imitation wooden doors on the kitchen units. They needed to be brightened up with yellow paint or something.

He put teabags in cups, his back to me, stiffness in his shoulders. He didn't want to discuss the car. He was adamant that other children shouldn't see me. He said they would make it impossible for him to give me his full attention. He said I needed to be more logical and insightful. I could understand his reasoning. But still.

'I'll knock on the door like anyone else. Who cares what people think? They're all going to know soon.'

'You haven't told anyone, have you?' He turned, his hand reaching his chin, stroking it softly.

'No, but I don't –'

'We've been through this Carol. People will talk.'

'Let them.'

He stirred the tea, then placed the cups on the table. The smell reminded me I was hungry. As if reading my mind, he got out some chocolate biscuits and crisps. 'People are funny, Carol. *You* know you're painting and *I* know you're painting, but others won't understand. People get jealous.'

The smell of lemon soap wafted. We stared into each other's eyes for a moment before I looked away, unable to hold eye contact. He stepped toward the sink as I continued, determined not to let the subject go.

'I can't see a problem. I mean, what's strange about a teacher teaching. Okay, so it's outside school time but – oh, I've got an idea: we can use the school building.'

'We can't. The head won't allow it.'

'Well, what do they expect us to do, then? If anyone wants to say anything, they'll have to say it to my face. They don't want to mess with me...'

He turned around; a muscle twitched in his cheek. 'No need to get so excited, Carol. Try not to over-analyse it. You're getting stressed. That is bad for an artist.' He picked up his cup and studied the rim. 'You haven't told your brother, have you?'

'No. We said it would be our secret. Surprise them when I get into uni. It's what's going to happen, isn't it?'

'Yes, of course. That's what will happen. Why don't you go on up now? We've wasted enough time.'

I headed upstairs to my 'studio'.

***

The smell of lemons alerted me that Schmidt was lurking outside the bedroom. The door was now slightly ajar. His snooping was unnerving, but Schmidt promised to get me into university, saying that I would gain admiration and respect. My brothers had taught me everything a boy should know, but I was a girl with aspirations, and I was going to show them what a great artist I was.

'Eight-thirty, Carol.' He came into the room. 'Don't worry about your brushes. I'll clean those.'

'Okay, thanks. I'll clean myself up.'

The lemon smell was stronger in the bathroom. After checking myself for telltale signs of paint, I made my way onto the landing. Schmidt's back blocked the view of my painting. I felt a surge of pride at my accomplishment, and I expected him to turn and congratulate me. Instead, I noticed his stance was odd. He was rocking slightly, hands in front of him. Something about his demeanour stilled me. Last week, he'd sat in the kitchen with my dirty gym kit across his lap. The sight had unnerved me, and now this odd behaviour unnerved me again, so I hurried downstairs shouting that I was ready to leave. That image of him ran like a film through a reel. It was just my wild imagination, I thought. He probably had an itch in an uncomfortable place that was embarrassing for him.

Slipping through the connecting door to the garage, I waited as nerves jittered my teeth. As he entered, I panicked, and, frantic for something distracting, I remembered that the drama teacher had been attempting to chat him up the previous week.

'Miss Francis has the hots for you. Are you going out with her?'

'Hum. I will reply with one of your sayings: "Don't be daft."' His mouth tightened, but I couldn't shut up. 'Wasn't she brave to ask you? Girls don't ask men out, do they? Did you turn her down because you think she's too forward?'

'No, of course not. I'm not one of these men who live in the past. I don't see women as ... how do you say ... "sluts".'

The word spat out of his mouth. His face was rigid, his eyelids hooded over pin-prick irises.

'Sorry. I'm nosy. My brothers are always up for any girl who makes eyes at them, even though they complain that those types of girls are easy. I ask you. You can't win. What's that all about, Mr Schmidt – um, Erik?' I drew in a breath and held it, hoping he wouldn't notice my frail composure under his unremitting gaze.

'You haven't done it with anyone, have you, Carol?'

Crossing my arms over my stomach, I rocked on my feet, guilt rising for no reason. 'I don't think you should ask me that. Can we go now, or Mum will worry and ask questions? I can walk ...'

'Sorry, I shouldn't have asked you. Forgive me.'

We got in the car. I knew I should stop these visits.

But I desperately wanted to go to university, and he was so confident that he could get me there.

Chapter 5

Friday, 20 March 1970

My hands shook as I knocked on Sarah's door. Mrs Burcher opened it; surprise lifted her eyebrows. 'It's a bit late, Carol…' She trailed off.

I itched from foot to foot, hoping sweat wasn't seeping through my clothes. 'Please, Mrs Burcher. I need to ask Sarah something important. To do with school.'

'On a Friday night? Okay. But Matthew will be here in a minute, so you must leave then. It's nearly nine o'clock.'

The Burchers' were our next-door neighbours. Their house was spooky. Its closed doors, velvet curtains and heavy furniture shrouded it in darkness. A crucifix loomed on the hallway windowsill; its substantial size blocked out the sun, seeming to censor its right to cast light into this dreary home.

'Sarah. Carol is here,' Mrs Burcher shouted upstairs before turning, 'Go on up. Tell her to pack up Chrissie's things.'

'Thanks, Mrs Burcher.' I walked up the stairs, ears alert for the sound of Schmidt's knocking. He's certain to come here after what I'd just done. Sarah's mum retreated into the dining room, back to the soft sound of the radio. Thank God Mum was out and Schmidt would get no reply when he knocked.

'Hi, Carol. Thought you were babysitting Julie?' Sarah looked around from her desk.

'Got cancelled. Your mum wants you to pack up Chrissie's things.'

'Oh. You should've come round earlier. Just finished another letter. You'll never work this one out.'

'Thanks. I'll take it home.' She handed me a letter. We'd been doing these letters for years – notes to each other using secret codes to disguise messages.

I stuffed it in my coat pocket as she stood, and we went to her old bedroom at the front of the house where her niece Chrissie was asleep. Sarah picked up a nappy and cardigan and dropped them into a bag.

'You don't want to do them anymore because I'm getting good,' she whispered over the carry-cot on the bed. I shook my head and went to the window to look for Schmidt as Chrissie sucked at her chubby thumb: a cute one-year-old slumbering in rosy-dewed innocence.

'No. It's not that. It's… I took Schmidt's car.' I pulled back the curtain. Schmidt was at the top of the road.

'What do you mean?'

'He locked me in his house. I panicked. Got in his car and locked the doors. Was afraid to get out in case… Had to threaten to drive through the garage door. But he opened it, so I drove off. Had no choice. No way I was going to stay in that house with him.'

Sarah gaped through the soft glow of the shaded night-light. 'Schmidt? The German teacher? Locked you in? You were at his house?'

'Yes. I've been going there… a few weeks… months.' I wanted her to say something, but she didn't. 'He's been teaching me… stuff… to get me into uni, but he… got spooky.'

She shifted her weight and checked that we hadn't woken Chrissie. 'Spooky? So you stole his car?' She looked towards the stairs as though checking for her mother. 'Carol, you're in so much trouble.'

'Don't think so.' Nerves had got the better of me, but deep down I knew he wouldn't report me to the Headmaster. I feared other consequences, but I wasn't sure what those were.

Her eyes darted back to mine. 'What made you scared? You're never scared.' Her brow furrowed, uncertainty crossing her face as she contemplated this reversal of our usual roles.

Taking her arm, I pulled her out of the room and into her

bedroom. 'He made all these promises about getting me into university. I'd surprise everyone when I produced this thing, a portfolio thing. Said my dad would be proud of me. It was our secret. That was the weird bit. Having a secret with a teacher. And he bought me stuff, paint and notebooks.'

'Gosh. Weird. But good. Like he was helping you.' She opened her arms as if to hug me, but then brought her hands back together.

Listening at the door for Schmidt's knocking, I told her, 'He made me hide on the back seat of his car under a rug because no one could know.' Her mouth opened in an O. 'He had my dirty games kit spread over his kitchen table. He said he was getting my hockey boots out to clean, but he wasn't. Then he was doing something in the bedroom as he stood in front of my paintings. And today... all the creepy things ...' Tears stung my eyes as panic threatened to erupt.

'Do you think we should tell someone? Your mum? A teacher?'

'No!' I rocked myself to control my nerves. 'I can't, Sarah. I can't. I'm so stupid. When I think about hiding in the back of his car, I... I can't believe I did that. Why did I? It was so...'

'But you're not afraid of stuff. You're brave. You don't worry because you... just... don't. If you want to do something, you do it.' She pushed my hair off of my face, but it dropped again. 'Like taking the twelve-bore, or fishing in the lake. You're... um... impulsive. And you never get caught. And if you do, people just say "Don't do it again", because you're not really bad.'

'Then why do I feel... strange, panicky? Like I've done something wrong, but I don't know what exactly. I feel weird inside. I had to get out. Had to take his car. Had to. Left it just down the road a bit. On the hill.'

She put her arm around my shoulders. 'Then he'll see it if he comes here, won't he? So it'll be fine. But stay away from him from now on.'

'But he has all my work. All the stuff I did before… I took it to show him. I've left everything. My poetry, everything.'

'Maybe ask your mum to get it…'

'No! No, Sarah.'

She squeezed me as I sobbed. 'It'll be all right. You can do more stuff, better stuff.'

'It was sooo creepy in his house. And it smelt of lemons, and *he* smelt of lemons. I knew something was wrong. Except I didn't… but, it has to do with… sex … I think.'

'Oh.' Her cheeks flushed. 'What, to do with… um… you know. What happened?'

'Nothing – not actual… you know. He crept about when I painted. And he asked me if I'd "done it". Then I couldn't concentrate. And keeping it a secret. He was annoyed every time I said that I wanted to tell people.'

'Mummy says I have to tell her if a man asks me to keep a secret. Should I tell her?'

'No! God, Sarah, don't you dare.'

'Okay. Don't worry, I won't tell. It'll be our secret. Oh, I didn't mean…' She laughed and suddenly Schmidt seemed silly, so I laughed too. Mr Burcher shouted upstairs for us to keep quiet.

Sarah's brother, Matthew, arrived to pick up Chrissie. Matthew's voice drifted up, 'Some guy outside Melissa's is looking for Carol.'

We froze. Matthew bounded up the stairs and beckoned me into Chrissie's bedroom. 'Who is that guy? He told me his name, but I couldn't make it out.' He moved to give me room to look out. As I stepped beside him, he moved closer; his breath distracted me as it flowed over my head. The adult Matthew entranced me, although I couldn't fathom why. He was repulsive and attractive at the same time. A moody boy, stomping off in a strop if he didn't have his way. My brothers fell in and out of friendship with him continually. Now he called my mum Melissa instead of Mrs Cage and spoke with a deep male voice that purred along my neck.

'Um… looks like Mr Schmidt.' I tried to sound uninterested as my body struggled to stay upright.

'Well, he's looking for his car. Seems to think you might know where it is. Do you?'

'No… I, oh, that looks like it just over there, down the hill towards the school.'

His look told me he knew something was going on. 'Right, well, I'll tell him. Strange that he forgot where he'd left it.'

He picked up the carry-cot and bag as he left. We watched him walk the front path and speak to Schmidt, who looked across the road and ran towards the hill. Matthew placed Chrissie in his van, then turned to look up at us.

'I'd better go before he comes back in. See you tomorrow.' I rushed downstairs and out the back door, startling Mrs Burcher from her knitting.

Mum would be home soon, but luckily Schmidt and his car had gone. Something told me he wouldn't be back; that he was doing something that he shouldn't be; that I could relax because he wouldn't bother with me again. I should have felt relieved, but I didn't. I felt guilty because I should have spoken to someone about him and I hadn't. Pretending that nothing had happened was easier, even though I knew he was evil.

Chapter 6

Easter Saturday, 28 March 1970

Easter Saturday. Tired and fed up, I'd trudged home from the supermarket. Stacking dry goods since eight that morning was boring, and the muscles in my back were complaining. Mum expected me to be grateful, as though that was to be my life. Leave school to work full time, she said. She didn't know I was going to uni, so there would be an argument. Another one.

Mr Philips owned the supermarket. He'd given me a job because Mum was sleeping with him. I didn't care that I was ungrateful. Shop work wasn't going to be my life.

As if that problem wasn't enough, Denny was dating Rosemary Major, Sally's older sister. What he saw in her, apart from her enormous chest, was incomprehensible. She was prettier than Sally in the same way that a piglet was cuter than a sow. Mum and Denny were pushing me to invite Sally home so that we could become friends – a little family. Unease accompanied every journey home expecting that bitch to be sitting on our settee, smooching with my brother. I hadn't wanted Denny to leave home, but now I couldn't wait for him to move in with our older brother, Gerry. Life was so awful all the time.

The memory of meeting Frankie would slip through my dreams each morning, and I'd worry that I had only imagined how gorgeous he was. That if I met him again he would be ordinary. My daydreams had turned him into an impossibly desirable man and my longing for him was so great that I believed my life would end without him in it. Fantasies in which he reached for me and drew me to him playing in my mind, hours spent daydreaming about marrying him and living in Thora's house – without Thora, of course. Lust and longing had replaced common sense as the rooms of Oaktree House became my imaginary home. Frankie was by my side and in my bed. Frankie, my gorgeous husband, took me in his arms, and we lived in eternal ecstasy.

As I trudged closer to home, I saw someone standing on our front path holding a bunch of flowers. The sun broke through, and its low rays illuminated my dream. It was Frankie. He turned and waved. My footsteps faltered as my heart raced. He couldn't see me like this: sweaty, no lipstick, my hair a mess.

Sarah opened her front door and stepped onto the path. She waved before noticing him. He turned, and they talked. She giggled as she stroked her hair and pushed it behind her ears. They turned together to watch me. As I approached the gate, he walked towards me.

'At last!' He smiled, but I didn't; I was horrified that I smelt. 'You've forgiven me for not having petrol, haven't you?'

'Yes. Of course. Where's your car?' I glanced around hoping for another chance to drive it.

Sarah looked up and down the road. 'Oh yes, where's your car? I didn't see it last time.'

'Oh, nice!' he said, 'The pair of you would rather see my car. I'll go then.'

'No. I want to see you … as well. We both do.' Moisture oozed over my body.

He winked. 'I could get used to being second best. Thought I'd walk.' He stepped closer, 'For you,' he said quietly, his back to Sarah as he offered me the flowers. His eyes searched for my reaction. The flowers reminded me of my dad's funeral. Repulsion mixed with gratitude and each rendered me dumbstruck.

'Well, are you going to take them before my arm drops off?' My reaction had disappointed him.

'Take them, Carol.' Sarah walked to the front door, easing away from us.

Red roses and white gypsophila lay in my sweaty hands: flowers Mum used in the wreath for my dad. The sight of them itched bad memories. Dad bought her these flowers for every special occasion.

'Have I done enough to get a cup of tea before I walk back?' He smiled and brought his hands together in a praying motion.

'I ... there's no one home.' My knees trembled at the thought of being alone with him.

'I'm sure Sarah will join us. She can protect you from me if you need it.' Another teasing smile before he turned to her.

Sarah said, 'I've made scones. I'll get them,' and ran into her house.

'Are we going to be poisoned?' He pulled a face of mock horror, and I caught my breath at how lovely he was.

'Course not. Sarah's a good cook.' She couldn't make scones, but we'd only get indigestion.

He followed me into the kitchen and sat at the table. Dropping the flowers onto the draining board, I contemplated them, mummified in cellophane. The simple process of making tea eluded me under Frankie's watchful gaze.

'D'you like your flowers?' His voice was soft yet strong.

'Yes, they're lovely, thank you.' I'd no idea how to react and hoped that I sounded both grateful and used to receiving flowers.

Sarah opened the back door and entered with scones and a pot of jam. We placed butter and cutlery on the table. Frankie watched as I spooned tea in the teapot, and asked Sarah, 'Do you work?'

'Not yet. I'm going to work at the baccy factory with my dad.' She hadn't told me that, so she avoided my stare.

'What's a baccy factory?' he asked.

'Tobacco factory. My dad's a foreman.'

He turned to me, 'And you, Carol, are you going to be working in this "baccy factory", or are you staying at the supermarket?'

'No.' I drew in a breath and came straight out with the truth. 'I'll be staying on to do my A-levels. I'm fifteen.'

His eyes skimmed over my breasts, astounding me that he would do that. 'You're very mature for fifteen. Both of you.' He looked at Sarah, who rewarded him with a blushing grin, and I worried that he had assessed her breasts, too.

'I would say you were both seventeen.' He picked up a scone and put it on a plate.

'Well, we're not.' The dream of us together disappeared. As I took the teapot to the table, I noticed that my hands had stopped shaking now that the chances of us dating had gone.

'When are you sixteen?' he asked me.

'May,' I said, pulling my shoulders back to ensure that he knew I was proud of myself.

'Oh, not long then.' He nodded.

Sarah handed him the butter dish and a knife. 'I was sixteen last December. How old are you, Frankie?'

He took the knife and butter and said, 'Nineteen. These look delicious, Sarah.'

She blushed. 'I hope you like them.'

We busied ourselves eating. Frankie's hands were smooth, with tiny hairs glinting as he deftly sliced his scone. He spread butter then lifted it to his mouth. Unable to watch, a piece of scone clumped dryly on my tongue, refusing to budge. My dreams did not feature Sarah, tea and scones.

He asked me, 'Where are your parents?'

'Mum's at work. My dad's dead.' I'd found it easier over the years to admit that he was dead, but my body still froze in grief.

'Oh, sorry.' He hadn't asked Thora about me – hadn't been that curious. He wasn't interested.

'So where does your mum work?' He swallowed the last bit of scone.

'At the supermarket. She's the manager.' He didn't remark about her being a woman and a manager; instead, he picked up his cup and drank, before looking back at me and asking, 'Are you going to put those flowers in water before they die?'

'They're already dead.'

'Are they?' He went to the drainer and picked them up.

'They're not. Why did you say ...?' He looked at me and a smile spread across his face. 'Ah, I see. They're already dead because ... they're cut ... so they're dying.' The triumphant gleam in his eye cut to my heart. He was pleased to read me.

'Carol, you're rude. You can't tell Frankie his flowers are dead. They're lovely. I would love to get flowers.'

He turned to her. 'Then *you* have them, Sarah. I'm sure Carol won't mind.'

Sarah looked at me and asked, 'Can I have them?'

As I nodded, glad to see them go, he handed them to her with a flourish and said, 'There's one condition.'

'What?' She waited for an answer, but he didn't reply. Seconds ticked by before she said, 'Okay, I'm going. See you later Carol.'

As the door closed behind her, he walked towards me.

'I promise I'll never buy you flowers.'

Then he leant down and kissed me.

Chapter 7

Sunday, 29 March 1970

W e went to Glastonbury for our first date. I'd not been there before. We'd talked about the place at school, about it dating from the Iron Age and King Edmund being crowned there in 1016, and that there was a church dedicated to Saint John the Baptist.

Frankie enthused about pagan ways of life and living outside the constraints of the Church and indoctrinated living practices. About how there were many ways to live that allowed you the freedom to explore, to experiment in ways that made you feel good and set your soul free. He said that Glastonbury represented freedom. I wasn't sure what he meant but I smiled at how animated he was. His enthusiasm was intoxicating.

He talked with authority about ley lines and the Holy Grail, King Arthur and Guinevere. He'd had an education far better than mine, and I worried that I'd show my ignorance. Nevertheless, excitement zinged my nerves.

We walked around in the cool March air, past shops full of souvenirs, with adverts for fortune-tellers. As we climbed up the Tor, billowing clouds raced across the sky creating a moody split of brilliant sunshine and threatening darkness. It was as if we were inside a kaleidoscope where the forces of nature fought around us. We walked in silence, absorbing the atmosphere and the newness of our togetherness.

The impressive Tor, a natural wonder associated with mystic influences, had an amazing view. We were in the heavens surveying our kingdom. He lit a cigarette as he gazed around and I watched his hands and the movement of the match as he shielded the flame. He scrunched his face, pouted, and inhaled deeply. Mysterious forces surrounded us, capturing us in their embrace. We were together in a new world – our world.

'It's amazing. Look at the view.' I opened my arms and spun around. He laughed and grabbed me, saying, 'You're so enchanting and innocent. You bring the place alive.'

'Do I? It's great. Love it. Can I visit one of those psychics we passed? I want to find out about my future.'

'Why? You know your future: it's what you make it.'

'What if they *know* about something? Something good. Or maybe something that could help.'

'Like, "You're a girl so will waste your time at uni and may as well do something else …"?'

'Ha-ha. No – or maybe yes … something like that. I want to know what's out there.'

'Well, trees and grass and roads and cars …' He ran his finger down my arm. 'And people.'

'Funny! Don't you think there may be more, something bigger than us?'

'Like God, you mean?'

'No, not God … something … *out* there … around us … bigger than us. Like an angel, taking care of you.'

He put his arm around my waist and crushed me to him. 'No. Never. I have my angel right here.'

Blushing, I wished it to be true. I ached for his love, and my head spun in a maelstrom of emotion as his arms held me. The heat of our bodies fused us, and the recognition that this could be normal from now on hit me as we gazed into each other's eyes. He threw away his cigarette and took my hand. We were a pair, a couple, a joining of spirits. He kissed my forehead and his lips melted on my skin before he pulled back.

'Hungry?' he asked. I nodded. He led me back down the Tor, ensuring that he walked ahead, his body supporting me so I didn't slip. He was my saviour. I hadn't known I needed one.

***

We found a pub for lunch. As I picked up the menu I felt his eyes on me as I checked the selections.

'Let's have a roast,' he said.

'It's a bit expensive.'

'I'm paying. What do you want to drink? I presume you drink even though you're underage?'

'Babycham, please,' I said with confidence, hoping I'd like it.

I watched his backside as he walked to the bar, then looked away in case someone noticed. He returned with our drinks and placed his pint glass down, already half empty.

'Am I driving home?' I asked, flicking my eyes to his glass.

'No, sweetheart. I'll only have a couple.'

'You can have more than a couple if you want. I don't mind driving.'

'Ah, is she saying she wants to drive my car, or is she saying she doesn't want me to drink and drive?' He placed his forearms on the table and leant towards me.

'What do you mean?' I took a sip of my drink. 'And who's *she*, the cat's mother?'

He didn't reply but cocked his head to one side in his endearing manner as I placed my glass down. 'I don't fancy being stuck here if you can't drive.' The thought was unnerving; like I was in his control.

'I'd have to drink a lot more than two pints before I couldn't drive.' He lit a cigarette.

'Maybe so, but if you do drink more than two, I won't be getting in the car with you.'

'Oh, Miss Bossy.' He reached out to run his finger down my cheek. As he sat back, his grin gave him a distasteful impish quality.

'I'm not bossy,' I objected.

'You are, sweetheart. You're telling me what to do.' He flicked ash into the ashtray.

'I'm not. You can do what you want.'

'You said you wouldn't get in the car with me if I drank more than two pints.'

'That's not being bossy. I'm not telling you what to do. I'm telling you what *I* will do … or rather what I *won't* do.'

'Clever little thing, aren't you?'

Sarcasm didn't suit him. Meanness overrode his gorgeous looks. He had to be teasing me.

'Excuse me.' A middle-aged woman in a floral dress placed plates in front of us. I thanked her, but he said nothing as he picked up his paper napkin.

'I don't see what's clever. It's simple,' I said.

'It's manipulation.' He picked up his knife and fork and let the paper napkin drop to the floor. 'Do you know what that is?'

If we had been outside I'd have smacked him for his cheek. This wasn't the sort of conversation I'd anticipated during our first meal together. All my friends talked about snogging and pushing away wandering hands. His manner had turned him ugly, and the adage about beauty being skin deep came to mind. How could he be so gorgeous yet have such an annoying way about him? All pretence of being ladylike flew away in my irritation.

'If you think I'm stupid and don't know what that means, or I don't know what I'm saying, or I don't know my mind, or what I want, or …' He was laughing. I pushed back my chair and stood.

'I'm going to the Ladies; if you want we can leave when I get back. Or you can go on your own if you want to risk the wrath of my mum. Is that manipulative enough for you?'

'Carol, Carol,' he said between breaths of laughter, 'sit down. I'm joking.'

'Well, if you don't mind I'll go to the Ladies and give you a chance to stop laughing at me. Then I'll decide if I want to stay or not. Hope you've heard about women changing their mind. My brothers try to say it's because girls are flighty. Huh! I say it's because we have to put up with boys changing what they've said to suit which way the wind blows.' Taking a deep breath, I stumbled away in my heels, my head held high.

***

Sitting on a strange toilet was not the best place to gather my thoughts. Sure that I'd blown it, I felt lost and homesick. His teasing was annoying, different from my brothers' straightforwardness. Frankie's charm had disappeared in an instant. Our conversation ran through my head causing uncertainty about my attitude; could it be my Achilles' heel? Mum said that girls needed to stand up for themselves. Be assertive and not let men walk over you.

There was enough change in my purse to phone Denny, but I thought I'd better not. Denny would punch him, and that would be the end of us. If there was an 'us'. Sarah had said I'd be a disaster at dating, and she seemed to be right. I flushed and went to the mirror. Lipstick and mascara made me look weird. The gunk on my skin was going to cause spots. Now I was a woman I was to wear make-up forever. Much too complicated. I pressed some damp toilet paper over my face to dilute my foundation. Taking a breath, I pushed the door open and went back to him.

'Ah-ha, here she is.'

Ignoring him, I ate my cold food as he watched me, and then he said, 'I'm going to the bar. Do you want another drink?'

'Thanks, but I'm fine.' I tossed my hair and looked up at him. He'd dump me now for sure.

As I pushed my plate away, he returned with his pint. He leant across to take my hand.

'Shall we start this date again? He moved my hand softly from side to side; a nerve twitched against the smoothness of his palm.

'Well ...' I didn't know what to say. I could have ended it right then. He squeezed my fingers and batted his eyelashes, then pulled a face as if he'd cry. I burst out laughing at the ridiculousness of him and relented. 'Okay … let's start again.'

'I solemnly promise not to tease you, and you can promise not to tell me what to do.'

'Maybe we should promise to respect each other? That's what my mum says.'

'I'll drink to that.' He sipped his beer, wiped his mouth, and said, 'Phew! You're a challenge, Carol Cage. A lovely challenge.' He got up and sat next to me. 'Can you see the landlady?'

'No – why?'

'Because I want to …' Then he kissed me, and any doubts about him disappeared.

Chapter 8

Saturday, 11 April 1970

T he lovely sound of Thora playing the piano greeted me as I approached Oaktree House. Thora was an excellent pianist and often played for us. Sarah wanted to learn, but Thora said that she'd need a piano at home to practise, so we had only learnt some simple scales.

The music stopped when I knocked on the door then started up again. Thora opened the door, noting my confusion. 'Oh, that's Frankie,' she said. 'I'll make some tea. We're in the library.'

Frankie had a look of intense concentration as he played. He swayed back and forth at the piano. I moved closer as his fingers slowly stroked the keys, belying the passion and melody that assaulted my ears. He smiled at me for a moment before returning his concentration to the music. With a flourish, he stopped, stood, and bowed. As I clapped, he pulled me to him, kissing me passionately.

'Wow!' I said catching my breath. 'You're incredible.'

'And guitar.' He pointed.

'Play something then.'

He laughed but fetched it anyway and sat back on the piano stool. He played the same tune. His fingers mesmerised me, and I sank to the floor, crossing my legs. He stopped. 'You look cute – like a pretty Buddha, but slimmer.

'What's a Buddha?'

He didn't answer but raised his eyebrows without missing a beat.

Thora brought in two cups of tea. 'I'm going now. I'll be back in a couple of hours. Eat the quiche and salad in the fridge.'

'Thanks, Auntie. You don't look well enough to go, though. Should we drive you?' Frankie asked.

'No, I'm fine. It'll do me good to get some fresh air. When will Sarah get here?'

'She'll be here in a minute. She had to go back for her Biology homework. She wants you to look at it.' The lie slipped out easily.

'Okay. I'll be off then.' She looked at us as though about to say something, then turned and left.

Frankie leapt on top of me and wrestled me. 'Got you all to myself now!'

I pushed him away. 'Behave, Frankie. Thora hasn't guessed we're dating, has she?'

'No. And well done you, thinking that up so quickly.' He jumped up. 'Come on, follow me,' and dragged me out of the room.

***

The cellar in Oaktree House runs underneath the back half of the building. I was uncomfortable being down there without Thora's knowledge. Frankie said she'd gone to a private hospital appointment and not the NHS. I wasn't sure what he meant. She didn't know that we were dating, as Frankie had said to keep it between us, although Sarah knew. Mum was getting suspicious about us, but she'd rather I neglected my schoolwork. Marriage was a better future for me, and I still hadn't told her that I wanted to go to uni.

The movement of his muscles enthralled me as I followed him down. He opened a door and turned on the light. We were in a large room with another door at the far end.

'Are we under the dining room?' My sense of direction was good.

'Yes.' His shadowy figure moved about in the dim light, creating an intimate sensation. I was completely in love with him but fought against showing him. He found my being obnoxious amusing (I'd realised from our first argument that he wasn't

41

easily offended) and didn't call me on my behaviour. He preferred to find me humorous and refused to take me seriously. This made me love him more, this man who took me as I was. Suspecting that my contradictory behaviour was a challenge, I'd catch him pausing, but instead of being irritated he'd take my hands and kiss them, acknowledging that I was a tease.

The floors were concrete, and the walls are brick. It smelt of dust, with a faint odour of things long abandoned. The room was full of junk: suitcases and trunks, and in the corner, a gramophone. The large horn-like speaker fascinated me, as did a pile of unappealing classical records. Frankie opened a chest and scrabbled through its contents. I looked through a pile of factual books. Most of them were medical digests, obviously Thora's father's; the eminent surgeon Mr Russell Kent.

'Look out – spider!' Frankie shouted.

I jumped and headed to where his finger pointed.

'What are you doing?' he asked.

'Looking for the spider.'

He had an amused look on his face as he said, 'You're supposed to scream and run.' He laughed and pulled his hands through the length of his hair over his ears.

'Why would I do that? Oh, because I'm a girl. I've probably seen more spiders than you have. I'm not afraid of them. They're harmless.'

'Okay, so you're not afraid of spiders.' He walked towards me and took my hands.

'No, and you could've asked me. You made me jump. I could've dropped one of those massive books on my foot.'

'What about rats? Are you afraid of rats?' He softly squeezed and then released my fingers; the sensation disarmed me.

'Not particularly. I don't *like* rats, but I'm not afraid of them. I wouldn't like to be bitten by one, though. Are there rats down here? There are lots on the farm.'

He pulled one of my hands to his mouth and kissed it. I held my breath to counteract the dizziness.

'Do you mean Perry's farm? Is Perry your boyfriend?'

'Of course not.' I shuddered theatrically.

Frankie chuckled. 'You spend a lot of time with him on the farm, though, don't you?'

'Not with him – ugh! And not so much now that he doesn't board at school anymore. Sarah and I help with stuff when he looks after his gran. She's very ill. He says she'll be dead soon. Are you jealous? You needn't be. He's about seventeen but acts like a child.'

'Of course I'm jealous. Checking out the competition.' He dropped my hands and stepped closer, placing his hands on my face. 'You're the most incredible …' He kissed me softly on my lips before pulling back and whispering, 'You didn't have sex with him, did you?'

My face flushed as I pushed him away. 'I told you, he's not my boyfriend.'

'I need to … know … it's the image …' He pulled me back and kissed me again. It was the most passionate kiss, simply wonderful. He moved his hand to my breast, and I pushed it away. 'Does that answer your question?'

'Yes.' He laughed and stepped away from me before pausing and laughing some more until I wasn't sure if he was laughing in a good or a bad way. 'I brought you down here to scare you, but you don't scare easily. Anyway, let's go back. You can make me lunch.'

'Make yourself lunch! We should wait for Thora to get back.'

'She'll be gone ages. Come on, race you up. Better be quick, or I lock you down here.' He slipped past me and headed for the stairs.

'If you lock me down here, I won't be able to make lunch,' I shouted as he disappeared upstairs. As I followed, I noticed a boy's school sock stuck underneath a closed door. There were spots of dried blood splattered on it. Perry used to wear similar ones, so I presumed it was his, part of his school uniform. But it couldn't be Perry's, it was too small. I couldn't pull it out, and the door was locked. I was puzzled by the oddity of it.

Chapter 9

Saturday, 11 April 1970

Frankie made himself comfortable at the kitchen table and picked up the newspaper, staring at the crossword. I put the kettle on the stove. It was cosy in the kitchen; the two of us in domestic bliss. The sandalwood musk of him, fresh like the woods in spring, zinged at my nostrils.

'What are you going to make me?' he asked, pulling a face that was meant to show me he was concentrating.

'Thora's left us something, remember? I'm not making you anything.' I smacked the paper out of his hands.

'Oi, what are you doing?' He scrambled to catch the paper.

'Didn't your mother teach you to look when someone's speaking to you?'

'Not that I remember. She wasn't bothered what I did.'

'Well, my mother would be. She said not to pander to boys. I have older brothers, remember.'

'Your mother sounds like a … um … strong woman.'

'She is and she … she's getting married again in September.'

'Oh. You don't sound happy about that. Who's she marrying?'

'Mr Philips. He's okay. He owns the supermarket and other stuff. It's just everything is going to change. We have to live in his big house in the city centre.'

'Oh, poor you!' Frankie laughed. 'The shame of moving from a council house into a private residence. Such a comedown.'

'You don't understand. That's the house where my dad died. The only home I've known. Where my friends live. Where I can walk out of my back door and straight into the countryside.'

'But you'll be living in a smarter place, and I expect Mr Philips will increase your pocket money.' He reached for me, but I stepped back. He didn't understand the seriousness of the situation. He started to say something, but there was a knock on the door, so I made my way through the hallway.

The shape of a man showed through the glass surrounding the front door. Opening it, I came face to face with Erik Schmidt. Fear and confusion mixed at the sight of his smirking face.

'Hello, Carol. You spend your time here? You have abandoned your art, yes?'

'No, I haven't. What d'you want?'

'I came to see the lady of the house – and you're not her.' He looked me up and down.

'She's not here. Goodbye.' I wanted to shut the door in his face but was afraid it would show Frankie how lower class I was.

'Ah, well, never mind. Please let her know I called and tell her that I'll see her soon.' He looked at my chest and pinched his eyes as he pressed his mouth into a thin line.

Shutting the door, I ran into the front room and pulled back the curtain to check that he'd left. He was making his way across the driveway, towards the lane. A car engine vroomed, gears crunched and the sound of gravel spit-pinged at metal as he left.

'What are you doing?' Frankie had crept up behind me.

'Jesus, Frankie, don't *do* that!' I said as I collapsed onto the chair.

'Do what? Who was at the door and where's my lunch?'

'No one.'

'No one? Well, Mister No One has certainly spooked you. Who was it? Someone selling us Christ the Redeemer? You took His name in vain.'

'A teacher.'

'What, Schmidt? Smutty Schmidt?'

How could Frankie know Schmidt? He noticed my confusion and said, 'Oh God, does he teach you, sweetheart?'

'Yes … well, no … why?' The look of horror on Frankie's face sent my pulse racing.

'Steer clear of him. He's one of Auntie's ex-patients. Pity they can't lock him up.'

'Lock him up? I don't understand.'

'He's a paedo. Paedophile, sweetheart.' He sat on the arm of the chair and put his hand on my shoulder. 'You don't know what I mean, do you? Schmidt has thoughts of sex with little girls.'

'What? He's a teacher at my school, why isn't he …?'

'He has thoughts; he doesn't act. At least, there's no proof that he does. You can't do anything to someone who just has thoughts. When he *does* something, he'll be locked up and they'll throw away the key. At least, that's the theory. Whether it happens, we'll see.'

He squeezed me and kissed my hair. 'Luckily, you're too old for him, or I would have to keep *you* locked up. With your small frame and innocent face, he could mistake you for prey, although you've grown up since Christmas. I mean, you're a lot taller.'

He laughed, looking at my chest. I was nauseous. My God, how did I let Schmidt entice me?

'What's wrong, sweetheart? You look like you've seen a ghost.'

'I have to see him at school … every day … and he … he … has some of my work, my poetry …'

'Too bad. Stay clear.' He stroked my hair behind my ear and I shuddered. 'Something's wrong, isn't it?'

'I went to his house.' I felt sick. The anxiety that had first started at Schmidt's house was once again coursing through my veins.

'What?' He squeezed in next to me and pulled me onto his lap. 'Tell me.'

'I … oh God, Frankie, you won't believe it … I went to his house. He took me there in his car. I had to hide on the back seat covered by a rug. He … he … bought me all this … art stuff, and he was … well, creepy. He crept around the house when I painted and wrote.'

Frankie's lips wrinkled in suppressed mirth, and his shoulders shook as he laughed so hard that he ejected me from his lap and said, 'I can't believe it. What were you thinking? Men want sex, Carol. That's all they want. How can you not know that?'

'But he's a teacher.'

'He's a teacher asking you to go back to his house on your own.' He slapped his thigh and then wiped tears from his eyes. 'God, you're easy.'

'Easy? You think I'm *easy*?' My brothers use that word about girls they call "slappers", but I'm not sure exactly what they mean.

'No. Of course not, sweetheart. Stop worrying. You'll be out of there soon doing grown-up things like making my lunch.'

Men want sex. He made it sound functional, devoid of emotion. Wasn't love involved? Escaping to the kitchen to get away from Frankie's mirth, I wondered if I'd known all along, somehow, and my determination to better myself had allowed me to mitigate his, now obvious, sickening persona.

'Need a hand, sweetie?' Frankie called after me.

'No, I'm fine.'

'Yeah? I'll have to get him to call round again tomorrow lunchtime.'

The sound of his laughter followed me into the kitchen, where pulling out plates and cutlery and generally moving about helped me to control my anxiety. The world was a strange place, and there seemed to be many rules to follow if you were going to survive. When would I learn them all?

Chapter 10

Sunday, 12 April 1970

Sarah wanted to go to Oaktree House to visit Thora, but I'd persuaded her that she couldn't and told her that Thora was too unwell for visitors. Frankie was uncertain how long Thora would allow him to stay and was doing everything to keep her on-side. He thought that if Thora felt she could rely on help from Sarah and me, she would send him away. There was no way I was going to put that in jeopardy, so we had to stay away.

She sat at her desk and I slouched on her bed, itching to tell her about my dates with Frankie, although my cheeks burnt with embarrassment at sharing these intimate details.

'I wrote you a coded letter,' she said and passed me a piece of paper.

'We've grown out of doing those. You're sixteen. It's childish.'

'Have we? Since when? 'She snatched the paper from me, screwed it up and dropped it on the floor. 'You don't want me now you have that Frankie.'

Her slouched shoulders seemed to reinforce that we were growing apart. I had a boyfriend and was making decisions about whether I should let him touch my breasts. She was where I'd left her before I met him.

'Shall I tell you about my dates with Frankie?'

She sat next to me on the bed. 'Not interested. He's ugly and too old for you.'

'Don't be like that. He's really lovely when you get to know him. You'll get a boyfriend soon. It can happen in an instant.'

'Oh, tell me then. But not too much detail.' She collapsed in giggles, and normally her sniggers would make me laugh and I'd join her, but I couldn't.

'We've been to loads of pubs. Luckily Sadie Fisher wasn't in the Cleave Inn when we went – that would be embarrassing, getting thrown out like a child. We drive around –'

'Does he let you drive? You like to drive.'

'No, but I'm working on him. I tell him that if he wants to drink more than two pints, I'll drive. But he drinks more than that and still won't let me.'

'You should make him.'

'He's not one of my brothers.'

'No, but. Do they like him?'

'Don't know. Don't care.'

'Bet he knows to take care of you. Matthew says if any boy treats me bad, he'll beat them up.'

'Yes, well, my brothers aren't like Matthew.' She was going to say something, but I cut in. 'I mean, they don't care as much.'

'Has he got brothers?'

'No, he's an only child and goes to private school. He's pretty rich. He's got a cleaning lady for his student digs.'

'A cleaning lady?' She sat up. 'Amazing.'

'He says his mum doesn't know how to clean.'

'Really?'

'And he plays piano and guitar. He's taking Music at university, though he's going to jack it in. He could be moving here if Thora lets him.'

'Oh.' Sarah got up and went to her desk.

'He's a bit of a joker. Always teasing me, and if I react he says I'm "too cute for words" and "a challenge". Anyway, thanks for doing my nail varnish, Sarah. Frankie thought it was great.'

'Did he?'

'Yes. He said he'd never seen nails like it.'

Sarah smiled and asked, 'Are you coming to Alice's party with me?'

'Not sure. Depends on Frankie.'

'Tell him you're going. You're my best friend and we need to do stuff together.' There was disappointment in her eyes, and

I felt estranged from her

'I ... can't ... I have to see him every chance I get because if I don't see him, he might dump me and get another girlfriend. And Thora could ask him to leave any day ...'

'I wish she would. I hope he buggers off tomorrow.'

'Sarah! Your mum could hear!'

'Don't care. Don't care anymore. Anyway, homework to do. You'd better go. I'm not the one in the A stream getting A's.'

Before I could protest, she went to the bathroom leaving me to see myself out.

***

Back home I select one of the books of my dad's that I'd claimed after his death. I tried to concentrate on reading, but the text swam in and out of focus. Thoughts whirled in my head about telling Sarah how Frankie looks at other girls all the time, about his incessant teasing; that he wasn't interested in my three brothers, or my driving, or the fact I could change a tyre and strip an engine.

Sarah needed to know that I felt stupid stumbling around in heels and wearing make-up that gave me spots, so that she could help me.

And how he smelt of musk and woodland and the fresh smell of spring water trickling through peat-lined streams ...

That he lied to us about his age because he was twenty.

That the hair at the back of his head flowed down past his collar, a golden mane like ripples of sand etched on the beach by the receding tide.

That he had a leather tie around his wrist with the word 'peace' etched into it.

That he wasn't afraid of my mum, and was going to convince her that we were good together.

And how he rested his hand on my thigh as though it was

natural, and kissed me with so much passion that I couldn't breathe, or think, or remember who I was.

And how I was going to die, if he returned to London.

I threw the book at the wall. Sarah couldn't help me. No one could. It had always been my dad's dream that I'd go to university. Mum had always shrugged and said 'we'll see'. As I ran my fingers over dad's wonderful books the way that he had, I longed for him to come back and guide me. But my dad's dream of me making something of my life crumbled in the pull of Frankie's magnetism. Frankie was winning because Frankie was with me. He was the man in my life now.

Chapter 11

Saturday, 25 April 1970

Frankie's bedroom was at the back of the house. He'd been at Thora's since Easter. His clothes filled the wardrobe and his shoes lined the wall. He'd brought his record player and records down from London. His aftershave sat on the dressing table, along with his car keys, lighter and a cigarette packet.

Listening to records was our excuse to go to his bedroom. Thora didn't like it but relented, treating me more like an adult than my mum did. Besides, she was ill and didn't have the strength to argue. Her visits to the hospital left her drained, and for some reason she'd started wearing a wig.

Frankie selected a record and put it on the turntable. He never asked what I'd like. His bedroom was three times the size of mine. An art deco theme ran throughout the house. A mirror with square bevelled edges sat on an oak dressing table that also had squared edges. The headboard matched the rest of the furniture. (This room is the same even now.) The room was feminine because Thora's mother was an interior designer. Interior design was a career I'd not heard of, and, after quizzing, Thora promised to investigate which exams were needed as interior design was my new career aim. This house inspired and delighted me, as it still does.

Frankie's hair was tied back, damp from washing. I was allowed to see him 'look like a girl'. He shuffled through his records, and I imagined the flow of his hair when he removed the band. He was an absolute dream.

It was hot in there in the April sunshine. He turned and smiled and said, 'Sit down then.'

As I sat on the chair in front of the dressing table, I said,

'Don't shut the door.'

He let out a long sigh. 'You're a spoilsport.' Then he threw himself onto the bed as music played quietly.

'Thora's downstairs. I don't like the door being closed.'

'She won't mind; she's very open-minded.' He put his hands over his face in mock dismay. 'You worry too much.'

'I'm not worrying too much. I don't like it.'

This room was nothing like Schmidt's bedroom, and Frankie was the absolute opposite of Schmidt, yet that same queasiness stirred in my stomach. Men only want sex. But surely women liked sex as well?

'No one gives a monkey's what we do. We don't have to tell anyone.'

'I hope not. Have you told your parents about us yet? Your friends, anyone?'

'No, not yet.' He shifted to sit up.

'So your mum and dad don't know about me? You didn't tell them when you went home?'

'No. I'll tell them next time they phone.'

'Every one of my family and friends knows.'

He shrugged in casual dismissal, which grated. My dating a posh boy from London, who lives in the witch's house on the hill, had fuelled the grapevine.

'So, we're not serious?' I sat on the dressing-table stool.

'Oh no, not that old chestnut. You are important to me. You know that. But I don't tell them everything about my life. Never have.' He lifted his arms, inviting me in. Who tells their parents everything anyway, I reasoned as I stayed put, wondering about chestnuts. His eyes clouded in dismay.

'God, Carol, you think too much. Does your pretty little brain hurt?'

'What do you mean?'

'That pretty little brain whirling around.' He grinned, and his fingers pattered the top of his head.

'Huh, how can it be pretty? It's hidden in my skull.' Maybe I was too standoffish. I went to him and flipped my hand across his shoulder, 'And it's not little.'

'You're exasperating, darling. Always starting rows over nothing.'

'I'm not starting rows.'

He made a grab for my arm but missed as I stepped back. 'You're lovely when you're angry.'

'I'm not angry. Why would I be angry? After all, I have a pretty, and pretty big, brain.'

'Come here and let me kiss you better. I'm sorry for saying your pretty brain was little.' He pulled a sad face and wiped a pretend tear from his eye.

'Frankie, I'm going to hit you in a minute!'

'You won't hit me when you know what I've found out.' He looked away towards the window, his face solemn. I thought of Thora's ill health and dreaded what he was going to say. 'I've found out that my mother isn't my mother.'

'She's not your mother?' I leant forward to take his hand, but he shook me off.

'No,' He wriggled away towards the window. 'Forget it. Forget I said anything. I shouldn't have told you. I'm not allowed to tell anyone. You won't say anything, will you? Promise me.'

'Of course I promise you.'

He knelt next to me, taking my hand, and pulled me down to kneel beside him as he whispered, 'It's nice talking to you. These last months have been hard. I'm not allowed to talk to anyone in London. If it got out that my father had an affair, it could ruin him. Not that Mother will let that happen.'

'She raised you even though you're not hers?'

'She can't have children, and she wanted a child so …'

'Are you saying that your real mother gave you away?'

He sobbed at my thoughtless words.

'Do you *know* who your mother is?'

'Yes. But I can't tell you, or I'll be disinherited, damned to hell, or whatever. Would never have found out but I needed a passport. They hadn't thought about that.' He pulled away and plucked at his leather bracelet. I pulled him back, and he cried on my shoulder. 'You mustn't tell anyone. Promise me you won't say a word. Mother and Father don't care about me. They only care about their "position" and their friends.'

'Is that why you came here? To get away from them? Does Thora know this.'

He nodded as I spoke and said, 'Yes.' He brushed the hair off my face. 'You're very clever, sweetheart. I need time to think. Work out what to do. This has messed up my degree. I can't concentrate, can't study. It's all so …' He collapsed against me. I rocked him softly, his face close to my breast.

'Don't worry my darling. I'll look after you.' My knees creaked, and I wanted to get up, but I hung on to him, taking his pain to make him better. I'd make him see how much he needed me.

Chapter 12

Saturday, 9 May 1970

The fields and woods surrounding Oaktree House awakened new sensations within me as I walked through them with Frankie. We watched as the paired magpies squabbled and squawked before swooping up over the lone maple at the head of Dawnview Field. My monochrome life had slipped away over the months since I'd met Frankie and I was as fresh and delicate as a butterfly.

Colour now drenched my world, dripping over Dawnview Lane and sliding down the branches of the sycamores and hawthorn bushes so that even the dandelions shone bright orange. We made our way home wearing daisy-chain crowns, woven in our hair; we'd had a mock coronation, crowning ourselves King and Queen of Oaktree Estate. Stealing one last kiss in the hallway, we congratulated ourselves on returning just as the threatening clouds burst and rain clattered down upon the driveway, clapping at the leaves of the oak tree.

We were impervious to the inconveniences of ordinary life and rose above the mundane. We were the chosen pair. We untangled reluctantly; our lips separated, but the honey taste of him remained at the back of my throat.

Thora was in the kitchen making a pot of tea. A well-risen Madeira cake sat on a plate in the middle of the table. When we congratulated her on her success, she gave a half smile and sat, motioning for us to sit with her.

'How's Sarah?' she asked as she cut the cake.

'Fine.' I'd hardly seen Sarah, and my guilt at neglecting her was growing by the day.

'I was wondering why she doesn't come here anymore.'

'I don't see much of her now Frankie and I …'

'You mustn't neglect your friends, Carol.'

'She's not neglecting her friends, Auntie.' Frankie bit off a piece of cake and cupped his hand under his chin to catch crumbs.

'Sarah's only next door, so I see her all the time.' I hadn't spoken to Sarah for weeks. She didn't bother knocking anymore. I'd turned her away too many times. Thora looked like she could read my mind.

'It would be nice to see her, so bring her with you next time.'

'Yes, I will …'

'It depends on what we're doing Auntie. We −' Frankie coughed as he choked on his cake.

'Don't let Frankie, or any man, stop you from seeing your friends.'

'But he *doesn't* …'

'Good. Make sure it stays that way.'

Thora had a bee in her bonnet about something. She'd been moody for days.

'I have something to tell you.' She poured the tea. 'I've decided to spend some time travelling. I leave next Tuesday for a cruise, then go on to visit some distant relatives in New Zealand.' She ate some cake. 'So, Frankie, you will have to leave this weekend.'

My world crashed. Frankie must not leave me. Not when I loved him so much. Not when I was nearly sixteen.

Frankie asked, 'Won't you need someone to take care of the house? I'm happy to stay.'

'The house will be locked. Mr Cutler has the key and will take care of the place, with Perry's help.' She picked at her cake. 'I appreciate that you two have spent a lot of time here, but things have changed. I intend to see some of the world before I … and I don't want the worry of you living here. So you have to leave, Frankie.' There was a dismissive tone in her voice. She didn't want us to be together, but I wouldn't let her stop us.

'Frankie can rent a place nearby.'

'I'm sure he can – can't you, Frankie?'

He straightened and said, 'I was thinking of changing to Bristol Uni anyway.'

'I thought you'd abandoned university.' Thora's cake crumbled, spilling onto her plate.

'Not abandoned. I've taken time out. As you well know. After what happened at Christmas.'

He was angry. Thora stiffened as I asked, 'What happened at Christmas?' belatedly remembering.

'Nothing.' They said it in unison, their eyes locked on to each other. Fearing an argument, and annoyed with Thora, I said, 'Just because you're leaving doesn't mean we won't be together.'

'I'm not asking Frankie to leave to thwart your relationship. What I'm doing has nothing to do with the two of you. I want to spend the remainder of my … oh, I don't have to give a reason.'

'You can move in with me, Frankie. Denny spends most of his time at Gerry's so you can have his room.' I smiled in encouragement and at the thought of us together on a more permanent level. 'At least until Mum gets married. She'll want some rent, of course.'

'I can't pay rent.' There was a mean tone to his voice. 'My home is in London, so it looks like I'm moving back, if Auntie insists.' His words were cold.

'There must be something we can do?' I stared at the tablecloth and allowed the red and white checks to swim before my eyes in a watery haze. Frankie drained his tea and left the room. The front door slammed.

'You'll be fine. Forget Frankie.' Thora put her hand on mine. 'Listen, Carol, Frankie's no good for you.'

'What do you mean? He's fine for me.'

'You have a future, a different future, without Frankie. You're smart and must go to university. You need to be yourself for a while before you tie yourself down to someone like Frankie … Boys hold you back. They'll stop you from being you.'

Her words reminded me of Schmidt. Anger bubbled. 'Frankie would never do that. He loves me. He loves everything about me. That I'm feisty and different and a challenge.'

'A challenge?'

'Yes. He likes that about me. I mean ... he tries to, sometimes – you know, get me to change my mind about things; but I ignore him. I'm used to bossy boys.'

'You're not dealing with your brothers. Your brothers look after you.'

'He looks after me.'

'No, he doesn't. He looks after himself.' She took my hand. 'Frankie's father, Frederick, is an eminent London psychiatrist. He holds a certain position in society. His mother Catherine is, how can I put it ... a snob.'

'A snob?'

'They move in high places, know people, rich ... the borders of royalty. He's being knighted for services to mental health, which I have to say he deserves. I worked with him for years, before ...' She lets go of my hand. 'So you see, their son's involvement with a girl, a fifteen-year-old girl from a council estate, won't be entertained.'

'Frankie can do what he wants. They can't stop him.' I took my cup and saucer to the sink and placed my hands on the worktop for support. My words sounded hollow. Frankie and I were worlds apart.

'Frankie will be persuaded against you. His parents support him, both financially and emotionally, and they will withdraw their support.'

The world had ended. She was telling the truth. Frankie had not only left the house, he'd also left me. An hour ago I had fought off his advances, but now he wouldn't bother with me. The council-house girl was not good enough.

Thora stood behind me. 'I did try to warn you.' She put her hands on my shoulders. 'I'm sorry, Carol. I've been distracted with my health, but I should have made sure you knew. I feel awful about not intervening.'

She *had* warned me. And I hadn't listened. That was why he hadn't told his parents about me. I was an idiot.

'I'm going home.' I fetched my bag and coat and slammed the door as I ran out. The fresh air hit my face like a long overdue slap.

Chapter 13

Saturday, 9 May 1970

My anger turned to full-on rage as I reached the track, stumbling in my heels. The heavy rain had turned the path into a mudslide. Belatedly, I'd pulled a torch from my bag just as I'd tripped and hit my head on a log. Blood seeped from my knee. My limbs were weak, and my anxiety reached a new high.

Covered in mud and bracken, I arrived at the corner of my road to find Frankie's car parked outside my house. He ran towards me.

'Carol! What happened? Oh my God. Are you hurt?'

I cried with relief as he crushed me to him and cried 'Sweetheart, sweetheart,' as he kissed my hair. We clasped each other until I pulled away, and then his passionate kisses attacked me. Desperate for him to love me, I responded eagerly, clutching and clinging to him. He mustn't leave me again; he must never leave me. My body was on fire, and we were fused, no longer separate beings. My desire for him flowed free at last, and my sadness left on the wind. Despite all reason or convention, we would be together. Frankie took my hand and led me to his car and we got in.

'What happened to you?' I asked.

'What happened to *me*? What happened to *you*? I went to the car to fetch a present for you, and then to the bathroom. By the time I got back downstairs Thora said that you'd bolted from the house like a bat out of hell.'

'Oh.' How silly and pathetic to presume that he was leaving me. Thora had been lying to break us up. She'd never liked us being together. Frankie didn't care about her, or his parents, or anything else. All Frankie cared about was me. Frankie loved me.

'So … where's my present?'

'Close your eyes and put out your hands.' Something small was placed on my palm. 'Open your eyes.'

The light was fading under heavy cloud cover, but the earrings glinted. They were the ones from the shop in Glastonbury. He'd noticed me admiring them and had gone back to buy them. He had done it to make me happy. I admired the three gold drop chains, each with a different charm: a sun, a moon and a star. I was speechless at the beauty and the expense. It proved he loved me.

'Put them on.'

'I can't. I don't have pierced ears. We can go and get them pierced tomorrow.'

'Sorry, sweetheart, not tomorrow.' He looked out of the windscreen. 'I have to go back to London to sort some stuff out.'

If these were a parting gift, he could have them back.

'I'll be as quick as I can. Need to sort out my student digs. Got to move all my stuff back home and see the parents. They miss me.' He grinned as he took my hand.

'Can I come with you?'

'No,' he said, too quickly for my liking. 'I mean – yes, you can come with me next time, but not this time, too much to do. Have to convince Thora to let me stay before she leaves. I'll work on Dad. Dad's always good at talking to her. He'll make her see sense. I'll tell him about you, and he'll support us. He's an old romantic at heart.'

'But what if Thora won't let you stay? What if she says no? What will happen to us, Frankie?'

'Listen, sweetheart.' He swivelled around to face me. 'When I want something, I get it, and I want you. We'll get through this. I'll be moving into Oaktree House soon. Trust me.'

'I do, Frankie, but …'

He put his finger on my lips.

'Trust me.'

Chapter 14

Tuesday, 12 May 1970

It was the end of lunchtime. The road was teeming with children making their way back to school. A group hovered in the doorway of the chip shop as I pushed past.

'Al'right Carol? Not with lover-boy? He packed you in?' Sally Major was, as usual, in bully mode, hanging around with her two favourite mates. The three of them blocked my way. I took a step towards her, clenching my fists. She had to get the message that if she said one more word, I'd attack her. Her bravado faltered, as she knew I wasn't afraid to fight. Fifteen years old yet we were like children. Impending womanhood hadn't changed anything. Just one word was all I needed to attack her. She opened her mouth but, sensing imminent danger, wavered, then turned and said, 'Better keep back from china-doll, girls. Don't want those fat cheeks to burst all over us.'

As they left, the temptation to batter the back of her head grew. I smashed the door to the chippy into the wall in frustration as I entered.

'Oi! Watch it!'

'Sorry, Mr Chippy. Don't know my own strength!' He grunted at my smiling apology. 'Chips, please.'

'Gonna have to wait. Just put a new batch in.'

He swept my coins into the till as I sat in the bay window. The walls were greasy. A young man walked in. 'Chips, mate.'

'Be five minutes.'

'Okay.' The young man dropped some coins on the counter before turning, 'Al'right, Carol?'

Matthew stood in front of me. My heart skipped a beat at the sight of him. He was sweaty and hadn't shaved. His cruel mouth and soft eyes with their long lashes captivated me. My heart banged as moisture formed between my thighs. He was well-built, not as slim as Frankie, but sturdier and a bit older. He moved towards me.

'Hi, Matthew.' His name rolled off my tongue and I liked it. He moved closer, towards my quaking knees.

'Not with our Sarah?'

'She's at school.'

'Is she? Oh yeah. Why aren't you?' He laughed and added, 'Only teasing. I have a certificate for bunking off.'

My skin was on fire; I was a schoolgirl in a woman's body, out of place and out of time. He looked at my legs then looked away. I uncrossed them and crossed them again. My skirt was short: one that Sarah gave to me that had belonged to Paula, Matthew's dead wife.

'Still with that chap?' he asked.

'Frankie? Yes.'

'That's been a while. Want a lift back?' He glanced around. Mr Chippy dropped the shaken chips back into the fryer before he returned to the back of the shop.

'Oh, no thanks.' I didn't want to be alone with Matthew, him and me in his van.

'You sure?' he asked. His blue eyes twinkled.

'Yes, but thanks.'

'I'm going to Mum's anyway to take Chrissie her doll.'

'Okay then.'

He sat and our legs touch. The back door opened, and Chippy came back.

'Ready now, folks.' We went to the counter as the chips got a final shake. Matthew was behind me; his hip strong against my trembling hip. Our hands touched as we reached for the bags. We got into the van, but he didn't start the engine, so we ate.

An image of Paula came to mind as I chewed my greasy chips. The memory of how he had kissed her on their wedding day, his face a mixture of awe and respect, a look I'd never seen a man give a woman. Nineteen years old and a year later she died giving birth to Chrissie. At her funeral, I'd cursed God, before quickly saying a prayer for my sin. But still, He couldn't exist. Depriving a baby of her mother was cruel.

Paula's clothes sat abandoned at the bottom of Sarah's wardrobe where her mother had dumped them. We passed them between us on the instruction not to let them 'go to waste', and altered them to suit us. We should have felt uneasy, but the excitement of fashionable, grown-up clothes at our disposal overruled that.

Outside my house, Matthew asked about my mum getting married, but I didn't want to talk about it. We didn't open the van doors to get out, but sat, neither of us moving. He didn't light a cigarette. He didn't smoke. Frankie smoked. He picked at a fingernail then lurched forward, switching on the engine.

'I need to fetch something from home. It's something I don't need any more, and you may as well have it.'

I said, 'Sure,' and we pulled away; his legs jerked between the accelerator and brake, throwing me against the door as we cornered. I wanted to ask, 'Where's the fire?' but was afraid to distract him.

His house was at the other end of our estate. Its position was the same distance from Oaktree House as ours was. He unlocked his front door and I followed him in.

'Up here.' His bed was unmade, the sheets in a tangle, as though he had thrashed around in the night. He pulled a jacket out of the wardrobe. It matched my skirt. 'Here. She'd want you to have it. Slip it on.'

As I slipped off my jacket, he held out Paula's, his face set hard. I hesitated, expecting him to pull it away and return it to the wardrobe, shut it away from the cruel light of day. But he was resolute, so I turned and slid in my arms. He pulled it up, catching my elbows in his haste. His hands lingered on my shoulders before he turned me to face him. He studied the fit; his eyes assessed my chest.

'You're the same size. Paula was small.'

A vision of Paula: heavily pregnant, pulling herself into his van, matchstick arms and legs. Then of her coffin inside a hearse. 'I'll alter it if that's okay?'

'What will you do to it? I see the skirt is half its length.' His smile didn't reach his eyes as he pushed my hair back with his fingers, making my breasts tingle.

'The sleeves are a bit out of fashion,' I said, 'so I'll cut them off above the elbow and hem them.' His fingers played with my hair; smoothing the strands around my ears. 'And I'll put denim pockets on, and do the same on the skirt to match.' His hands lay on my face, and his eyes moved from my chest to my eyes.

'You're very good with your hands, Carol.'

'People tell me that.' I couldn't breathe; my lungs wouldn't work. If he'd kissed me, I would've passed out.

'Yes, you are. You'll make someone a good wife.'

'Depends if I get a good husband.'

'Oh, you will.' His face softened, and the release enchanted, so I reached up to touch his cheek before leaning in to kiss him. He dropped his hands and stepped back, tipping his head away from me and asking, 'What are you doing?'

'I ... I ... um ... you had something on your face.' I pursed my lips and blinked as he stiffened his shoulders. We stood still. An ice-cream van played, 'Girls And Boys Come Out To Play'; its eerie chimes echoed along the street.

'Come on. We'd better get back. Shouldn't you be at school? Oh, forgot: you bunked off. Where d'you go?'

'To the doc's.'

'Women's trouble is it?' He laughed then turned to me, his face serious with what he had assumed. 'You're too young, so don't.'

How could he know I'd gone to get the pill? The thought of it brought heat to my face, as it did when my doctor told me that I was too young. Matthew took my hands and squeezed them together in a kneading motion and said, 'Don't let him ruin your life. You're too young to get tied down. Believe me; I know what I'm talking about.'

My skin crept with cold from the ghost of his wife. He walked to the window to open it. The light cast him in silhouette, and his strong outline stirred excitement and fear in me. Fear of what he could do to me. Excitement at what that would mean.

'Time to go, Raven. D'you, mind me calling you Raven? It suits you. All your beautiful long wavy hair.' He lifted a strand and rubbed its silkiness. Before I answered, he strode out of the room saying, 'This room's too bloody stuffy.'

He crashed downstairs, so unlike Frankie's gentle manner. I promised myself that when Frankie got back, he'd be the only one for me. Matthew had to be forgotten.

Chapter 15

Monday, 25 May 1970

A blob with pupil-less eyes and a toothless mouth made of bright pink bubble-gum floated through my dream. Its semi-formed shape fought a battle to reach an unknown goal. Reaching for it, I attempted to pin on the eyes and ears I'd stolen from Frankie. Curled in my dream-bed, snug beneath candyfloss sheets, Frankie slid into a tank where hundreds of purple tadpoles surrounded him. Each had an eel-like tail, with a barbed end flicking in frustration. They swam towards him as he drowned, his fish-mouth gasping for air, and his hands groped for mine, but fear rendered me unresponsive to his predicament. Jolting awake, I gasped for breath as sweat ran over me.

Thoughts of yesterday's visits to the doctor and Matthew's house rushed in as I made for the bathroom. A long walk through the countryside should restore some balance to my soul, I told myself. It was my birthday; I was sixteen.

***

Frankie was back! He'd left a message with Sarah that I must go to Oaktree House at six o'clock to celebrate my birthday. Thora has gone on a cruise, he'd said, and he'd moved in until she returned.

'Oh, it's you,' he teased as he opened the door. 'Here she is, the birthday girl. Sweet sixteen.' He kissed me then abruptly let me go. 'Better not get into that, sweetheart. Now, where did I put your birthday present …'

I followed him into the kitchen. The table was covered with crumbs and dirty crockery and told the story of a shared meal.

'And now,' he mimicked as he played a drum roll on his leg.

He picked up a square box and handed it to me.

It had to be an engagement ring. Savouring the moment, I asked him, 'Do you want to say something first?'

'Say something first? Um, happy birthday – again.'

'You're a tease, Frankie! I'll remind you of this one day.'

He seemed more confused than excited, and I felt idiotic. It wasn't a ring. The box was too flat and heavy. Much too heavy. But tearing off the wrapping did reveal a jeweller's box, lavish, solid, with the maker's name in gold lettering.

'Open it; it's not a bomb.'

Inside was a heavy gold chain with a solid, heart-shaped locket and a padlock closure. The gold necklace my mother bought me hung around my neck; the 'C' shaped charm was flimsy.

'Frankie it's beautiful! I love it. Thank you, darling.' I threw my arms around him and kissed him, breathing in his intoxicating smell.

'Glad you like it. Let me help you.' He took the box and lifted the chain from its cushion. 'You'll have to take the other one off.'

'Do I have to? Mum bought it, so I want to keep it on.'

'She mentioned she was buying you a necklace.'

'Did she? When did you talk to Mum?'

Mum loved talking to Frankie on the phone. She giggled like a schoolgirl, reluctant to pass him to me. She kept telling me that he was charming and quite a catch.

'I phoned her to check what you'd like.'

'So now I have two necklaces.'

'You're a woman, Carol. You need jewellery. Ask any woman.' He moved behind me and looped the chain around my neck. Then he unclasped mum's chain and dropped it on the table. 'Gorgeous. Look in the hallway mirror.'

The large heart-shaped locket sat amongst heavy gold links. All I could think was, *He loves me.*

'It opens. Let me show you.' He slid his finger along the edge

70

of the heart and eased the two sides apart. The look of concentration on his face, so close, so intent on pleasing me, was thrilling. 'You need a picture of us to put inside.'

'We'll get someone to take one. Maybe when Perry comes ...'

'Perry's not coming here. Don't need *him* poking about. I'll manage things.'

Back in the kitchen, I placed my mother's chain around my neck.

'You can't wear both.' His sharp voice jarred. 'It looks odd. They clash.'

'Clash? How? They're both made of gold.' Holding his against my lips, I smiled assertively; I would do what I wanted.

'Mine's a special gift. I want you to wear it on its own.' He was telling me what to do again, but he wasn't going to get away with it.

'Not today. I'm wearing both.' I released the heart from my grip and let it drop onto my throat.

'Okay. For today, birthday girl. But wear mine on its own when we're together.'

'When will I get the chance to wear my mum's chain?'

He registered the implication and pulled me into his arms, saying, 'I have a feisty one here. Okay, sweetheart. You're the boss.'

He kissed my cheek and ran his hands around to my bottom. I disengaged myself. 'Has someone been here?'

'No. Why d'you ask?'

'Two cups, two saucers, two plates.'

'I'm lazy. Anyway, you're early. I said six.'

'Thought I'd surprise you. Don't let me stop you doing the washing-up.'

'*You're* here now, so ...'

I smacked his arm and we grappled in laughter as he tickled me. His hands moved near my breasts, and I pushed him away, asking, 'Where are you taking me?'

'You choose. It's your day.

'Chewton Lakes, then. South of here, about six miles. There's a nice pub in Chewton.'

'Chewton Lakes it is. Whatever my birthday girl wants she gets.'

***

Frankie was driving us home and had turned off the main road.

'Where are we going?' I'd been dozing, unsure where we were.

'Back to Oaktree.'

'It's late, Frankie. I need to get home.'

'It's too early for the birthday girl to go home.'

Slumped in a woozy, happy state, I watched branches whiz past as the headlights swept along the lane, creating the sensation of us drifting in a verdant light show.

'Have another drink. The night is young.' Frankie rubbed his hand along my thigh and under the hem of my skirt. I didn't push him away.

In the kitchen, I filled a glass with water.

'Here. Have some vodka.' He picked up a bottle of colourless liquid.

'Vodka. Is it alcoholic?'

'No, it's like water.'

Taking the glass, I sipped, 'Oh? Then I'll stick to water.' I giggled.

'Don't be boring on your birthday. You're sixteen. The world is yours. You can get married.'

My heart skipped a beat. He was going to ask me to marry him after all. Pure happiness heated my blood. Frankie was lovely, and I loved him – he was gorgeous and lovely, and I needed to get very close to him. I removed my jacket.

'That's more like it. Relax, darling.' He took me in his arms and kissed me so hard I couldn't breathe, but I liked it. He picked

72

me up, and I giggled; I couldn't stop giggling as he walked out of the kitchen and up the stairs. He put me down beside his bed.

'I need the bathroom,' I said.

'Don't take too long.'

I returned to find his room full of candles. They flickered enticingly, reminding me of the safety of the church, and hymns, and Christmas. Frankie was naked on the bed. He pushed himself up onto his elbow. 'At last, sweetheart. What kept you?'

'Nothing,' I said as I lay down beside him and pulled his golden face to mine.

Chapter 16

Sunday, 14 June 1970

F rankie's naked back curved away from me as I traced my fingers softly along his spine. He trembled but didn't wake. The past three weeks had been a blur of kissing, hand-holding and lovemaking. I wondered why I had ever worried about 'doing it', and was pleased to be grown-up at last. I couldn't stop smiling to myself, and Frankie admonished me, saying that I was competing with the Cheshire cat from *Alice in Wonderland.* Sarah couldn't look me in the eye for the first week but had finally accepted that Frankie and I were a couple. Each day I'd crossed my fingers and hoped that Thora stayed away on her cruise. She'd said that she might island-hop somewhere in the South Pacific and come back on a different ship. She could be gone forever, I thought, and I could be waking up in bed with Frankie forever.

The telephone was ringing. I groaned, knowing that it would be my mum and what she would be calling to say.

The cool morning air seeped around me as I slipped on one of Frankie's discarded shirts and went out onto the landing. Sarah looked out of the bedroom opposite and gave me a resigned smile before retreating. I crept downstairs. Frankie had fought with Denny last night at Mother's fiftieth birthday party. Frankie's bloodied clothes lay abandoned on the hallway floor. The sight of them reminded me of all the shouting. My head hurt as I remembered Denny's ugly face, angry and snarling, and the disgusting language he'd shouted. Lies about Frankie kissing his girlfriend. As if he'd kiss that ugly bitch when we were in the next room. If he had, I would have killed him. Sally would spread the details all over the estate. I'd be a laughing stock.

Rosemary had slunk around revelling in the assertion that

Frankie found her attractive. A sly, winking expression on her face as she watched Denny jostle in drunken anger against the cool detachment of my Frankie. Mum would not allow any explanation from Denny that painted Frankie as anything less than perfect.

The ringing had stopped, so I waited and grabbed the phone as soon as it rang again.

'Carol, is that you?'

'Yes, Mum.'

'Where's Thora?'

'Over at Mr Cutler's. They're planning a kitchen-garden project for Perry.' The lie slipped out easily.

'Now, before I forget, Peter says he can't employ you anymore. You've missed too many shifts.'

'Well, it's no loss, is it? I wasn't any good at it.'

'You weren't any good because you didn't apply yourself, young lady! And no, it's no great loss because someone who needs a job now has one.'

'Well, that's sorted then, Mum. Shall we forget it?'

'Carol you're exasperating. Your wages are here waiting for whenever you decide to come home. And Mr Jessop stopped me at the supermarket yesterday saying that you'd missed school. Where are the letters they've written because I've not seen any?'

'Well, if I'm not staying on there's no point in my going.'

'Not staying? For heaven's sake, girl! You said you wanted to be an interior designer and Peter said he'd help with that. Have you changed your mind again?'

'No. It's just that … Can we talk when I get back?'

'We will, young lady, mark my words. Anyway, how's Frankie? What did the hospital say? Sorry I couldn't stay.'

'You didn't need to. I can manage Frankie. Matthew drove us home, and Sarah and Alice stayed over.'

'That was good of Matthew. I must thank him. What did the doctor say?'

75

'His nose isn't broken, just swollen. And no concussion, but we have to go back if he starts being sick or something. He has a black eye and a couple of stitches in his eyebrow. He may have a little scar there.'

'Oh no! Not on his handsome face. My God! He has *such* a handsome face.'

'Yes, Mum, he does – but it's fine.' Mum's words irritated with their intimacy about Frankie's looks. 'He says he's not worried and it'll make him look tough.'

'Oh, I can't believe Denny! After Frankie arranged everything and paid, and then he does that, I just … Where on earth did Denny get the idea that Frankie would kiss a tart like Rosemary Major? Oh, wait until I see him!'

'So it's okay for your son to go with her, but not Frankie?'

'What? Oh, Denny's not going to *marry* her, is he? He's just … having fun.'

'Fun? He's sleeping with her.'

'We don't know that. Anyway, perhaps I'll question him about that as well. We don't want her sort in our family.'

'Don't be hard on him, Mum. It was a misunderstanding. Frankie didn't help by saying Rosemary was attractive. He was irritating Denny.'

'Well, that's a fine thing to say about your boyfriend. Denny's not perfect. He's got a temper on him …'

'I'm not saying –'

'You'd do well to remember where your loyalties lie, young lady.'

'I do … I –'

'Let me speak to Thora and apologise.'

'I told you, she's gone to Mr Cutler's.'

'Oh yes.' Mum paused, and I could almost hear her thought process. 'I haven't spoken to Thora for ages. Is she okay?'

'She's fine.'

'Well, tell her that I apologise on behalf of my hot-headed son who needs a smack …'

'I'll tell her.' I jumped as Frankie reached around me and took the handset.

'Melissa. Good morning. How are you?' He turned his back to me as he stepped away. I remembered how he had flirted with her before, and how he kept saying how good she looked for her age. Ten years younger, easily, with a figure wasted on an old goat like Peter Philips. 'No, don't you waste your time, Melissa. I'm fine. Yes. Don't be too hard on Denny. I'd be the same if I thought someone was messing with Carol. Yes. You have a beautiful daughter. We both know where she gets those charming looks from, don't we? No, I'm not teasing you. Why don't you and Peter come over for lunch on Sunday? Of course Thora will be here. She'll be delighted. Okay, and don't worry, I'll survive. I've had worse playing rugby. And I have Thora and Carol spoiling me. See you Sunday about one – no, let's make it twelve, and we'll have a swift half in the Cleave Inn first. It's a date, Melissa. Bye.' He replaced the telephone and dropped onto the stairs. 'Phew. She wanted to come over now.'

'She's going to turn up one day and find out Thora's not here. And that we're … um … together. You invited her for lunch on Sunday, or did I misunderstand?'

'Ah, but I'll have a bad headache Sunday and cancel.'

'But they'll see each other soon, and we'll be in trouble when they work out what we've been doing.' I sat next to him and touched his swollen face, gently running my fingers across his cheek.

'Don't worry about it. What your mother doesn't know won't hurt her. She abandons you when she stays at Peter's, so it's her lookout if you get up to mischief.'

'Yes, but –'

'Stop worrying, my naughty girl. Your mum is easy to charm. If she finds out, I'll just have to make an honest woman of you.' He pulled me close and kissed me and kept kissing me to stop me arguing with him until I moved against his nose.

'Ouch! That hurts!' He gently pressed his face.

'Don't do that. I'll get you a cold flannel.'

'You do that, sweetheart. And while you're about it, a cup of tea and some aspirin. Then come back to bed and see if you can do something to take my mind off this pain.'

'Behave! … I didn't know you played rugby.'

'I don't. Wouldn't look this good if I'd let a bunch of hooligans at me. Now hurry up.' He slapped my bottom as I headed for the kitchen.

Chapter 17

Sunday, 14 June 1970

W hen we eventually went down, Sarah and Alice were clearing away their breakfast things.

'Hope you were okay sharing that room?' I asked as I put water in the kettle and washed the teapot. Frankie liked his tea freshly brewed.

'Yes. Fine.' Sarah sat as Alice left the room.

'What's up?' I whispered.

She shrugged and picked at some crumbs. A horn tooted and Alice rushed back in.

'Thanks for letting me stay, Carol. Have to go. Dad's waiting. See you.'

'That's okay. Bye, Alice. See you soon.' She slammed the door and the sound vibrated through the hallway.

'What happened?' I asked Sarah again.

'Nothing. We had a row. Well, not a row, just a sort of …'

'Disagreement?'

'Yes.'

'What about?' I didn't want to know. Sarah could be so strait-laced and proper. I imagined her chastising Alice for drinking too much. I made the tea, glad that she didn't reply.

'Morning, girls. How are my two favourite girls in the whole world today?'

Sarah giggled and blushed. 'How's your face, Frankie?'

'It's sore Sarah. Come and give it a little kiss to make it better.'

'Stop teasing her, Frankie. Go and chop some wood.'

'What do we need wood for?'

'Keep the range going.' He looked at me as if I was mad. 'I can always call Perry.'

'No you don't. I'll do it. She's such a slave-driver, isn't she,

Sarah. She's got me running around at her beck and call. It's exhausting.'

'Hardly! What do you do that's so exhausting? Play the piano?'

'Well, I can't say in front of Sarah, can I? It's exhausting being that good.' He winked and skipped over to squeeze me. 'Those lessons from the drunken gynaecologist have been worth their weight in gold.'

'Frankie!' I hit him hard on the arm and pushed him away. Sarah glowed bright red and didn't know where to look.

'You weren't pushing away from me last night. Okay, I'm going.' He left, grabbing a piece of toast and humming the 1812 Overture as he banged his other arm in rhythm against his leg.

I took my tea to the table and sat. 'Sorry about that.'

'It's okay. I'd better go. Leave you to it. Oh – I don't mean …'

She looked so sad that I reached for her hand. Huge sobs quaked her body. She collapsed into herself, clutching at the air before covering her face.

'What on earth? I'm sorry about Frankie. Just ignore him. He can be insensitive sometimes. Well, actually, all the time. But that's just him. He's not unkind, just … selfish, I suppose. But not in a bad way. He always lets me win arguments and … What on earth is it?'

'Alice.'

'Alice? What did she do?'

'Nothing.'

'Nothing? I don't understand.' I knelt and hugged her.

'It's just that she … she kissed me,' Sarah whispered in my ear, her breath so quiet that I was sure I'd misheard.

'She kissed you?' I flinched and drew back. 'Last night?'

'Yes, she ...'

'Gosh, I didn't realise you were that drunk. We must get you both boyfriends! Bet that was awkward, sharing a bed.' Sarah

put her hands over her mouth. 'I mean, she knows you aren't …
um, like that … doesn't she? D'you want to phone her when she
gets home and sort it out?'

'No!'

'Oh, okay. Well, I'm sure it's nothing.' Alice had been a
godsend since I'd been dating Frankie. Keeping Sarah busy and
going out with her.

'I think I imagined it. I don't know what happened. I don't
know why I did it. I don't know what I was doing. Oh, God.'

She clutched me and sobbed into my shoulder, her hot tears
wet against my neck. I breathed in the smell of her; summer roses
plump with the smell of Turkish delight. 'You'll still be my
friend, won't you? Please say you will, Carol. I … I don't know
what I'd do if I lost you.'

'I'll always be your friend, Sarah. We've been friends forever.'
She choked back some final snotty breaths. I handed her a tea
towel.

'Thanks.'

'Is there something else? You seem a bit confused. She did
kiss *you*, not the other way …?'

'No! It's a mistake. I'm being … stupid. It's so embarrassing
being that drunk.'

'Well, I'm sure Alice feels the same.'

'It's just that I thought she …'

'She what?'

'Liked me.'

I took the tea towel and threw it through the doorway into the
utility sink. 'Of course she likes you. Who doesn't? You're sweet.
And just the best friend. We do stupid things when we're drunk.
I've done a few …'

'Yes, you're right.'

'Shall I drive you home?'

'What's upsetting my two girls?' Frankie dumped the logs in
the basket, picked up my tea and downed it.

'Sarah's had a … disagreement with Alice.'

'Oh. Well, I disagree with Alice as well, Sarah. So you're not alone. She needs to pretty herself up a bit. At least try to be attractive. Does she ever smile? Does she have legs? Will we ever know?'

'What do you care how Alice looks?" I said. "Anyway. Can you run Sarah home while I clear up?'

'There she goes again. D'you see? I'm run ragged with her demands. Come on, let's get out of her beautiful hair. And can I have some food when I get back? A proper meal?' He kissed me hard. 'Try not to miss me. Won't be long, sweetheart.'

Then he was gone. Sarah followed meekly behind, the pair of them an odd mixing of water and oil. They were never going gel and never going to complement each other. And I knew then that I wouldn't keep both of them.

Chapter 18

Sunday, 19 July 1970

A large white horse disappeared before turning and rushing back to hit me. I lay against the pillow panting as the nightmare faded. The cool air in our room didn't stop me from sweating. Bile rose. The luminous hands on the clock read six thirty. This early waking and needing a wee was worrying. And all those weird nightmares. It's as if something had taken over while I slept and changed my brainwaves. I prayed for a period as I made my way to the bathroom. It was weeks since the last one. Waves of nausea flowed as I sat on the toilet. The girls at school said the pill made them feel sick and made their breasts bigger. My breasts were tender. Probably because my bras were too small.

Frankie's friends were arriving on Saturday, and I couldn't wait to meet them now that we were a couple. Frankie stirred as I got back into bed and rested my head on his back. Mum didn't like me staying here because it was too isolated. A new bus service had started in April with a terminus not far from our house. The bus stopped on the main road by the Cleeve Inn so mum could be here quite quickly. It was handy for me even though I preferred to walk and the early bus meant I could slip home before mum returned home to get ready for work. She stayed at Peter's all the time now but kept up the pretence that she lived at home. She didn't want her workmates to know the full extent of their relationship. I didn't have the heart to tell her that everyone knew. Hopefully, she wouldn't have time to visit as she was packing for her holiday in Spain with Peter. Giving up on sleep, I went to phone Sarah.

'Hi, Sarah.'

'Oh, hello.'

'What's wrong? You're still gonna be Mum's bridesmaid, aren't you? Please say you will. I don't want Rosemary Major to be one, so you have to do it. Or I'm not doing it either, and Mum will have to go without.'

'Can't Sammy's wife do it?'

'No. Valerie had a miscarriage and isn't well. I'm not flouncing about like a fairy on my own. We've bought bridesmaid dresses now.'

'Your mum told my mum I let you down by not staying with you last night. She's annoyed that I let you stay at Oaktree on your own without telling her. Now I have to do all the housework.'

'Sorry.' I heard her draw an exasperated breath. 'Please, Sarah. Mum knows Thora's on another cruise. Don't forget: if she asks you, Frankie's still in London as his mum's ill.'

'When are you coming home?'

'I'd better come back just until Mum leaves on Saturday.'

'Are you staying with Frankie for the whole fortnight she's away?'

'Yes. You can go to my house every evening so your parents will think I'm there. Then Mum won't know.'

'But you're *not*. You're with stupid Frankie. He's making you a liar.'

'No he's not!'

'He is. Why don't we do things like we used to?'

'Look, I'll come back tonight, so come around.'

'I'm babysitting Chrissie. You can come with me. Matthew won't mind. He's got a new girlfriend.'

As I said goodbye, I thought about Matthew's new girlfriend: was she pretty and would he fall in love with her? I didn't know why I was bothered, but thoughts of him played on my mind as I prepared to go home.

Chapter 19

Sunday, 16 August 1970

Mum was finally coming to accept that Frankie and I were together. I wasn't sure what he'd said to her, but it had worked. That we were 'living in sin' she strove to keep quiet. I wasn't to tell people.

Frankie's friends had been staying with us for three weeks. Ben, Augustus and three girls, Grace, Vicky and Celia. They made three couples without me. If I hadn't been with Frankie, I'm certain he would have been with one of the girls. I thought Ben was with Grace, but the day before Grace was in Augustus's room, and Vicky was with Ben. Celia had slept with both of the men; she'd told me neither was that good 'at it', then laughed at my embarrassment.

Another of their friends, Mario, had moved to Bristol and was staying in a flat above the restaurant owned by his father. The restaurant where mum's disastrous fiftieth birthday took place. Mario came every day for a few hours because they were forming a rock band. Celia no longer slunk after him since he'd made it clear that his ideal woman was dark-haired and well rounded.

They lazed around discussing the band and who wrote the best lyrics. There had been several drunken and drug-fuelled arguments about whether to emulate Cream or The Beatles. The dining table was against the wall to accommodate Augustus's drum kit. Frankie behaved like a temperamental teenager as they tried to outdo each other's outlandish playing. Mario avoided them and sat quietly playing his acoustic guitar to such a high standard that Frankie became jealous when I complimented him. His rage was as refreshing as our making up afterwards.

Playing hostess, making cakes, sandwiches and salads, was

my role. Sarah refused to help because Ben put his hands on her breasts and forced his tongue in her mouth.

Dealing with them was tiresome. When not 'jamming', as they called it, they lounged around the garden smoking dope, drinking alcohol and talking about Joplin, Hendrix and Lennon as though they knew them intimately. Intrigued initially, I'd wanted to be 'cool' and fit in and be part of the crowd, but soon became bored by their repetitive droning on and the continual 'Yeah man's'. Three of them had gone to Woodstock and repeatedly mentioning it made me want to throw them out. It seemed that all you did at music festivals was get drunk and stoned.

None of them knew what day it was. They had no hope of writing meaningful songs because they hadn't a clue about life outside their tiny minds. We all needed a good trek through the countryside, but my suggestion met with incredulous stares and remarks meant to belittle the poor girl from the housing estate who couldn't afford anything except free walks. Arrogance on this scale was something I'd not encountered before. My brothers had not prepared me for retaliating against people who thought they were something special, who lived 'better' lives. Sarah and I knew who we were, though, and that surety was comforting. Sarah found them hysterical and mimicked Vicky saying 'Dah'ling' until we collapsed in laughter.

These friends of Frankie's seemed lost and bewildered; they needed drugs to enable them to relax. The need for drugs was a mystery to me. Frankie had given up suggesting I partake. There was a limit to what I would do for him, which surprised me. At least that confirmed that he didn't control me utterly, that there was still a little place reserved for me. Sarah was frightened of drugs and threatened to tell Mum. Her solidarity comforted me when I wavered under pressure from the five of them. Mario would not dream of forcing his views on anyone and was so sweet. He would have been a good match for Sarah if only she'd had taken my hint and dyed her red hair brown.

Thora phoned now and then and was suspicious each time I answered. She complained that I was there too much and said to let Frankie deal with taking care of the place. I wasn't to do the housework. She asked if I'd been to the doctor to get contraception, but I stonewalled her. I wasn't going to tell her that I'd managed to get the pill the week after my sixteenth birthday.

Although I was the lady of the house, I was also the servant. The place was a mess, and keeping it clean was a never-ending task. When alone with Frankie all he wanted was sex. I gave in because Celia took every opportunity to cosy up to him and share her smokes. Her behaviour highlighted that she was after him. She started arguments between us and I hated her. She walked into our bedroom one morning and asked for a towel. She was naked. Frankie couldn't take his eyes off her and jumped up so quickly to fetch one that I banged my head. My mind was in a frenzy as I flailed around trying to hang on to some sense of normality. The world was running full speed away from me.

The pill was making me ill, too. Nausea and headaches all the time. My breasts were tender, and I needed to buy new bras but couldn't leave Celia alone with Frankie.

Then, just when I could no longer stand them, something happened. Everyone was in the garden. From my deckchair I noticed that the roses needed deadheading and the borders needed weeding – Frankie had banned Perry until his friends had gone. Why Frankie hated Perry so much was baffling. Perry had always done the gardening for pocket money. He was going to be a horticulturist, and Thora was helping with the cost of his education. I refused to do the garden as well as everything else, so I decided to ring and ask him to come early the next morning, as none of the others got out of bed until midday.

'I love your earrings, dah'ling.' Vicky propped herself up on her elbow to lean closer to me. Her breath stank of gin. 'Moon, sun and stars, very pretty.'

I pushed myself up and slipped my feet into my sandals.

'Let me see.' Celia walked towards me, knocking her glass over as she rose. She fingered an earring as I shrank from her, trying not to inhale her perfume. 'I used to, I …' she stuttered.

She let it go, and a snarl of distaste crossed her lips as she walked away.

'Carol,' Frankie called me from the kitchen doorway; his eyes flicked between us as he walked towards me. He stared at my stomach and said, 'You can see through your dress.'

'Can you?' I looked down, blushing; it was too hot to wear an underskirt.

'Yes, you can. Your breasts are massive.'

'What! Frankie, please!'

He looked at them as though he hadn't seen them a few hours ago. Ben collapsed with laughter and fell off his deckchair. The other four looked up to see what was going on.

'What's this? I didn't catch …' Celia padded to Frankie, laughter sprinkling her pretty face. She pulled her shoulders back, thrusting her braless nipples forward.

Ben sat up and snorted. 'Frankie just told Carol her breasts are massive!'

Celia looked at Frankie and said, 'Frankie! All pregnant women have big breasts.'

Stunned, I retorted, 'I'm not pregnant, Celia. I'm only sixteen.'

'You may only be sixteen, darling, but I know a pregnant girl when I see one. And I've seen many pregnant girls. My father's a gynaecologist.'

Frankie turned and walked back to the house.

'Frankie.' I shouted after him.

Celia laughed and shouted, 'Oh dear, you've done it now. He doesn't look happy.'

It had to be a mistake. I couldn't be pregnant because I was taking the pill. Frankie was sitting in the front room with his head in his hands. It was refreshingly cool in here, on the northern side of the house.

'Frankie. I'm not pregnant. Celia's wrong. I don't care what she says.'

I sat next to him and took his hand. 'You know I've been taking the pill ... The reason my breasts are ... and the sickness ... that's side-effects.'

I kissed his forehead. 'You know I can't be pregnant. You can't get pregnant your first time anyway. You told me that.'

He relaxed as I squeezed his hand and smiled at him. He smiled back. 'You're right, sweetheart,' he pulled me onto his lap and kissed me. 'It's time my friends left us alone. We haven't been alone for ages, have we? Time to get back to normal.'

He went to the garden and shouted, 'Okay everyone, the party's over. Time for you lot to go home. First thing tomorrow ... so go and pack.'

There was a chorus of complaints. Finally!

Their last supper was a joy to prepare.

Chapter 20

Monday, 17 August 1970

Frankie was not in bed. He'd got up earlier, letting light through the curtains as he peered out. He had to be in the bathroom. His friends were leaving. Happiness filled me as I stretched in the warmth of our bed. Soon we would be alone. As I moved, bile rose to my throat. Grabbing his shirt, I ran to the bathroom. As I vomited, I prayed that no one else was sick. What had we eaten?

His shirt was tight across the mound of my stomach. I'd eaten too much since they'd been here. Waiting for my nausea to calm, I contemplated driving into town to buy bigger clothes. I had some money and Frankie could lend me some, too. Or maybe if I let him choose the underwear, he'd pay.

A bedroom door opened then a female laughed, and then a male said, 'Shush,' and the sound of bare feet scuffled on the landing. Easing the door ajar, I saw Frankie and Celia with their arms around each other. Her blonde curls shimmered and waved softly down her back onto her expensive blue silk negligee. He pulled his hand through them, resting it on the back of her neck as he pulled her lips to him.

'What about Lisa?' she asked.

'She's fine. She knows I need time alone.'

'She's going to be mad when she finds out. And your mother. You are naughty, Frankie.'

'Yes, but I'm good at being naughty.' He kissed her and ran his hands down her back to cup her buttocks. 'Those lessons your drunken father –'

She smacked his chest, 'Frankie, behave. I doubt my mother had any benefit from his knowledge.'

'Ugh, please don't.' He kissed her forehead. 'Now shush,

sweetheart. We'd better go.'

'Just as well you're so good. Not sure I've forgiven you for the earrings. You let me think I'd lost them, you cruel man. They don't suit her. Make her look like a demented pixie.'

'Don't call her that. She's grown up in these last months.'

'She certainly has. You know she's like Lisa, preg –'

He put his finger on her lips, and she gazed at him. It was clear that they'd been making love; she had seduced him. Her expression was so intimate that I glanced away in embarrassment. How could they stand there like that? Their hands move across each other's bodies, and I could see her nipple stiffen under his touch as he slid her gown away. She pulled it back and said, 'She's so young. You like women.'

'Ah, but Thora likes and respects her.' He kisses the top of her head.

'So ... oh Frankie you ..'

Closing the door softly, I crumpled to the floor. He was going to leave me; he didn't love me anymore. I'd lost him and this house.

Who is Lisa? I wondered.

Doors closed and silence resumed, but just as I judged it safe to leave, the door rattled and Celia asked, 'Is anyone in there?'

'Me. Be out in a minute.' She'd be leaving soon, and I would have to concentrate on waving her goodbye. Maybe this sleeping with one another was acceptable and forgivable. Maybe I should aspire to be in a higher class where immoral behaviour is normal. As long as he didn't leave, as long as I could stay. Facing her with a smile was the best attack.

'Morning, Celia. Are you packed and ready to go?' She'll see I'm the mistress, I told myself. She's a nobody here. This is our home.

The reality of our situation registered and her grin disappeared. She was only a distraction, nothing more. She pushed past into the bathroom.

91

'I'm going back to bed for a while to wake Frankie.' I giggled and turned away. 'See you in an hour or so.' Shutting our bedroom door on her, I crawled in beside him, careful not to touch him.

They could make their own breakfast for a change.

Chapter 21

Tuesday, 18 August 1970

The morning light filtered through the curtains as I woke to find myself alone again in our bed. It was only eight o'clock, but Frankie's side of the bed was cold. Celia had gone home, though, so I could relax. Nausea stirred me. The day would be grey as the forecast was rain. The garden needed some to freshen the flowers and stop the grass browning.

A car was approaching along the lane. The awful thought that one of them had returned crossed my mind. Getting out of bed, I held my stomach and crossed to the window. A taxi pulled up and waited with its engine idling. The front door opened, so I stood on tiptoes to peer down. The top of Frankie's head bobbed into view. The taxi driver got out and opened the boot. Frankie walked to it and dropped in three suitcases before getting into the passenger seat. The taxi pulled away.

As the car disappeared, I was afraid to move, afraid for time to carry on ticking in the relentless way it did. The stairs jolted through me, each step towards what I'd refuse to acknowledge.

The early sun cast a glow through the clouds onto the trees opposite, bathing them in an ochre light. I watched from the front door as the sun's beautiful rays tripped through the branches. Had he told me he was going somewhere? Had I forgotten, during these last few busy days? He must have left a note, a reminder. This side of the house was cold. I shivered as I closed the door and headed for the kitchen. Glancing around, a feeling of uncertainty that I was alone assailed me: a sense that Celia had returned to collect her missing things – things that included Frankie. The thought that he had gone after her lingered as I swung about peering into the shadows and opening doors. He couldn't leave me, this house, our life, our future. He must be visiting his parents to tell them about me. He must be planning something: a surprise; a long overdue engagement ring.

As I filled the kettle, I remembered the clothes he'd emptied from the wardrobe yesterday. He'd said they were old and needed to go in the bin. I'd persuaded him to give them to the charity shop and had packed them into his suitcases. What he called old and out of fashion would suit someone short of cash just fine. I'd laughed and said he'd have nothing left to wear. He had run his fingers through my hair and said that he didn't need anything to wear when he was with me. Then he took me back to bed and made love to me so perfectly that we cried.

There was an envelope on the kitchen table. Only a coward would leave a letter. Frankie was not a coward. Tearing it open with shaking hands, I could barely read his writing. He said he was going back to London, and then to France with his friends. He couldn't live with me anymore. He wanted his old life back.

Well, that was fine, I told myself. He needed some time alone. He'd soon miss me and come home. He loved me, and he loved Oaktree House. The pair of us would draw him back. I'd keep the house nice and wait for him to come to his senses.

The burnt note dropped into the bin. I retrieved the duster and polish. A few hours cleaning would pass the time until he returned. Then I could have a bath to freshen up.

Perry arrived earlier to deadhead and weed, both of us thankful that he could sort the garden before it became unmanageable. The money Thora had left in the cash box had gone so I couldn't pay him. He'd have to wait until Thora returned, and having to tell him that was embarrassing.

My freshly washed hair smelled divine. Celia should have looked harder for her shampoo; I'd stored it with the bleach under the sink. There was a bottle of her perfume on my dressing table; she wouldn't miss it. Her cashmere jumper had been hand-washed along with her pale mauve silk dress and silky blue negligee. She was careless with her things – but then, she could afford to be.

His parents might know where he was but his address book wasn't in the dresser drawer. Before I could think what to do there was a loud knocking on the door. He was back! Running down the hallway, I threw open the front door. But it was Perry. He shuffled from one foot to the other as though he was about to burst out laughing.

'Do you want lunch? I have plenty of food.' I smiled and opened the door wider to allow him access.

'No, thanks. Been home for lunch.' He shoved his hands in his pockets and looked into the hallway. 'Dad had a message from Thora.'

My heart sank; she must be coming home. 'What is it?'

'She wants the house locked up. So you have to leave. She says Frankie has left.'

'He's gone home for a few days, that's all.'

'That's not what Dad said. He said Frankie has left.' A smile played around his lips.

'What does it matter? I'm living here.'

Perry drew in an exasperated breath. 'But you shouldn't be here. You must leave now that Frankie's left you.' There was a look of malicious triumph in his eyes.

'Frankie has not *left* me. He's gone to his parents'.'

Perry held my gaze and hooked his thumbs into his pockets, rocking on his heels. 'Frankie is going to France with those friends. Then he's going back to university in September. In London. That's what Thora told Dad.'

'But that's not ...' My grip tightened on the front door. Before I could protest, Perry cut in. 'Thora knows more about what Frankie's doing than you do. Pack your things. I'll bring the car round at six and run you home.' He walked away shouting, 'Don't be late.'

Tears pricked my eyes as I slid to the floor and rocked myself on the hallway rug. Perry was lying. How dare he speak to me like that? Frankie had better come back and wipe that smirk off his face. I needed to find him quickly, so I rushed into the study and frantically scanned through Thora's address book until I found Frederick and Catherine Dewberry's number, and dialled it.

'Hello, Blanchard Place.' A young woman had answered.

'Hello. I ... need to speak to Frankie.'

'Frankie? He's not here, Miss. Who's calling, Miss?' She spoke slowly, enunciating each word.

'It's Carol. His girlfriend.'

A muffled noise, and then, 'Who? Not another one! Give me the phone. Hello. Who is this?' The woman was older, her refined voice natural, but annoyed.

'Hi, um, hello, I'm Carol. Frankie's girlfriend.'

A long sigh. 'Frankie has lots of girlfriends. Who did you say?'

'Carol. We've been living in Thora's house since May. His Aunt Thora's house.'

'So *you* have been with him. Ha! I didn't think he would be living there on his own. Celia's mother mentioned something about a girl. What do you want?'

'He was on his way to visit you. Just wondered if he's there yet as I need to speak to him.' The lie burns my face, and a tremor runs through my hand. She's rich and powerful.

'Visit us? I'd be surprised if he did.'

'Well, um ... can you give me the telephone number and address of his digs? I've lost them and must contact him urgently.'

'My dear, I cannot do that.' A mocking laugh cackled in my ear.

'But I'm his ... fiancée. We're engaged.'

'Engaged?' Her voice had risen in pitch and panic. She was going to send someone here. The police, to arrest me. 'I doubt you're engaged to Frankie. What on earth has he been telling you, because – well, it's not my place to say. I'm not getting involved. We've not long found out ourselves that, um, so there will be trouble. And I can do without it. I can't help you.'

'But I must speak to him.'

'You're not … you're not pregnant, are you?'

'No! I mean – I don't know …'

A continuous purring tone signalled the end of more than my call.

Chapter 22

Friday, 21 August 1970

Living back home with Mum was horrible. She went out with Mr Philips most nights and slept over. So much for keeping yourself whole before marriage. Sarah was staying with her Gran in Ireland. I missed her. I missed Frankie.

Matthew's van pulled up outside. He carried Chrissie along the garden path; his strong arms held her close as he kissed her cheek and rubbed her nose with his, making her giggle. It was eight thirty. Matthew had dropped her with his mum every day since he split with his last girlfriend. I opened my front door.

'Hi, Matthew.'

He looked around. 'Hi. Didn't know you were back.'

'Only temporarily. Hello, Chrissie. Haven't you grown? Isn't she just the sweetest darling?'

'Yes. And she knows it.'

'Shall I take her while you fetch her things?'

'No, it's okay. We're fine.'

'It's no bother. I can … oh, that's my phone. I'd better go.' My heart sang as I rushed in. Please be Frankie ... After a delay, a voice said, 'Carol?'

'Frankie! Darling, where are you? I've been so worried.' My breathing failed to match the gasps I drew.

'I'm in France with the others … listen …'

'What are you doing, Frankie, disappearing like that?' I had a vision of Celia and gripped the handset.

'Carol, listen … I don't have much money.' The line crackled. 'Don't phone Mother.'

'Well, I don't need to now, do I? Tell me where you are and the phone number. And when you're coming home. I'll meet you.' I grabbed a pen, my hand sticky.

'I'm not. I'm not coming back to Oaktree House.'

'What d'you mean? Oaktree is your home. Why won't you? What about Auntie Thora? She needs you. She's dying. She needs us to take care of her.'

'I'm going back to London. Listen, Carol –'

'Okay. I'll come with you. Then I won't have to move to Mr Philips's house. I wasn't looking forward to that. But London, Frankie! Wow! Great!'

'No, Carol. I don't want you to come to London. Didn't you read my letter? Please understand that it's not working for me – oh, my money's running out. Please don't phone my mother.'

'But Frankie ...' The line bleeped, and a continuous tone droned in my ear.

He didn't know what he was saying. He'd be back. Thora was dying. She needed both of us to take care of her. He'd be back when he came to his senses.

But as I filled the kettle, the pretence evaporated. Everything he'd said to me was a lie – a line he'd spun to get me into bed. How dare he treat me like this? How dare he disregard my feelings and use me, and then cast me off like some outdated shirt. I smashed the kettle into the sink. I was pathetic: too poor, too mundane, too boring. He wanted to travel. He craved things I couldn't give him. I wasn't good enough. Smash, smash, smash. Blood dripped from my hand forming cloudy patterns in the dregs of water in the sink. They swirled and spun, a dizzy river winding in a maelstrom. As I stared at it, a vision of Glastonbury Tor appeared. We stood entwined, new, together. He'd fallen in love with me as we'd walked through its mystical healing atmosphere. Help would be in that place of spells and magic and charms – help from a higher source, from a fortune-teller, someone with magic. I had to go back to the beginning, make him mine again. A medium or a witch would help me charm Frankie. They must not fail.

Thora's car sat in her garage. Her house keys were in my bag.

The signs were on my side. It was fate. The heart on his necklace gave me strength and the charms on his earrings cast an aura of magic to shoo away any bad omens. Frankie must return, no matter what I had to do to make it happen. Somehow, I would make my dreams come true.

Chapter 23

Monday, 24 August 1970

My bed was the only safe place. I lay under a sheet, unable to rest without the tight comfort of my cotton tomb. The August sun sweated through and dehydrated me. I couldn't leave, afraid that more misfortune would manifest should I venture out of my confinement. Psalm twenty-three rapped through my head, and each time I lost my place in its mesmerising chant I had to repeat those holy words or risk the Devil visiting me. This ritual would place a charm on my father's house and protect it. The place where my dad died would not have another family living in it. Mum must not marry Mr Philips. Mr Philips must jilt her at the altar when my dad returned to take his rightful place, once again, as husband and father. Dad would ensure that I would not be made homeless or left at the mercy of a stranger who, at a whim, could cast me out. None of my brothers would let me live with them. I hated them all. My life had ended.

Hate, hate, hate.

The Lord is my Shepherd.

The day before, a mystic called Ruby Silver had clinked and chimed around me as hundreds of fine silver bangles shimmied from her wrists to her elbows. Some were jewelled or fashioned like snakes and other animals. Chiffon cascaded from her head to the floor, and as she moved she glided through the smoky atmosphere of joss sticks and musk, impervious to the air that caught my throat in an acrid claw.

She took my hand and sat me in her chamber of dreams and showed me how to take back control of my life. Putting a halt to my powerless state by the laying on of her hands, she spoke of the unknown authority that was trapped within me, waiting to set me free. I possessed power in my physical and intellectual being, but I needed to take control to overcome disaster. A serious assessment of my life and my place in the universe was required.

A crystal ball sat in the middle of the table, sparkling with glorious beams of future joy. After clearing the mists within the precious orb, Ruby Silver told me that she saw my life stretching out to infinity. She said there were many obstacles to overcome to find my path. But when she told me that a man was not a necessity in life, she corrected herself on seeing my distress. The universe was listening. My heart's desire was a breath away, just beyond my grasp. Whatever I wished for, I could attain. Frankie's love. Oaktree House. Everything. The gifts he had bestowed upon me, the necklace and earrings, were love tokens that captured his desire and spirit. I was the holder of these talismans, and they had to remain on my person forever. Believe in my future, picture my dreams, and most of all, desire them above all else. The power to make things happen was with me. Marriage, children, even the world, were there to take.

Her books of spells were too expensive, but she assured me that faith in her would be sufficient. She could see the truth; she had seen the future for thousands of people. My part was to believe in myself.

This morning I awoke traumatised and bereft. My power had gone, my dreams were now nightmares, and my future was too big to grasp in my insignificant hands.

The letterbox rattled, stirring me from my bed. A letter lay on the doormat. The stamp was foreign. It had to be from Frankie, writing to tell me that he was returning, as Ruby Silver predicted. Frantically I tore it open.

Dear Carol

Catherine (Frankie's mother) informs me that you're pregnant with Frankie's child. I can't believe this after the warning I gave you. I'm coming home to sort this out before you ruin your life. I urge you to abort it. I have arranged for an excellent gynaecologist to carry out the procedure: Celia's father. You will be in safe hands. I'll pay for your travel to London, and a private room, etc. He assures me your fertility will not be affected, so you will have children when the time is right.

Please believe me when I tell you Frankie does not love you. Frankie only loves Frankie. He has many 'girlfriends'. I don't doubt that you believe you're in love with him, but you have no experience of men like him. Your family are loving and protecting, and are honourable people. Do not make the mistake of thinking Frankie is like your brothers, or your father – he most definitely is not. Frankie abandoned you because his parents threatened to disinherit him should he continue a relationship with a girl from 'the working classes'.

You must continue with your schooling. Erik Schmidt brought your work to me. He let slip that he was 'nurturing your talent'. I'm sure you can guess how we know each other. Frankie told me that he'd warned you what Schmidt is, but thankfully you already knew before I needed to intervene. Anyway, I can see you have talent so please believe in yourself and go to university. You will make an excellent interior designer. I'm prepared to leave you enough money to cover your education. As you're aware, I'm dying of cancer; I'll alter my will for you. Time is of the essence. But this money will not be available if you keep the child, or if you continue your relationship with Frankie.

Unfortunately, Frankie has gathered some information on Schmidt from my confidential files, and he's blackmailing him. I wouldn't be surprised if he tried to blackmail me, too (although he'll have to hurry up!). Did you know that Frankie's father and I used to work together at Maytree Hospital? That's why I'm Frankie's godmother, although he calls me Aunt.

I must catch the post. Please destroy this letter. I shouldn't be writing it, but my life could end soon, and you need to make an informed decision. Don't worry, I will make sure that my solicitors are aware.

Yours sincerely,

Thora

I read it again. Why did she think I was pregnant? The writing looped and curved along a strange trail from the beginning to the end. A ship's monogram sat resplendent at the top of the headed paper, and told me of adventure and exciting journeys. But the letter burnt my hands, and the sensation made me vomit into the sink.

Chapter 24

Thursday, 27 August 1970

Storm clouds gathered and brought a steady rain as I made my way to Thora's. The promise of thunder and lightning loomed, threatening to dissipate the crushing heat. My burnt skin, hot and pink, trapped sunshine on my naked arms and legs. It tightened and stung. Restless yet apathetic, it seemed that my brain couldn't decide between living or dying. A storm suited the day's mood perfectly. Longing for my dad's arms crushed my spirit and agitated my feet. I stamped on the dry grass, squeezing the fragrance from cracked and desiccated stems into the air.

Mum came home as I was clearing up the vomit, and found Thora's letter. She had no right to read it. We tussled over words of shame, guilt, regret. Her eyes were crazy with impotence as I revealed how deep Frankie's love was for me. She hesitated when I pointed out his redeeming features, which continued to seduce her. She waved her arms and stuttered as the truth dawned. His wealth, status, good looks and charm were irrelevant without a ring on my finger. Gifting Frankie my virginity was my right. I was taking the pill and wasn't pregnant. She turned from me, her face flooded with so much anger that her ears throbbed on her head.

Hindered by my stonewalling, she then insisted I try on my bridesmaid dress. As expected, because of the side effects of the pill, it was tight. Again, the pestering questions. Again, my denial that I was pregnant. Then an onslaught of strange myths and methods to bring about the death of this imaginary clump of cells. Hot baths, alcohol, and running uphill. Other possible ways to abort it, with disposal down flushing toilets. She made me pee in a bottle and had taken it to the chemist for testing. The result

would be back today.

All through her rant, she regaled me with Peter's feelings. Peter will *withdraw his support for my education*. Peter will *not be happy*. Peter will likely *change his mind* about me. Peter will *share her shame*. Peter will not have his *doorway darkened*. This man my mother deemed fit to replace her previous husband. A husband who had lost his inheritance for her love and made himself and his family poor; a man who overflowed with compassion and regard for all humanity; he should be her one and only husband.

I'd be homeless if I were pregnant. The adults had changed into patronising judges bent on eviction and murder. If there was a baby, why did everyone want to kill it?

***

Erik Schmidt had his back to me as I approached Oaktree House. A roll of thunder rumbled in the distance and the baked ground awaited the patter of cool rain to soothe it. Thora straightened, her demeanour changing, and Schmidt turned to me. He was saying he'd report her as his eyes slid over me, his lizard tongue flicking against flabby wet lips. It seemed that Thora was incapable of stopping him from pestering her. She was powerless, and not, as she'd professed in her letter, an adult and a doctor with authority.

'Carol. Nice to see you. Looking lovely in that little, um, dress. Ouch! You've burnt your delicate skin. You'll need to rub cream into that. Is there someone who can help do that?'

'If he's bothering you, Thora, we should call the police?'

'It's fine. Erik's leaving, aren't you Erik?'

'What's the matter, Carol? Don't you like your teacher now? You have forgotten how I helped you?'

'You haven't helped me … you …'

'I've shown you how to develop your talent. Are you putting

on weight?' He appraised my stomach, his fingers rubbing his thumb. Thora's face twitched.

'As you've done so much for me, we should go to the Head and tell him. About me hiding in your car …'

'What's this?' Thora threw her hands up to her ears.

'It's nothing. Carol's dramatising, like all girls her age. They're all attention-seekers.'

'How is Christine Allbright getting on under your private tuition, Mr Schmidt?' I remembered that Sarah had said something a few months ago and had wondered if we should talk to a teacher in case he was now targeting this other girl. But I'd not followed it up with her; Frankie consumes every waking moment.

'Christine's doing well. She has talent, much more than you. She's easy to … teach.' His smile faded as he turned and walked back to his car. 'Lovely talking to you. I hope we can chat again soon. Very soon.'

He drove off, grit spraying as he crashed the gears. Thora followed me into the kitchen, where she filled the kettle. Schmidt's presence had been unnerving. Anxiety bubbled under my sunburnt skin, and I'd wondered if the bubbles would escape if I cut it. These emotions had never swirled and raged before to conspire such a level of uncertainty. Eight months ago I knew who I was. Thora turned and leant against the sink.

'When you went to Schmidt's house, he didn't …?'

'No. I stopped going; I didn't like it … him … something.'

'Okay.' She swirled the water in the teapot. 'He brought some of your work here. That's when I found out. I mentioned to Frankie that he taught at your school and Frankie said he didn't teach you. So I didn't say anything to you. We need to tell the Headmaster.'

'No. I can't. There's nothing to tell. Nothing happened.'

She turned to me, but before she spoke, the phone rang. She went to answer it.

'Carol, it's your mother.'

Mum told me I was pregnant. As I slid to the floor, Thora stood over me.

'What on earth is wrong? Has someone died?' Anxiety darkened her pale-yellow skin.

'I'm pregnant.' It was like a dream, or rather, a nightmare. I didn't *feel* pregnant; I just felt bloated. Frankie's baby was growing inside me, a part of Frankie that was mine, yet I hadn't thought it possible.

'Carol ...' Thora rubbed my back in a circling motion. 'Take a breath, take a deep breath. Come on, that's it. Sit up.'

My stomach clenched, so I ran to the bathroom and slumped over the toilet, heaving. Thora handed me a wet cloth to wipe my face. 'You didn't know? That you're pregnant?'

I shook my head. 'I'm taking the pill.'

'I'm sorry. I thought you knew. Does Frankie know?'

'No. I mean, yes. I don't know. Celia said something, but I thought it was the pill, but then he left and ...' I retched and my stomach hurt.

'Calm down. Come on, sit back and relax. This isn't good for your baby.' She gently pulled my arm until I sat against the bath.

'What does it matter? Frankie ran away because he guessed about the baby.' For the first time I said aloud why Frankie had left. I shouted at Thora, 'How dare he! How dare he get me pregnant and leave me!'

'Listen, Carol. There's a way out of this. Let me help you. Let's sit somewhere more comfortable.'

She helped me into the kitchen and fetched a glass of water, 'Drink some of this.'

I shook my head.

'You have options and the best option, although you won't see it right now ... is to abort the child ...'

'What? No ...'

'But if your health was at risk, say ... because your pregnancy was making you mentally unstable … I could refer you to the best gynaecologist … as I've said … and everything will be taken care of …'

'What do you mean by *mentally unstable*?'

'Let's just say that I can fix it for you to have an abortion.'

'But I'm not mentally unstable. Who do you think you are? Speaking to me like that. You're a bloody witch. You're the one who's mentally unstable.' I ran to the hallway certain that she could see inside my head; that she was a witch and knew my thoughts. I had to get out of the house to stop her from forcing me to do something against my will. The walls were breathing; the rug was moving; the door turned black as I grabbed the handle, and smashed it against the wall. *Get away, get away, get away. Be free of it, all of it.*

Across the driveway, across the main road, across the lane. Away from home, from Oaktree, from weird people, killers. Rain hammered down as I slipped and slid along. Past the church and on towards the village. Taking the right fork, towards the edge of the Cleave, away from people, away from judgment and murderers and dictators. *Away, away.*

The sky dropped, heavy with the weight of clouds. Thunder clapped overhead, and although the area was familiar it seemed strange, as if the trees and the vegetation had morphed from another planet. Only one residential path weaved around the village, and this one wasn't it. But I didn't care. I wanted to be lost and never found.

Lightning flashed and the sky ignited in a yellow glow. Stars sparkled amongst the clouds as though the heavens were peeping down.

'Go to hell, go to hell the lot of you.' Why did these people hate me? Thunder roared, reinforcing how insignificant I was – a no-one, with no power. There was no reason to live. My life had finished. My mother was marrying, abandoning our home. My brothers didn't want their little sister hampering them, getting in the way of their futures with their sensitive partners. And Thora wanted to lock me up.

The edge of the Cleave dropped sharply away. I steadied myself inches from the edge. Could I jump? Could I kill myself? What if I ended up in a wheelchair?

Thunder reverberated. Lightning exploded in a forked burst and zig-zags lit the sky. The drop before me was not sheer enough. It had sloping sides and was slippery and ...

I fell.

The ground flew beneath me. Rocks hit and jarred me. Excruciating pain seared through my left arm and shoulder – each thump-crack sent agony through me. Hitting my forehead then my leg, fresh pain, more pain, new pain assaulted me. The world was a kaleidoscope of agony and fear.

At last, my body embedded itself in the ground. My arm was twisted behind me and my shoulder didn't work. My left leg was numb, and the pain, the pain! Sleepy, dizzy, wet and cold, I moved my right hand and felt around my left side. Something was wrong with my shoulder and arm. Pain cramped across my stomach making me curl up. Oh God, my baby, my baby. Please let me die. I couldn't take any more of the pain. Even the Fates believed I should die. How did Ruby Silver get my life so wrong? Sleep tugged me away.

Chapter 25

Friday, 28 August 1970

There was a memory of a man standing in the rain on the hillside: then a needle pressing into me, and a facemask, and dragging, and cold, but most of all pain. My shoulder hurt, my arm hurt, and my leg hurt.

'My baby! Is my baby …?'

Mum sat next to my hospital bed. She tried to put her arms around me, but I pushed her away. 'Leave me. Is my baby …?'

'Your baby is fine. We already told you. Though God knows how you didn't kill it.'

My baby survived. No one was going to kill my baby.

'You're disappointed …'

'That's an awful thing to say, Carol.' She pulled out a handkerchief and dabbed her eyes.

'But true. That's what you wanted. To get rid of it.'

'Carol, Princess, you don't understand. I was angry. Surprised. I wasn't expecting you to … It was a shock …'

'Oh, and it wasn't to me? Finding out I'm pregnant, and my mother's telling me how to kill my baby and myself, too.'

'It's because I love you. I don't want you to ruin your life …'

'You love me? Then please go if you do.'

'All I can say is sorry. And I *am* sorry, you must believe me, Princess. When we couldn't find you, and it was so cold and wet and … well, my God, Carol … I love you so much. You're my daughter. I never wished you harm. You don't realise how upset I've been. Peter says the baby is welcome. Peter loves me and whatever makes me happy makes him happy. You can have the baby, and you can live with us. You can even go to university if you want.'

'Go to …? Oh, so everything is okay because Peter says so.

Well, tell Peter he can go to hell.' A sharp pain shot through my shoulder as I pushed myself up. 'Please leave, I want to sleep.'

A nurse announced that I had another visitor, but Mum had to leave before she could come in.

'Is it Sarah?' I asked. 'Don't tell her ...'

'She's still at her gran's, and I'm not telling anyone our business.'

Before I insisted, Mum said, 'Okay, I'll go.' She dabbed her eyes. 'If it hadn't been for Perry –'

'Perry?'

'Yes. Thora phoned Mr Cutler, and Perry answered. He and Mr Cutler went out to look for you. They drove to the village. Perry guessed where you'd be. He told me you were likely to be outside walking in the fields and woods. He walked that path looking for you.'

She stood. 'This is obviously the wrong time to remind you, but those books need to be packed up. Only a month until we leave. Shall I do it for you? I know that you don't like me cleaning or moving them.'

'Okay, but take care with them, Mum. They're Dad's books, not "those" books.'

'Don't worry, I will. We're moving everything we can to Peter's now. You should see the amount of rubbish he burnt yesterday. Gerry got into a state about some old toy and some school reports of his, but we've had to be tough. We can't expect Peter to have our rubbish in his beautiful house. I've told the lads they need to make time to sort it all, otherwise, it'll be binned or burnt. If they can't be bothered, then neither can I.'

She stopped to talk to Thora on her way out, and there was a promise between them to meet for tea soon. Then Thora came up to me and placed a hand on my shoulder.

'How are you?' Her yellow skin hung on her face. She pulled at her skirt then rubbed her tired eyes as I failed to reply. 'I'm so sorry. I didn't think ... that you would react like that. I was trying to help.'

'Help? By suggesting I was mental?'

She sat and shifted uncomfortably. 'No. If you had listened to me, I would have explained.' She wept, and tears fell onto her lap before she retrieved a handkerchief from her bag.

'I'm changing my will. You can have the baby, and if you want you can live at my house. I'll sort it out with my solicitor tomorrow. You'll have the money to support you, so you can stop worrying. You can have the baby *and* have somewhere to live.'

'I don't believe it! I have an accident, and suddenly everyone changes their mind. What's going on?'

'Accident?'

'Yes. What did you think happened? It was very slippery, and I couldn't get a grip.'

'So, you didn't try to ...'

'If I had wanted to kill myself, I would have chosen a better place. It wasn't high enough.'

'But you thought about it.'

'Everyone wanted to kill my baby, so why not kill myself?'

'I didn't. I said that was one option I ...'

The nurse came in. 'Have to do observations now, sorry.'

Thora took my hand. 'There are things you need to understand – important things. I needed to be sure about you. That you wanted to keep the baby for the right reasons. Hurry up and get better. And don't worry about anything. There's plenty of money.' She squeezed my hand and rubbed it before picking up her bag and leaving.

The nurse held my wrist and looked at her watch and said, 'That's nice. Wish I had a gran like that.'

'She's not my gran. She's a witch.' I watched Thora hobble away and wondered how long she had to live.

The doctor breezed in and told me there was no serious damage from the knocks to my head, and although concussion was a concern they were happy that I was okay. My arm would be in a sling for a while until the pain from my dislocated shoulder settled. Bruises covered my body, and I had to go to my doctor if I was concerned about any aspect of my recovery. Stiffness inhibited every movement. But he assured me that my baby was fine. They wanted me to stay another day, and I could go home tomorrow.

Now, instead of being homeless as threatened, I had to decide whether to live with Thora or Mum. I decided to go to my childhood home before it – the place where my dad had lived and died – was taken from me.

Chapter 26

Sunday, 30 August 1970

Thora arrived at Mum's to take me to Oaktree because there was something important to discuss. It couldn't wait, she'd emphasised on the phone.

I settled at the table as Thora filled the kettle then stirred a pot on the range before bringing it to the table.

'There's something I have to tell you before we visit my solicitor tomorrow.' She sat and ladled soup into dishes.

'I'm seeing your solicitor? This soup looks delicious. Did you use that recipe I gave you?'

'Yes. Thanks very much. It's so easy to make that I virtually live on it. Just vary the main vegetable, and … Anyway, we have important things to discuss. You must keep this to yourself, so please promise me. There are only a few people that know what I'm going to tell you.' She took a sip of soup. 'In 1949, when I was thirty-nine, … I was raped.'

I swallowed and the hot soup burnt my throat. 'Oh God, Thora.'

'It's okay.' She placed her spoon down and rubbed her hands. 'There was internal damage, and that's why I don't have … And I've never married … Anyway, a long time ago.'

She tore a piece of bread and dipped it into her soup. 'It happened at work. I was on placement in … well, that's not important. I didn't tell anyone. Couldn't risk losing my job. I left it too late to do anything about the baby. So I … had him. I had Frankie.' She held my eyes and pursed her lips. A tremble shook her hair.

'What do you mean … Frankie …? *My* Frankie?'

'Yes. Frankie is my son.'

'You're Frankie's *mother*?' I said the words and they left my lips as though I'd just learnt a foreign language. I'd known that there was a secret about someone finding out who their mother was. That was in the letter I'd glanced at on my first day here. And Frankie had told me that Catherine wasn't his mother. But this was unbelievable. That meant Thora was about sixty yet she looked ancient. Why didn't he tell me? He should have told me when he guessed I was pregnant.

She acknowledged my confusion by opening her hands. 'Which means … your baby is my grandchild. Apart from a few long-distance cousins in New Zealand, your baby and Frankie are the only blood relatives I have.'

'Does Frankie know that you're his mother?' I already knew the answer and flushed.

'Yes. He needed his birth certificate for a passport. I'm listed as Mother and Frederick as Father. Frankie thinks that we had an affair, but we didn't. It was easier at the time for Frederick to say he was his father even though he's a few years younger than me. Frederick knew I was raped and that I didn't want to keep the baby. We had a few months to sort out what to do. Catherine was desperate for a baby, they'd been trying for years, so everyone was … well, not happy but … They moved back to London. Catherine insisted – in case I changed my mind. But I didn't. I never wanted children.'

'So Frankie doesn't know who his real father is?'

'No. So please don't tell him any of this. That would be cruel, don't you think? If you do love him, save him the anguish, please.'

'Well … Yes, okay.' I wasn't sure that I should keep this promise.

Thora went to the kettle and filled it with water before putting it on the range. She brought a cake to the table.

'Frankie suspected something when he was about sixteen. Him being fair, and not a blond hair anywhere in Catherine's or Frederick's ancestry. Me being blonde. When he found out, he came to get some of what he calls his "inheritance" out of me last Christmas. Told me Catherine and Frederick were awkward; that they were trying to stop him from living his life. He has trouble understanding responsibility. But you know that.'

It was all too much to take in, but I needed to know something else, something much more important. 'Why did you want to get rid of your grandchild?'

'I was testing you. Making sure you wanted the baby and that it was Frankie's. I'm going to tell you more about Frankie to make sure that you still want to keep the child.' She ate some cake and a minute dragged by before she said, 'Frankie's father was an inpatient. A man with severe mental health problems, a psychopath.' She paused to make sure I understood.

'So my baby's grandfather is …' The thought was unreal and disgusting that I had unknowingly inflicted these genes on my innocent child.

'You're sure Frankie is the father? Okay, sorry, I need to check, you appreciate that, don't you?'

'Yes, he's the baby's father. And I'm keeping the baby.' My baby would have all the love it needed.

'Well, that's sorted then.' She patted my hand, then took my cup and saucer to the sink.

The air had changed with this revelation. It was as if my history had stopped and I'd stepped into a new world.

'I love Frankie and want to marry him.' Frankie was half Thora, I mused, so there was some good in him. And it was down to me to nourish it.

Her shoulders stiffened. Something clattered and broke in the sink. 'That's not a good idea, Carol. You should raise your baby alone.'

'My baby needs a father. My dad died, so I know that. And Frankie loves me. When he's sure about our baby, he'll be back, he'll … change. Together we'll be his family and we will –'

'Children survive without their fathers. A child can grow up perfectly well without its father, and your baby need never know its father and so will not miss him. And you will marry a nice man, and he'll be its father. Forget Frankie.'

'But I love Frankie.'

Thora turned and shouted, 'Frankie must not be part of your baby's life!'

She faced me: her yellow skin fought to be pink and the woman I'd shown how to bake morphed into an alien. My child had her genes, and the fear that I would cause it harm if I chose Frankie as its father shook me. I had done this. I wanted to run away, but I'd tried running before and didn't succeed.

'I'm going home. I'll see if Mr Cutler can give me a lift.'

'No, don't. I'm sorry. That wasn't nice. It's the opiates. They make me short-tempered. Forgive me.'

I knocked my shoulder as I sat, and groaned in despair. A feeling of claustrophobia overcame me.

'Let's start again.' Thora fetched a pen and writing pad and sat back down at the kitchen table. 'I thought Frankie's children would be the responsibility of Catherine and Frederick. I'd not thought I'd be involved at all.'

She picked up the pen. 'Let's get started. Frankie will not inherit any of my money or property. Even if you marry him, and I hope you won't, although I won't be able to stop you. He won't get his hands on this …' She waved a hand around. 'He's got enough money coming his way from his adoptive parents, so he's provided for.' She smiled. 'Now I have a grandchild there is someone to inherit. I won't be leaving it to you directly.'

'Are you saying you're leaving everything to my baby?'

'To my grandchild, yes. In trust for now, but later on he, or she, will inherit – when they're twenty-one.' She scribbled something down.

'So my baby will get this house? And we can live here?' Thora nodded. 'But I *can't* live here. I can't afford to pay the electric or –'

'Don't worry. You'll have money for living expenses. Did you bring your birth certificate? We have a taxi booked for nine tomorrow. Let's go upstairs to your bedroom. I'm getting the decorators in next week so you must choose wallpaper and curtains.'

She had written a few lines on her pad, with the word 'Frankie' underlined at the top. As we climbed the stairs, each visiting step turned to a possessive one: my carpet, my handrail, my bedrooms leading from my landing. Maybe Ruby Silver had spoken the truth. You needed to want something badly enough to get it.

Chapter 27

Tuesday, 1 September 1970

The solicitors' office of Thwaite & Hamilton smelt of polish. Large heavy desks, bookcases and panelling crowded the narrow rooms and hallways. The stone flagstones, remnants of the former almshouse that Thora had told me about in the taxi, created a church-like feel. According to the brass nameplate on his door, Thora's solicitor was Archibald Thwaite. The 16th-century graves of plague victims lay beneath the office and its grounds. I shivered at the thought.

I was out of my depth in these auspicious surroundings and felt that I was about to commit some crime by agreeing to whatever Thora wanted Thwaite to do for us. She was suggesting I'd have access to lots of money, property and land. The enormity of it sparked feelings of guilt, as though I'd become pregnant on purpose and was blackmailing her. My throat shrank and I needed the toilet, but I'd not manage on my own with my arm in its sling.

Thwaite opened the door. A big man, his stomach strained at the buttons of his shirt and his tie strangled an engorged neck. 'There you are. Come in and sit down. You too, Hamilton. Take notes will you?'

A young man in an old man's suit followed us into the room. He wasn't much taller than me. He walked across and turned to look at me as he moved a chair for me to sit on. He had the most amazing eyes. Smoky, blue-grey circles dilated as they engaged with mine and then swept down my body. I wished I'd put a cardigan on over my faded summer dress. He smelt nice, had an air of freshness, of outdoors, horses and fields. His face glowed with health and he seemed strong judging by his unwavering stance. He hovered by the desk as Thwaite sat down behind it and indicated that we should sit.

Thwaite gestured towards the young man, his chair creaking under his weight. 'This is Hamilton junior, my partner's son.' Hamilton stepped towards Thora and shook her hand, then shook mine, the firmness in his fingers seeming to linger longer than necessary.

Thwaite shuffled through some paperwork and gathered a few more pieces from across his desk. The pages fanned out in a welcoming breeze from the window that overlooked an inner courtyard full of potted plants. Then Thwaite looked up at me and said, 'Now, Miss Cage, as you know, Doctor Kent wishes to amend her will to make provision for you. We need to sort out the details. I should advise you to talk to your solicitor and take legal advice from him on this.'

'She doesn't need to do that, Archibald, so shall we get on?' Thora sounded tired and irritable.

'I have to advise that Thora … Ah, tea. Be Mum, will you, Hamilton?' A lady in a blue tweed skirt and blue twinset placed a heavily laden tray on a table by the window. She nodded to Thwaite as she left.

Hamilton poured the tea. He wasn't at all nervous but deftly sorted the cups and saucers. He put my tea on Thwaite's desk, and then, assessing my sling, asked if I would like him to help me move closer. I declined. I was too nervous to drink. Hamilton settled back and picked up his pen and a yellow pad.

Thwaite looked up at us. 'Now, Thora, your will. Have you written to the trustees of Maytree Hospital to make them aware that you're changing it?'

'No, I haven't had time. Can you write to them for me? Tell them I'll leave them a thousand. They'll have to find another location for their halfway house.'

Thora crossed her legs, winced, and uncrossed them. 'The pieces of family jewellery I inherited from my mother, and the sum of three hundred each, go to my two distant cousins in New

Zealand. Everything else goes in trust for my grandchild until he or she reaches twenty-one.'

'But ...' Thwaite's face reddened. He sat back and pushed the tips of his fingers together. 'Not wishing to be rude but –' he looked at me '– how do you *know* that Miss Cage is pregnant with your grandchild?'

Hamilton looked up at me. His face did not convey that he was shocked. He wrote something down.

'For our purposes, Mr Thwaite, change my will, trust, whatever it is, so Miss Cage, for the rest of her life, can live in Oaktree House and have the benefit of the whole of the estate. Ensure that she can live comfortably and that all repairs, maintenance, et cetera, are carried out as they fall due. That is what we discussed yesterday.'

'Yes but –' Thwaite attempted to intervene.

'And when Miss Cage gives birth, her child will be registered as the inheritor of my estate, which will be held in trust until the child is twenty-one. The child shall enjoy the benefits until then. You know very well what I intend and how to process this.'

'Yes, but your estate is substantial ...'

Thora rubbed her hands and shook them before placing them on her cheeks and drawing in a long breath. 'Yes, and it's mine to do with as I wish. I leave everything to Carol's child, except a provision for Carol to live in Oaktree House with an allowance. In the unlikely event that the child is not my grandchild ... well, then, more fool me! But it won't matter to me or you or anyone else by then. Any mistake I've made will be my lookout. Leave in the provision for the Cutlers to have a continuing rental of the fields, and access over my land and the streams, at the price we agreed as before.'

'And when Miss Cage marries ...?' Thwaite assessed me, a curl to his lip suggesting that might never happen.

'If and when Carol marries, there must be no chance of her spouse inheriting – absolutely no chance whatsoever.

Specifically, Frankie Dewberry must not be allowed to inherit even though he's my natural son. This trust must be foolproof; otherwise he'll spend the lot in seconds. Also, exclude any children he has with other women. They can have Frederick and Catherine's money.' Thora looked at me, and I realised that Thwaite didn't know that Frederick Dewberry wasn't Frankie's father. I felt guilty, a party to a conspiracy.

'And if the child dies?'

Thora wiped her face and looked up out of the window, then shrugged her shoulders with an impatient gesture. 'Well, Carol still lives in Oaktree as before. Then the property would revert to the trustees of Maytree Hospital when she dies. Perhaps you can tell them?'

She watched Hamilton write, then became very agitated. 'No! Don't tell them that. The estate must not go to Maytree Hospital. Forget I said it.' Hamilton drew a line through what he had written. 'Someone might kill her. There are too many mentally unstable psychiatrists. Sometimes the lunatics run the asylum.'

'Are you serious, Thora?' Thwaite leant back and laughed.

'Very serious. I will not place anyone in danger. If the child dies, then the estate goes to Carol… in trust, for her lifetime. She can pass it on to whoever she wants. Who cares, I'll be dead and she'll be dead. Let someone else have it. Not Frankie Dewberry, though.' She looked across at me. 'You understand that, don't you, Carol?'

I nodded, not knowing what else to do, my mind numb with the enormity of it all. I looked at Hamilton, and he had a look that appeared tinged with awe and respect, and I guessed that the circumstances of my pregnancy could be overlooked as the enriching consequences played out.

Thwaite was not so enamoured and had turned a mottled shade of red, the capillaries lining his nose merging so that it appeared to throb with frustration. 'But Thora … your estate is worth hundreds of thousands …'

'Yes, and the trust will be paying you handsomely to ensure it's invested wisely. Is that clear? – because I'm tired.' She picked up her bag and retrieved another handkerchief before snapping the catch shut with impatience. 'Archibald, when you are dying you will realise three things. One, you have nothing to lose no matter what you do. Two, your wealth means absolutely nothing, and three, you're powerless to stop your fate from playing out. I thought my son, Frankie, would marry someone who his father and Catherine would approve of. Those children would inherit that family's wealth. I never thought that I would be involved in any grandchild's, or mother's, welfare. But now, in my dying days, there *is* a grandchild, and its mother, who are dependent on me and are my responsibility. I still have breath in my body and can make a difference. This is my legacy. Now, while you prepare this for signature, Carol and I will go shopping and get some lunch. We'll be back at, say, three?'

'Oh, I'm sorry, but it won't be drafted today. Far too complicated.'

'You have been aware of my wishes for a few days already. Surely you have started it when you know its importance and that time is of the essence? I was going to take the papers back with me to give to my witnesses.

'Yes, yes, I'm ... If you return tomorrow with your witnesses ...'

'I won't be fit enough. Can you come to me, or send Hamilton? I'll get William Cutler and Sadie Fisher to call in and witness it if you phone with a time.'

'Well, yes, we should be ready by late afternoon. Sadie Fisher's address is the Cleave Inn, Chewton Road?'

'Yes. Make sure it's completed and let's hope I don't die overnight.'

'No doubt Miss Cage will keep a close eye on you to ensure that you don't. I'll need your birth certificate, passport and proof of address, Miss Cage.'

I put my birth certificate and a wage slip from the supermarket on the desk. He noted that I didn't have a passport. Thora wobbled as we stood so I took her arm and she put her hand on mine as she clung to me. I looked back at Thwaite in an attempt to convey that I thought him a nasty snob, but inside I was panicking: what if Thora did die tonight? I'd miss my chance of becoming the mistress of Oaktree House.

Chapter 28

Saturday, 5 September 1970

The will and trust have been witnessed and remain in the safekeeping of Thwaite and Hamilton Senior forever. My imminent wealth helped alleviate the devastation of Mum's marriage to Mr Philips, which had taken place at noon at the registry office.

We were at the prestigious Kings Hotel for the wedding breakfast. My bridesmaid's dress, sleeveless and gathered under the bust, had soft fluid lines, minimising the small round of my stomach. Almost no one knew I was pregnant, and those who did wished it kept private. I'd no problem with that. Until Frankie was by my side, I didn't want to be talked about in derisory terms.

I was supposed to go to Sarah's house earlier so that we could get dressed together in our bridesmaid's attire, but I made an excuse not to go. Besides, Alice had stayed with her the previous night as her parents and Matthew had to make an urgent trip to Ireland because Sarah's gran died. Matthew had inherited the grandmother's hotel on the Irish coast, and Sarah was not happy that she only got some jewellery.

Peter Philips made a point of seeking me out between courses during the meal to ask for reassurance that his disappointment about my pregnancy had not caused my accident. What could I do other than nod and shake my head at appropriate moments during his self-centred dialogue? The thought that without my pregnancy I would be living with him and mum sickened me. They were so wrapped up in themselves that I didn't share the news of Thora's will with them. Instead, I told them that I was moving in with Thora to nurse her. Mum patted my hand and told me that I was a good girl with a good heart, and that I was welcome to live with them as soon as Thora passed. This loudly spoken sentiment was a speech made to impress anyone listening. She didn't hug me. She hadn't for a long time. She hugged Peter and his rich friends, people who could give her something that her failure of a daughter couldn't. It was amusing watching Mum struggle to be as snobbish as the wives of Peter Philips's business associates. They were to leave for their honeymoon at five, so I planned to leave before then.

Sarah walked past and lifted her hand to give a little wave as she headed out. She was going to the restroom. I wanted to join her for a chat but was afraid I might tell her I was pregnant, or that I was to become the 'caretaker' of Oaktree House. Sarah looked glamorous in her bridesmaid dress. She'd lost a little weight and seemed taller.

She made her way out, making small talk with all and sundry, seeming to have lost her shyness as she walked, perfectly balanced, on high heels. Then she stumbled in the doorway, and I realised that she was a little drunk. Alice ran after her and took her hand before putting an arm around her waist. Sarah gently pushed her arm away, but undeterred, Alice stayed with her. They disappeared, and I stared at the empty space knowing that when they returned they would be together. They had no plans to seek me out to share any part of their lives.

I was on my own, and even though I would soon have security for the rest of my life, my veins ran cold. I looked across to where my three brothers and their partners sat. A couple of crawling babies scooted on the floor. They held no interest for me even though I'd be a mother myself soon. Apart from exchanging basic information and updates on how my nieces were doing, there wasn't much else to say. Denny had invited me over next week, but Rosemary had given me a look that said I wasn't welcome. Gerry had told me that Peter was investing in a garage with him and that Denny would be his apprentice. Sammy was now a qualified carpenter. They all seemed sorted. I bit my tongue about my news as they crowed and preened.

There wasn't anyone here to make small talk with and I felt too tired to bother. The realisation hit me that since Frankie, I'd abandoned the circle of people that made up my small life. His friends had become my friends, and my friends had gone. They had new friends and lives that didn't include me. It had only been five months but people move on so quickly. My yearning for Frankie was back. I wanted to overlook his bad behaviour so that life could get back to how it was; Frankie, me and our baby. Thora had encouraged me to be strong and independent, but I longed for that closeness I'd had with Frankie and missed it so much. A desperate sense of loneliness sent me to the hotel reception to order a taxi.

As I waited for the lift to return to the room that was mine for the night, a movement caught my eye. Frankie was sitting in the bar nursing a drink, a mischievous grin on his face as he waved to me. My heart sank and soared as a tsunami of emotions assaulted me. Thora was adamant that I didn't need him; and a small part of me agreed with her, now that I was independent. I didn't need a man with his fickle ways to mess with my heart. But at that moment a flood of sentiment swirled in me and my resolve weakened. However, I wasn't going to run into his arms. I had more pride than that. Turning away, I entered the lift but my heart lurched in my chest and fluttered in confusion at my strong longing for him.

I quickly packed my things, panicking that he would leave because I'd snubbed him. But he was still there when the lift doors opened. The well-defined shape of his shoulders as he sat, his back to me, beckoned me in the seductive way they always had. Sarah had joined him and sat opposite him. They chatted like friends do, at ease in each other's company. She didn't hate him for what he'd done to me, why would she? She talked and sipped her drink and put her hand to her lips. I wanted her to be on my side: to find out why he'd left me; to tell him that he should apologise to me; to ask him if he loved me. I wanted her to be the friend I used to have. He seemed to be complimenting Sarah as he touched a strand of her hair and ran his finger down to tip her chin and examined her face. The action was odd but didn't seem flirtatious.

Alice arrived and stood over them. Sarah bowed her head as Alice placed her hand on her shoulder. Again Sarah shrugged her off, as she had done earlier. I slipped away to the reception desk with a glimmer of hope that their friendship was maybe not as strong as I'd thought. Maybe I'd get my best friend back as *well* as my boyfriend. Those two people in my new and better life would help chase away the fear of the loneliness I'd feel when Thora died. A house without a proper family living in it wasn't home. But that could wait until tomorrow, I decided, as I checked out.

As I turned to leave, I collided with Alice as she ran out of the bar. She looked at me and muttered, 'Sorry,' as she headed for the main door. Something about the look on her face made me turn and walk back to where I could spy on Frankie and Sarah. Sarah sat ramrod straight as tears flowed down her face. Frankie sat immobile, his hand rubbing his thigh. I recognised his frustration at not knowing what to do. He was always at a loss with any emotional display. He used to listen to me as I ranted about whatever was bothering me, before asking if I was okay, the helpless look on his face belying the fact that he hadn't engaged in any way with whatever was frustrating me. Then he would kiss me better, leading to lovemaking and the obliteration of my worries. He couldn't take that course with Sarah.

He pulled himself forward and gently wiped a tear from her face. His finger stroked her cheek and jealousy seeped into me as the intimacy of his touching reminded me of what I was missing. He must have said something because she nodded her head and drew in a deep breath. He took her hand and squeezed it. Nausea rose, suppressing my lungs, and the claustrophobic sensation forced me to turn away. I grabbed my case and stumbled out onto the pavement and into my waiting taxi. I'd contact Frankie tomorrow, but for now I'd leave and spend the rest of the day in my new home. It was the first day of my new life, and there were some decisions to make.

Chapter 29

Sunday, 6 September 1970

Frankie drove us to Chewton Lakes. The lakeside was quiet, with few people scattered about the popular tourist attraction. Frankie had brought chocolates. I walked ahead to the edge of the lake and looked out over the water. I wasn't happy with him, and a small part of me wondered if I should tell him that we were finished. But my baby needed a father and I knew how important that was for a child.

He touched my arm and asked, 'Am I forgiven?'

'Everything is not fine because you buy me a box of chocolates, Frankie.'

'Oh, Carol, of course not. But you know I've moved back because I miss you so much.'

'No you haven't. Sarah told me that you'd moved back because the uni course was better. And because Ben has agreed to move here with you. And Thora is leaving again soon so Oaktree will be empty...' I won't tell him I have moved in, or about the trust.

'You know that's not true. Well, it's partly true. But I switched courses to be close to you. That's the main reason.' He continued talking to my back as I walked to the water's edge. 'Sarah told me about your accident and about you staying with Auntie Thora. I should stop calling her that, but I can't call her mother. Catherine's my mother.'

'When did you speak to Sarah? You didn't tell her I was pregnant, did you?' A frisson of jealousy mixed with alarm at the thought that he'd spoken to her before Mum's wedding.

'I phoned her when I'd fixed everything to come back. I swore her to secrecy, so don't be angry. But I didn't tell her about the baby because auntie ... um ... mum said to keep it quiet for now.' He rubbed my arm. 'How can I convince you that I'm sorry?'

I wouldn't answer. He didn't understand how he'd destroyed my life when he left. What if he did that again? The thought made me nervous, and I rubbed my tired eyes fearing I'd slip back into the nightmare of conflicting thoughts I'd been having all night.

He linked his arm in mine, his mouth close to my ear. 'It's been like living in a whirlpool since Christmas. Finding out about mum, then falling in love with you. Then the baby … I couldn't … it all seemed to happen out of my control. Like I was living in a parallel universe. But I've had time to get my head around it all now.'

'You sound like a hippy, "get my head around it".' Mentioning hippies reminded me of his silly friends. 'How are your friends? Are they missing you? Are you going to run away with them again any time soon? Reject your baby again?'

'You know I'm not. I'm back to stay. I want to be a good father. I missed you so much, and I was an idiot to do what I did. I wanted to contact you before. Wanted to tell you how much I … love you. But I thought that you'd reject me. You had every right to, me running off like that. But I knew I had to do something to show you I was serious. I'm going to get my degree and get a job. Provide for us and be a proper husband. I do love you. You must know that.'

He grabbed me, pulled me to him, and kissed me so passionately that I forgot everything. I was back where I wanted to be, in Frankie's arms, and Frankie was my king. His hand slid to my breast, and I pushed him away. The next time we made love would be on our wedding night.

'Why are you pushing me away? A bit late for that isn't it?' His voice was soft and seductive.

'Are we engaged?' I asked.

His eyes widened. 'I suppose, what with the baby. Shouldn't

you wait for me to ask you?'

He laughed but noticed I wasn't amused, so said, 'Carol, you're so feisty, and that's why I love you so much. You're a challenge, and you keep me on my toes. You're so good for me. I couldn't live without you.' He dropped to his knees. 'Carol Cage, love of my life, light of my world, will you do me the greatest honour and marry me?'

In the softening twilight of a perfect early-autumn evening,

with the birds chirping,

and the waves of the lake gently lapping at the shore,

I said yes to the man of my dreams.

Chapter 30

Friday, 6 November 1970

Frankie was upstairs packing. He'd received bad news and had to travel home. I flinched when he spoke of London as *home* but held my tongue for fear of an argument when he was about to leave. His mother was gravely ill. It was two months since our engagement, and we were to go together tomorrow to tell them our good news and our wedding date.

Now five months pregnant, my swollen body had stretched beyond recognition, and I was glad that I had stayed relatively small and agile for the first four months. Once again, there was a reason not to take me with him to meet his parents and show off my motherly curves.

He was still spending most weekends in London as usual, which was getting tiresome, but he said he had to go to keep his parents happy. He said it would be best I didn't go with him as his father was distraught and his mother was in shock, so they had enough to cope with without dealing with our relationship as well. Packing a Victoria sponge in our best cake tin, I placed it next to his car keys, sure that they would not feel like baking. Frankie didn't want to take the casserole I'd made.

As he drove away, I stood for a long time staring at the place in the lane where his car had disappeared. My heart broke each time he left. Images of car accidents and beautiful women swirled in my imagination. How to stop these feelings of despair when he left was a constant worry. Cleaning our bedroom distracted me. And once I'd finished that I set about systematically cleaning the whole house. Moving about dissipated my loneliness and stopped desolation from lodging in my chest. I'd spent long periods alone because Frankie preferred studying with Ben. He returned smelling of a life away from me;

of foreign air puffing from his scented, ironed clothes; of conversations had with people I'd never met.

He was unhappy about the terms of the trust. I'd had to tell him the full extent of it when I could no longer keep him happy with the cash I obtained from Hamilton for non-existent household items. He'd wanted a new car, a holiday, clothes. Realising that I didn't have access to wealth he'd stormed off to London for a few days, only to return extremely apologetic about his shallowness. He'd been his normal Frankie self until a few weeks ago; then something had shifted into his eyes: a panic, a sense of dread. I worried that he was ill, that he had cancer like Thora, but he assured me he didn't, that he intended to outlive me. He promised that our child would always have him.

Left alone much of the time I thought of Sarah. We used to be so close. I mourned the loss of our friendship. We'd drifted so far apart. The last time I'd visited we'd sat in her strange and unfamiliar bedroom. It had new wallpaper and a snazzy bed throw, and smelt of peach and wood polish. The feeling of not belonging itched my nerves and twitched in my feet. Maturity was expected to separate us, but the stamp of that parting hung over us. Our new lives had barriers. Mum said it was part of growing up, that I was sentimental and was resisting maturing into a woman and a soon-to-be wife. The thought persisted that defining our lives in such a way was wrong. As if loyalty was separate instead of communal.

Sarah had hinted that she did not miss our friendship. She had a job at the factory and two new friends to replace me. I gained some comfort from her wounded tone and the news that Alice seemed to have deserted her. Perhaps Sarah wasn't such a good friend after all. But I did miss her. She was my best friend for many years, and I cursed that we had grown apart, that our lives were following separate paths.

Matthew had visited while I was there and Mrs Burcher insisted that we go downstairs for tea as a family. Matthew's new girlfriend, Lucy, was hopeless with Chrissie. Chrissie, sensing fear the way a dog does, screeched and threw a tantrum until they left. Matthew should have taken charge. It seems men like to delegate childcare to the nearest woman. That relationship would not last. He would walk all over her with his arrogance and sharp words. Any girl taking on Matthew needed to be as strong as an ox judging by how he spoke to her. He was testing in his masculinity and in need of a girl like Paula to put him in his place. The thought that he didn't respect Lucy enough to moderate his behaviour crossed my mind. Beauty did not conquer all, it seemed.

Frankie was a saint in comparison, and would never speak to me in that undermining and sarcastic, nagging, way with the continual suggestion that women were stupid. Frankie was open with his criticisms and easily tired of bad humour, bouncing back to hug and make up and forget. Even when we had terrible rows, he was up-front with his reasons; he would storm off to calm down, but always returned with his tail between his legs.

There were many lonely hours waiting for Frankie to come home. Strangely, I thought a lot about Matthew, which was disconcerting. Like a bad habit I'd not conquered.

My dad's books comforted me, though, and I remembered the first time Francine made her presence known because I was lying on my bed reading one. A strange sensation fluttered across my abdomen to jolt me and remind me that motherhood would be my new life.

Chapter 31

Tuesday, 24 November 1970

Frankie had changed. He seldom played the piano and left his favourite guitar at Ben's flat. He started arguments over the least little thing, and he spent many weekdays working with Ben. I'd recorded his absence and uninterest in our life in a small notebook I'd found in Thora's desk. Documenting our arguments had shown me a pattern, and I began to see that he made me into a nag or a simpleton purely to enable him to tell me how horrible I was, then use that as an excuse to spend time away from me. During his worst outbursts – provoked when I was strong enough to challenge him with a degree of resilience – he threw the fact that I had all his money in my face. The situation tested my sanity and I developed what I now recognise as panic attacks.

Arriving home late on many weekdays, he assured me he had been studying with Ben at his digs. But he came back drunk. Sometimes the smell of perfume, like apricots, leached from his clothes. He still went *home* to London every weekend but now added Friday's. The dutiful son visited his ill mother, keeping his father sweet, too, so he could collect his allowance. He was having a good time arriving shattered on Sunday night to flop into bed and sleep without giving me so much as a goodnight kiss. He never placed his hand on my stomach to feel the gentle movements of his child.

Bored of staying home, I fretted for fitness, freedom and long walks in the countryside. To be able to drive without wanting to pee each time I pressed the brake! Pregnancy had a heavy impact, draining me mentally and physically. Some evenings when Frankie failed to come home, I longed for Sarah but when I'd phone she was reluctant to meet up, being too busy with a community programme at the church, or going out dancing with her workmates. She still looked after Chrissie at Matthew's house when he took Lucy out. She complained that I only wanted to see her when I had nothing else to do, and it was tricky because she had a busy social life spending Saturdays with her friends in town, shopping at the new boutiques and having coffee. Sundays were spent in church and with family. She was making excuses not to see me after all those years of friendship, and the realisation that I had somehow lost her by spending too much of my time with Frankie saddened me.

She didn't know I was pregnant. That unnerved me. It was like not telling my hand it was wearing a glove. We used to share everything, and now we were strangers. When I phoned the previous week, she was distant. I'd try to tell her not to be jealous of Frankie and me. She'd soon have a boyfriend, for she was not unattractive and had a kind soul. I wondered if she fancied Ben, thinking that would be an excellent solution and make us a foursome, but she had not forgiven him for what she called his 'assault' on her in the summer.

For some reason, she'd thought that I was nursing Thora and became confused when informed that Thora was on another cruise. She seemed reassured when I told her that Thora had given up any hope of a cure and was dying. And that I would nurse her when she needed it. It was a strange conversation, and I had the feeling she hadn't listened to a word and was still confused about what I was doing living at Oaktree House, and how Thora was still well enough to travel even though she was dying. When I put the phone down, I had an intense feeling of loneliness. Frankie said it was best not to keep in touch as he didn't want Sarah upsetting me. He said that she was in my past and should be left there.

Frankie had not come home again, so I decide to phone Sarah to tell her we had booked our wedding and that I was pregnant. I'd become afraid to drive, as I didn't have a licence and Frankie kept telling me that I'd go to prison if I was caught. I longed to go to my old house, to get out of the car, walk up the path, open the front door, see my mum and my brothers – for everything to be as it was a few months ago. Tears came as I hankered after my old life. So much had happened that year, and I was not adapting well. Admiring my engagement ring didn't banish those blues. Frankie would be mad at me, but I had to tell someone, as I couldn't stay hidden away forever. There would be another row but I was prepared for it.

'Hi, Sarah. How are you?

'Oh. Hi, Carol. I'm okay.'

There was a long pause when neither of us spoke, and the silence told me that she wasn't interested. Anger at being treated badly by both her and Frankie rose to my throat, and I struggled not to shout at her. It seemed too much to expect people with whom you'd shared so much of your life to treat you with some respect: to allow you to make a few mistakes without condemning you. Life was showing me how uncompromising people could be. There was nothing to do about her apathy. At least I roused some sort of response from her as I said, 'Guess what? Frankie and I have set our wedding date for the nineteenth of December. Isn't that great? I wanted it to be sooner because … well, something else you don't know … I'm pregnant.'

She drew in a deep breath and expelled it before drawing in another. Then she said, 'What do you mean? I thought Frankie had –'

'Frankie had what? Are you okay?'

'I'm fine … I thought … Frankie had … *moved* … um ... Thora's very ill, isn't she? And dying people like to be alone, don't they?'

'Well, maybe, but she's still abroad, so I don't know. But Frankie hasn't moved. Why would he?'

'She's abroad? I thought she was almost dead; I thought you were … um, I thought you said something about Thora when you phoned last time.'

'Why are you bothered about Thora? You haven't asked about her for months?'

'Um … no reason. I thought … never mind.'

Silence returned as I waited for her to congratulate me.

'Sarah, what I just told you is to be kept secret. We must meet up and I can show you my lovely ruby engagement ring. Frankie is so generous. It's gorgeous.'

'That's lovely. When's the baby due?'

'End of February, I think. I haven't been to the doctor. That weight I put on that we thought was me "filling out", as Mum called it, you remember – when we were bridesmaids? Well, I was over three months gone. Can you believe it? And I thought it was the pill. Mum says it's a girl, as I'm big all over.'

'But that means … I thought …'

'What did you think?'

'Oh, nothing. I'm a bit confused because you didn't tell me – and Frankie … neither did Frankie. And your mum's not here anymore …'

'Why would Frankie tell you? He wants to keep our baby and wedding a secret.'

'I have to go. Sorry, Carol.'

She put the phone down. I sat on the hallway chair numb with rejection. There was no one to tell about how Frankie said that everything wrong in his life was my fault. How he'd apologise after forcing me to cry and made everything better only to destroy me again a few days later. There was no one to ask why I still loved him and panicked that he would leave me. I was on my own and had to be strong. I would be a mother soon.

Chapter 32

Wednesday, 2 December 1970

Frankie moved back into his digs with Ben on the twenty-fifth of November, when Thora returned. She was expected to die that night, but she survived due to improved pain medication and rest. Her doctor couldn't tell me how long she had. Frankie wasn't happy, but I insisted that Thora spend her remaining time in dignity and not having to deal with our relationship. He wanted us to be home for our wedding and Christmas. We had discussed whether to tell her about the wedding and decided not to, unless we married while she was still alive. She didn't deserve this conflict. Neither did I at six months pregnant.

As I set down Thora's cocoa, I noticed that she was ghostly still. The air shifted with a chill breath, as though a door had opened. Something moved at the edge of my vision, but there was nothing there. Air caught in my throat because I knew she'd gone and everything had changed. Placing her hand back under the cover to keep warm, I put my face close to her mouth to feel the breath that did not come. I drew back the curtains to let in the night, the world, the heavens. The silver slip of the waxing moon peeked out from behind clouds as we waited for the sun to rise on her first day free of pain.

Chapter 33

Sunday, 20 December 1970

We were married yesterday. The excitement tripped me into a state of euphoria. Frankie accused me of drinking, but I hadn't drunk anything, not willing to let the effects of alcohol sedate me. He found my joy hard to control as I wandered the house naked, stroking my wedding band. We were married – blessed and entwined forever. Let no man put us asunder.

Schmidt had turned up to our wedding reception. The memory of his creeping about outside the reception room spooked me. Frankie had chatted with him instead of asking him to leave immediately. Eventually, Schmidt left – with a cheery wave of his hand. I refused to believe what Thora had written in her letter was true.

At thirty weeks pregnant it was a struggle carrying out even basic tasks. Frankie had to chop wood and wash the kitchen floor. He wasn't happy doing 'women's work', but he did it rather than argue with me. He was happy to be banned from cooking and was compliant with my demand that the house must be spotless at all times. He complained that his studying was suffering so I offered to read his textbooks to him as he cleaned. He declined.

Frankie had gone *home* to tell his parents about our marriage but would be back tomorrow. They still didn't know what was going on in his life. He wouldn't allow me to meet those sensitive people who were unable to celebrate our choice. He was a married man, and they were about to be grandparents, yet he was unable to reason with them. He said that they cared nothing for his happiness and assured that they weren't interested in our child.

The weather was atrocious, with rain streaming down the

windows. The sound of the front-door knocker roused me from my cosy chair in the kitchen, and I waddled off to answer it. A car pulled out of sight, having left Sarah on the doorstep, trembling with cold. Obliged to let her in, she sloped passed me into the hallway.

'Go into the kitchen.' My voice croaked from lack of use. Sarah hovered, so I pointed to a kitchen chair, she wasn't having my comfortable one.

'Do you want a cup of tea? I've made a pot.'

'Yes, thanks. Is Frankie here?' She watched as I shook my head and placed her tea down. 'When will he be back?'

'Tomorrow.' I eased myself back into my chair.

She picked up her tea, blew on it, then placed it back down. 'I need to see him.'

'You can see me. We're married.' A sense of doom rose and wafted around. Something evil had entered the house with her. These last months of Frankie's distracted behaviour had flagged a suspicion that he was with someone else, but I had refused to entertain it. Now the lies were coming home to roost and I knew what Sarah was about to say. There had been something about hers and Frankie's body language during our wedding breakfast that told me they were more familiar with each other than they should be. A picture of Frankie touching her cheek at mum's wedding came to me; the gentle way he did it.

The wind howled through the house and the curtains billowed. Upstairs our marital bedroom door slammed shut, making us jump. Rain clattered against the windowpanes, like devil fingers tapping out secret spells of death.

'I'm pregnant.' Tears fell onto cheeks that were as pale as chicken skin.

'Who is the father?' I asked, hoping that against all the odds it would be Ben or Mario. Her hands flew to her face to capture her cries. And I knew in an instant who it was. 'I'm guessing it's Frankie's.'

'Oh, God. How did you know? Oh, you didn't. What have I done? I'm so sorry ...'

'Don't bother, Sarah. You cheated with him. How could you.'

'No. You don't understand ... I ... thought you two had split up. Frankie said you had. I didn't know that you hadn't split up, I swear ...'

'Really? I don't want to hear it.' Frankie's behaviour, the late nights and his lack of interest in sex. The sixth sense that he was cheating that I'd ignored – all of it rushed in like thunder pulsing in my head.

'Have you told your parents?' I asked. She shook her head. 'You'd better tell them. Find out how to get rid of it.'

'Get rid of it? That's against God.'

'Against God? And what was seducing Frankie then?'

'I didn't seduce Frankie! He told me that you knew he loved me. That he couldn't pretend to love you anymore.' She pulled a handkerchief from her bag and blew her nose. She had a touch of righteous indignation about her, as though telling me her lies had made them true.

'Do you realise how stupid that sounds, Sarah. One phone call was all that was needed. But you knew that he was lying, didn't you?'

'No! I didn't! He said you were staying here to take care of Thora. That day you told me about the wedding, and the baby, I was distraught. I went to Ben's the next day and was so angry that Ben had to pull me off him. He told me that you were fragile and he had a responsibility to his child so he *had* to marry you. He was afraid that you would kill yourself and the baby. And he said some awful things about you. Things I didn't want to believe. Like after your baby was born he'd get you sectioned. That Thora would help him. Then he said that we could get back together and look after your – um, his – baby. I didn't like that but he said it was the best thing for you.'

'Why would Thora help him section me when I'm the mother

of her grandchild? You know Frankie is Thora's son?'

'He told me at Thora's funeral when he inherited this place. He said he had to get married to you to ensure that his name was on the baby's birth certificate before he got you locked away in the looney bin. If he couldn't do that I just had to wait until you accept that he didn't love you anymore and moved out of here.' She pulled her shoulders back and set her mouth straight. I went to the sink.

'Frankie has not inherited this estate. I have.'

'I don't believe that ...' She stared at her hands before blowing her nose again. The wind rattled the window like a poltergeist trying to get in. 'You *can't* have ...'

'I'll fetch the paperwork, shall I? It goes to our child, and not a penny to Frankie.'

Sarah crossed her arms and pawed at her cuffs. I wanted her out of my house and far away. I wanted her baby dead.

Kneeling in front of her, I said, 'Maybe you can live with Matthew in Ireland and take care of Chrissie. He might need some help running that hotel.' She looked stunned that she'd not thought of that solution. 'Shall we go and tell your family?'

'Oh, God! Don't tell Matthew. What am I going to do? I don't know what to do.' She retched but luckily wasn't sick.

'You'll cope. Things will feel better after you talk to your family. They can help you get rid of ... it. Say you were raped or something ...'

'Raped? I would never say Frankie had raped me! Are you mad?' She grabbed another handkerchief from her bag.

'No, not that *Frankie* had raped you ... just ... anyone ... a stranger.'

'No, I won't do that. I'd have to lie. Dad would call the police ...'

That plan was not going to work. The only other way was to make her realise how awful Frankie's family was.

'No; of course not. Sorry, Sarah, I was trying to help but that was a stupid idea. Best to keep the baby. But Frankie is poor. He has no access to money so he can't support you. You will put him in an impossible position if he finds out you're pregnant. His parents move in high social circles in London. His father is a wealthy consultant about to be knighted. And his mother is an awful woman. Nasty, small-minded snob.'

Her mouth worked, but she couldn't find any words, so I continued. 'If word of your pregnancy gets out, you'll be in the newspapers, and they won't be kind to you. "Girl from council estate claims Sir Dewberry's son got her pregnant." Your parents will not survive the shame. Frankie's parents aren't nice. They will set a solicitor on you and have you in court for defamation or something. You had better not tell Frankie that you're pregnant. I promise that I won't.'

I knelt in front of her and took her hand. 'Sarah. You must get rid of it or move to Ireland with Matthew. You do understand, don't you? Frankie will not leave me or this house. He won't want to know you.'

'Don't worry, I already know that Frankie doesn't give a stuff about me. But I thought that he should know about –'

'No, Sarah. If they wanted to, his parents could take your baby away from you.' I wasn't sure where this insight had come from, but I was sure that it had finally got through to her how insignificant she was. She was already pale, but now she turned white as she leaned forward, resting her arms on her knees.

'I never loved him. Not properly … not how I should. Please understand that I never meant to hurt you. I need the bathroom,' she said as she ran down the hallway and up the stairs. I listened as she was sick and hoped that I'd done enough to convince her to either get rid of it or move to Ireland and live with Matthew. She needed to be as far away from me as possible now that she had destroyed our friendship.

Chapter 34

Tuesday, 22 December 1970

The telephone rang. It was Ben wanting to speak to Frankie, but Frankie was out buying cigarettes. A sense of foreboding fluttered in me. He was agitated, so I promised to get Frankie to phone him as soon as he got back. Had he found out about Sarah's pregnancy? As the call ended, there was a knock on the door. Opening it revealed a young woman in her low twenties. A large red overcoat dwarfed her. Her appearance suggested money and class. Parked behind her was a red MGB sports car, identical to Frankie's blue one. Another car's headlights retreated further along the driveway, towards the lane.

'Hello. Is this Thora Kent's old house? Is Frankie here?'

'Yes, but he's popped out for some fa – ... cigarettes.'

'Oh, great. Ben said he'd moved in. Bit desolate, isn't it? I'm Lisa.'

'Carol ...'

'So sorry about Thora ...'

A screech of brakes in the lane cut her off. I suspected that Schmidt was lurking again. 'Did you see a blue Austin when you drove in?'

'There *was* a car. Oh, there she blows!' A baby screamed through the open car window.

'D'you mind if I come in and feed Isabella? I've managed to drive down from London without feeding her.' She removed the baby from the car. Its cries made my baby kick.

'Of course. Come into the kitchen.'

She followed me; the cries were deafening, echoing around the hallway. As she sat in my chair, she opened her blouse, exposing a swollen breast, and let out a sigh of relief as the baby sucked. There was a gnawing sense of doom in my stomach. Was she one of Frankie's ex-girlfriends? She was smart and well-to-do, but too expensive for him to court.

'Wow, that's better. I didn't want to stop. When I got to Ben's, she was dead to the world, so I pushed on up here.'

'Would you like some tea and something to eat?'

'I would kill for a cup of tea, and anything you have to eat would be great, thank you.'

'I'll heat you some soup.'

As she fed the baby, I glanced at her. She was beautiful. Her dress, her shoes, and her bag were items of exquisite taste. She wore a massive diamond engagement ring next to her wedding band. Like a servant girl feeding the mistress, I stirred the pot. She overwhelmed my home. Her perfume filled the air, forcing me to breathe the alien smell. She pulled a muslin square from her bag and placed it over her shoulder before lifting the simpering baby onto it. The loud crack of a burp made me jump.

'Good old Isabella. She does fantastic burps, doesn't she? You can't believe they come out of such a delicate mouth.' She laughed and exposed her other breast. Blue veins threaded like spiders' webs around her nipple.

'How long have you got?' She pointed at my belly.

'About ten weeks.'

'It's a hard slog.' She cooed and wiped Isabella's mouth.

I dished up the soup. 'How do you know Frankie? Did you go to university with him?'

'Me? Go to university?' She laughed. 'Come on, Izzy. Mummy hasn't got all day.'

'So …?' I prompted her. The name 'Lisa' rang a bell that sent an icy shiver through me.

'Know Frankie? My father and Frankie's father are colleagues at the hospital. We grew up together, a street apart in Knightsbridge. Do you know Knightsbridge?'

'No. I don't know London.'

'Oh, you should come up. It's lovely. Wouldn't live anywhere else. Except for Paris. Do you like Paris?'

'No. I've not been out of England.'

'Oh.' My answer disappointed her. 'You should make your husband take you. We went in February for our honeymoon. Bloody freezing. So beautiful and romantic. It would have been better if I hadn't got pregnant. And if we hadn't eloped. But Valentine's is romantic for a wedding day. You wouldn't believe the trouble we're in now it's all come out. And Fran –' The baby pulled away from her and grizzled. Lisa lifted her onto her shoulder and gently rubbed her back. 'Come on, Izzy, there's a good girl. Daddy won't want to see you with a windy face.'

As I lifted the teapot, dread filled me at the thought of who this daddy might be. I didn't want to register what I'd surmised, because even Frankie couldn't be that stupid. There must be a better explanation for why she was here.

'So, are you related to Frankie?'

'God, no. That would be gross.' The freshly made Victoria sponge cake caught her eye.

'Would you like some?' I asked.

'Yes. Did you buy it from the bakery Frankie uses? It looks just like the ones he brings home with him.' She looked at my wedding ring, a frown creasing her face. 'Where is your husband?'

We looked at each other as the same thought exploded within us.

'He's gone to buy ciggies.'

'You mean he's gone with Frankie to buy ciggies?' She scanned my face and looked down at my neck. 'Where did you get that necklace? I had one like it, but I lost it sometime last May.' She blanched and stopped jiggling Izzy.

My legs gave way, and I slumped onto a dining chair. 'Frankie, my husband, gave it to me.'

'But … he can't be … Frankie? *My* Frankie? What are you

149

saying?'

Isabella let out a massive burp as Frankie's key turned in the lock and the front door swung open.

Chapter 35

Wednesday, 23 December 1970

Frankie was married to Lisa. He'd marched around the kitchen listing the faults of which Lisa and I were both guilty. Trapping by pregnancy, draining of money, demanding time and exclusivity. We'd sucked the life out of him, imprisoned him, and were she-devils. We had undone him. We would pay for our sins in every way there was: the police, the courts, the public shaming of our grasping intentions. We would suffer greatly for the injustice we had bestowed upon him by making him a bigamist. He no longer needed us, or his children, in his life.

He threw us out of "his" house.

Helping Lisa leave, I whispered, 'I'm sorry you lost him,' which confused her. She couldn't have Frankie; she must have known that. It was a relief watching her drive away. He'd married her and realised his mistake, then deserted her for me. He married me last, making me his chosen wife.

Locked out, I tried to get in through the back door. Sliding on the moss-covered path, I slipped into the lean-to. My icy feet burned as I stood in the place where Thora used to tend her seedlings. Continuous rapping brought Frankie into the kitchen, where he'd stood, calmly ignoring me. My pleas irritated him as I spoke into the mildewed air. *Stay away from Oaktree House or he would call the police and have me arrested.* He'd obviously taken drugs. He must think he was talking to Lisa. Retrieving my wellingtons and an old gardening coat of Thora's, I walked out onto the lane, lost and homeless. Allowing him time to calm down would be the secret to soothing his destructive outburst.

My mother was in Spain until the New Year. My inheritance had not gone down well with my brothers: they seemed to think that I'd got pregnant on purpose. None of them liked Frankie. They'd not befriended him, or spent family time with us since Mum's birthday. Denny said that he didn't trust Frankie. He wasn't willing to give him a chance. They were too busy with their lives; what did they care about their little sister? They would say 'I told you so', and talk with their fists and Frankie would be hurt.

Cars trundled past along the main road, and the sounds of hymns on radios reminded me that Christmas was only a few days away.

I'd arrived at Cleave Farm cold and dishevelled. Perry handed me a jumper and blanket. Mr Cutler settled me by the open fire. They seemed unsure of how to manoeuvre around their home as if I was a disaster they hadn't planned. But I could stay; it was fine. They paced; slips of conversation, of hankerings to resolve my circumstances with fists and force. They had keys and could enter the house at any time to throw him out, but I forbade them. The thought of them, or Frankie, being led away by the police was nerve-wracking. The situation was best left to resolve itself with time and calm thought. As we settled in for the night, Ruby Silver was again my counsel. Sweating in a bed of damp sheets and rough blankets, I prayed myself back into my bed in Oaktree.

As the morning sun fought to break through the winter cold, I couldn't contemplate anything other than the continuance of my ideal world. You had to believe it to make it happen.

Chapter 36

Saturday, 26 December 1970

Christmas Day passed in a surreal atmosphere devoid of joyous emotion. If Mr Cutler and Perry exchanged gifts, they did so out of sight. They had a glass of sherry in the evening before bedtime. Farm life continued like any other day. Animals were fed, gates secured, rats and rabbits shot.

Perry tormented me that Frankie might have a legal right to Oaktree as he was Thora's natural son and I'd allowed him to live there. He ensured that I registered blame for being the mistress of my misfortune, and acted as though I should agree to Frankie's natural position as the king of his kingdom. He said that women shouldn't own property and that no woman he knew had ever done so. Mentioning Sadie Fisher and the Cleave Inn displeased him. He immediately surmised that she must have inherited it. His words swam around my head compounding my anxiety, and I panicked again to think that maybe Thora had done something illegal. But Thwaite would have stopped her I'd hoped.

Perry's intimidation reinforced my impotence, and I cowered under the bedclothes. My 'kill or be killed' responses agitated me. Frustration burned as my brain twitched between tension and listlessness. My forehead throbbed and my fists reflexively clenched. I ran from my bed to wander the surrounding fields seeking solace in the fresh air. But the air was stale in my lungs, and there was no freedom to be found outdoors. Until I was back home, I'd not sleep. If I couldn't go back, then I'd go nowhere. My life would end.

At my insistence, Perry slipped out of the house as dusk fell to go and talk to Frankie. The wait was fraught with visions of fights and even death. Perry flew into a rage quicker than my brothers, and I imagined him fighting for no reason other than the enjoyment of injuring Frankie. Ruby Silver's words comforted me: *concentrate on what I want to make it happen. Trust in Fate, and visualise happy scenarios.* My necklace hung heavily around my neck; it weighed on my soul.

Perry returned to tell me it was hopeless. Frankie said that his parents had disowned him. As I was implicit in his downfall, and the impetus behind his criminal behaviour, they would pay for the best solicitors to acquire Oaktree Estate. He was the father of the child inheriting it; there was a legal claim. We had to wait until the New Year for Thwaite & Hamilton to check the trust. Perry was sure I would lose the house as these rich people had influence. I paced around the farmland, frantic, ignoring my bare arms and legs in the chill. Why was Frankie doing this? How could he be so cruel? Did he intend to take our baby from me? I couldn't contemplate that.

Instead, I made plans for the future, for redecorating, and upgrading the heating. These improvements were jotted in a notebook as I wandered around Cleave Farm. Mr Cutler was concerned that I wasn't coping, but Perry told him to ignore me and not humour me. Sheets of paper, filled with drawings of rooms coloured with fibre-tipped pens, piled up on the dining table.

Perry made me coffee and sat too close; his fingers lingered too long on my shoulders as he adjusted my shawl. He lit a fire and gave me baby magazines. Each morning he entered my bedroom with a breakfast tray that he placed on my bed. He adjusted the covers, his eyes lingering on my breasts. He insisted that he help me into my dressing gown and his hands touched me too much. His fussing felt comforting and threatening at the same time. How he could plan to take my affection away from Frankie was disgraceful.

That evening my head buzzed with heat, so I removed my shawl and slippers. Feeling more comfortable, I wandered around in Celia's thin dress; my bare feet hopped on the cold wooden floor as if it were a hot sandy beach. Perry grunted at my explanation that my baby kept me warm. Walking with a rocking motion would settle me, I insisted. Mr Cutler let out a snort as he left to attend to the animals. Perry eyed me with suspicion but followed his father.

Once they'd gone, I made my way through the dark fields to Oaktree House with the twelve-bore and a torch. It was so cold that the foxes let me walk alone. Owls hooted along my path and wished me good fortune. The sky was full of stars, but the new moon had no power to brighten it.

Light shone in the hallway of Oaktree House, illuminating the front sitting room. I was sure Frankie was recovering from his breakdown, so I sent him special magic to give him happiness and calm the fuzzy waves in his brain.

As my hands dug deep in the pockets of Thora's coat, my fingers touched the hard metal of a set of keys. Thora's spare house keys were in my hand. It was magic because the pocket had been empty. I'd let Frankie have one more night to rest and recuperate. I retrieved Celia's negligee from the conservatory and put it on.

Chapter 37

Sunday, 27 December 1970

Perry was at Honeydew Farm and would be gone ages. There was a problem with the stream. Mr Cutler was checking the animals before continuing the ongoing fence renewal. I planned to visit Frankie in the evening when daylight faded, and my thoughts drifted towards bedtime with my lover. The farm echoed with my footsteps, but loneliness sucked at my bones. The pull of him was irresistible. Clouds sat low on the horizon, their air-soft cushions ready to ensure that my chanting spells held close to the earth.

With the twelve-bore hooked over the crook of my left arm and wellingtons on my feet, I glided through the door and walked the fields once more towards my heart's desire. I was the redeemer on my way to take him and make him mine again. This time, he'd commit to me forever because I was his guardian angel, his talisman. He'd hear my voice and touch my body, and I would be the last woman to consume his soul.

And now my home lay before me, a shining temple waiting in answer to my prayers. The keys to my kingdom were in my hand. A rush of welcoming air surrounded me and tugged me into its bosom as I opened the front door and stepped into my hallway. Home. I swore I'd never leave again as long as I had breath in my body. The kitchen was filthy, but I fought the urge to clean. A noise from the garden attracted my attention, so I headed for the lean-to, through the kitchen.

Stepping into the doorway, I watched the gorgeous man that was my Frankie. He picked up a branch, and it struck me how off balance he was. He struggled with the simple task of chopping wood. He brought the axe down, making me jump. He was hopeless, pathetic. My gladiator swayed like a mortal, stumbling and swearing like an ineffectual nobody – then the man I wanted looked about with no sense of purpose I could see.

The passion that had sustained me dissipated. How could I settle for someone so inept? He wasn't good enough for me. Drawing the rifle snugly into my shoulder, I looked along the sight-line to his heart. My finger itched on the trigger as I slipped the safety-catch. My rage gathered pace, jittering at the edges of my concentration. He was attempting to set up the next log. As he raised the axe, I shouted,

'Frankie!'

He turned, jolted, and brought the axe down on his leg with a crunch. Blood spurted onto the cold grass as he screamed, before falling, grabbing his leg to stop the flow. He cried in agony. His life drained away, and he called my name, 'Carol … Carol …' It was the sweetest sound, and I sought to hold it in my memory, as it was the last time I'd hear his voice. He looked into my eyes as I raised the gun to put him out of his misery. For the first time I saw fear in my champion's eyes, and it wasn't an emotion that enamoured. He acknowledged what I had to do. He knew it was the best way, the only way he'd be at peace with himself. He must know how much it would hurt me to end his life and live without him.

The previous night I'd decided we had to make sacrifices, to achieve greater wisdom and be truer to ourselves. That's what Ruby Silver had meant. She'd meant for me to do everything I could to make my life happy. To overcome any problem that got in the way. To get rid of all the causes of stress and anxiety. And although I was doing the worst thing I could do, it would be the best thing for me. Frankie had to die so that I could be set free.

Chapter 38

Sunday, 27 December 1970

I ran through the house and out of the front door. I'd killed my precious, darling man. He'd never hold me again, or tell me he loved me, or lie to me, or sleep with other women.

Crawling amongst the sleeping lavender and rose bushes, I curled into a ball as angels arrived, their brilliant wings surrounding me. They had come to take his soul away. Freezing damp seeped through me and the urge to sleep grew overpowering. As I drifted off, the noise of laughter boomed out. The angels had changed into demons. They danced and poked and swooped, enticing me to return with them to their evil lair in the depths of hell. They mutilated him. His body was stretched to impossible lengths as they squabbled over his beauty. Their smell made me vomit and I dry-retched over the flower border. My baby, eerily silent up to now, cried out as the demons consumed its father. Mercifully, our blood stopped flowing, and we drifted away from the madness into unconsciousness.

The noise of wheels sliding on gravel roused me. Perry shook me, shouting questions in the sharp tone he always used. He removed his coat and wrapped it around me, dragging me into the passenger seat of his car. The heater blasted hot air.

'What did Schmidt do to you, Carol?'

'Schmidt do to me?'

'He's just passed me, driving like a maniac along the lane. What did he do to you?'

'He was here? Oh, God.'

'Tell me what happened.'

'I've killed him.' I sat up and pulled back to look Perry in the eye.

Perry screwed up his face. 'But he was driving away …'

'Not Schmidt! *Frankie*. I've killed Frankie. He's dead. In the back garden.'

'Don't be silly ...' Perry scrutinised my face and got out of the car. He'd not stomach this, no matter how much he hated Frankie. He'd not come near me now, be tainted with my evil. I should drive away, drive off a cliff – but my bones were rubber. I lay down contemplating my fate and considering ways to kill myself.

Perry returned with the twelve-bore and put it in the boot. He sat in the driver's seat muttering, 'What have you done.' His hands were soaked in blood. Blood streaked his coat. 'You'll go to prison.'

'I'd rather die.' He grabbed me as I tried to open the door.

'You're pregnant. Don't be stupid.' He was too strong, and he hurt me as he pulled me back against the seat, agitation and anger in his eyes and his grip. He shouted, 'You don't understand, the farm, the trust ... everything ...' Angry tears were hot on his face, and spit landed on me. 'What about your baby's inheritance?'

'I don't know ... let me go ... leave me alone.'

'Thwaite doesn't like you so he persuaded Thora to add something; I remember reading something ...'

'What's it to do with you?'

'*Our farm* is what it's to do with me! I was eighteen last Sunday. Dad told me about stuff ... The land. My inheritance. Thora and Dad were friends. Thora's parents and Dad's parents, they had an arrangement. We have access to this land and the stream indefinitely. Paying proper rent and access fees will bankrupt us.' He banged his hands on the dashboard before collapsing against the steering wheel.

'Shall we find Mr Cutler and ask –?'

'No! Dad – he'll call the police ...'

'I've killed Frankie, Perry. I've killed him. They'll find out.'

'Oh, keep quiet! Let me think.'

His pain and confusion were tangible. 'You have a copy of

the trust in the house, don't you?'

'Yes. In my desk, in the study.'

'I need to check it.' He came around to my door and said, 'You're coming with me,' and pulled me out.

The trust was clear. Thora didn't think I'd do anything criminal because she wouldn't have agreed to such a clause. Thwaite was a nasty man to think of this way to exclude Thora's grandchild from their rightful inheritance: if I was, or became, a criminal, then it was null and void.

'Oh, God.' Perry put his head in his hands and paced. 'We have to get rid of him.'

'He's not leaving me. I need him here.' I curled up on the sofa exhausted and frozen; my fingers tingled with pain as I closed my eyes.

'Get up, Carol. Listen. I'll start digging in the orchard. We need some stuff. Drive to Cleave Farm and fetch some heavy-duty plastic from the second barn. And the big ball of twine. Go by the outside route and don't let Dad see you. Wear my gloves and don't touch anything with your bare hands. Fetch enough to wrap a body.'

He shook me and fetched Frankie's coat from the hall. 'And don't come back through the house – go around the side, to the orchard. Quickly, Carol, or we'll both be going to prison.

I had to find strength and courage. As I held my necklace, Ruby reminded me that life gave us help, and Perry was here to help. Drawing in a deep breath, I set out on another deceitful path.

***

As Perry dug the grave in the orchard, I paced in frustration. He repeatedly shouted for me to sit in the car, but I had to kneel and pray. He feared I'd die of cold. We couldn't be sure how long I'd been lying in the front garden. If the cold killed me, though, I didn't have far to fall. Perry could bury us both.

The grave was ready. Perry put on his gloves and took the plastic sheeting and twine before making his way to the garden, to Frankie. He warned me not to follow him. He feared I would collapse and die of shock; then he'd go to prison for two deaths. He dragged Frankie across the grass, the smooth plastic aiding him. Frankie was bound up like an Egyptian mummy and slid into his final resting place with a *slosh* and a bump. We closed our eyes and prayed. He was resting peacefully beneath the apple and pear trees. The blossoming flowers would surround him with beauty in the spring and summertime. He was safe, and I was free to leave him there.

I could rest at last.

Chapter 39

Tuesday, 29 December 1970

Yesterday, as Perry and I whispered our plans about how to cover up Frankie's absence, Mr Cutler narrowed his eyes and looked on suspiciously. Better that he presumed we'd fallen in love and left us alone than that he knew the truth.

Perry would drive Frankie's car to Portsmouth. He'd abandon it with its keys in the ignition and logbook in the glove compartment. He'd travel as a foot passenger to France on Frankie's passport, wearing a shirt and jumper of Frankie's, as in the passport photo. His hair would be tied in a ponytail and covered with a pale woolly hat. It was shorter, and jet-black to Frankie's blond, but he would say he'd dyed it. It was uncanny how similar their noses were. Once in Caen, he'll get the next ferry back under his passport, then get the train. The problem is what to tell Mr Cutler to excuse his absence. That was my job.

***

Perry left early morning. Mr Cutler walked into the kitchen, so I put the kettle on and offered to cook eggs and toast.

'Where's Perry? I need his help with the fencing down Drovers Way.'

'He had to do something. He might not be back till late.'

'Late? Why?'

'Um … Frankie decided to go to France. To see in the New Year with his friends.'

'Oh, he has, has he? Well, that's very nice for him, seeing as everyone else's Christmas is ruined.' Mr Cutler stood, fists clenched. 'What has it to do with Perry? Don't tell me they're both going?' He let out a guffaw and coughed.

'No. Frankie forgot his passport. Perry has driven to Portsmouth to give it to him. Frankie couldn't drive back because he didn't have enough money for petrol. His friends will meet him in France and they'll have money for him.'

Mr Cutler's face reddened. 'What the bloody hell is Perry doing that for?'

'I persuaded him to, so blame me, because he didn't want to. I convinced him. I'd have gone, but ...' I opened my arms around my belly. 'It may do Frankie good to be away for a while. Have a rest, a change of air.'

'Rest? Change of air? What is he, some bleedin' woman with the vapours?'

'Please, Mr Cutler. I'm sorry. I thought it best. Perry has been so helpful. You have a thoughtful son who's a credit to you.'

Mr Cutler looked at me, assessing me. 'Yes, I have, and you'd do well to forget that two-timing bastard. Sorry, I didn't mean to swear. But you should forget him. We'll look after you, and the baby.'

My hands covered my face as I cried. 'I'm so grateful for your kindness. I don't know what I'd have done without your support ... I've paid for his petrol, by the way.'

'Get away with you. We've known you half your life, and I won't forget all you did for Elsie.'

'I did what anyone would've done. No need to thank me. She got me to the hospital after I fell off the gate.' I rubbed my forehead remembering the whack I'd got.

There was an awkward silence before Mr Cutler turned and left. I eased myself into a chair; my mind was racing in a panic but I hoped that when the police came looking for Frankie, Mr Cutler would back us up. As long as he didn't go to Oaktree House – because Perry's car was in the garage.

At last I gave in to fate and slept for hours because I knew I'd soon be back home.

Chapter 40

Thursday, 31 December 1970

A note on the hallstand reminded me of my anti-natal appointment, but I had already missed it again. My baby was fine and loved to kick and bruise my ribs. Relaxing in the cosy chair in my kitchen, book in hand, I felt wonderful. Frankie, resting close by, eased any isolation. The churning wheels of doubt and fear had slowed to manageable levels. For once my head felt in harmony with my body.

But convincing myself life was good didn't stop loneliness taking hold. The house was empty without Frankie. The rooms suffocated without his breath and shrank without his touch. No more meals to prepare, or body to satisfy. So many demands no longer required, an autopilot list that made me feel jittery with frustration. New behaviours jostled to replace my favourite ones. Grief was natural. But it would be put in a box, not savoured.

If only my brothers weren't so involved in their own lives, they could come for a meal and enjoy my home. We'd reminisce about our happy past and plan happy futures. There would be no reuniting with my mother either, as she'd replaced my father with an imposter.

If only Sarah hadn't betrayed me in such a deceitful way, I could have forgiven her. Maybe we could be friends again now that she couldn't touch Frankie. I went to the phone.

Mrs Burcher answered immediately, clearly disappointed that it was not Sarah. Sarah hadn't come home since the day before. They were distraught. The police weren't overly concerned, as she was seventeen. The Burchers had to admit that she'd a boyfriend, although they didn't know who he was. The police weren't interested, so they wouldn't look for her. Then it would be another night. Mrs Burcher cried and needed me to comfort her, but there was nothing to say. I asked if they had checked with Alice, but they hadn't seen Alice for a while. Matthew was home for New Year but had no idea where she was and had spent hours driving around looking for her. She'd phoned Mr Cutler yesterday. They decided not to tell me, as I had problems of my own. Thanking her for her concern, I made her promise to phone me when they found her.

The situation was bizarre. Sarah wouldn't stay out all night. The last time I'd seen her was the Sunday before Christmas. Before Lisa arrived. Before Frankie lost his mind and ruined everything. Maybe she was fretting, trying to pluck up the courage to tell them about the baby. Where would she go? To Alice? She told me that Alice was a favourite friend, but that was meant to hurt me. Would she come here to see Frankie? Would she dare, even though I'd warned her?

Returning to the kitchen, I sipped my drink before pulling on my wellingtons and heavy coat and grabbing a torch. Perry had dug-in brambles on top of Frankie's grave, completely obliterating it. He'd also mulched manure in, haphazardly over the orchard, the pungent smell enough to repulse keen noses. I asked Frankie where Sarah was, but he didn't acknowledge me.

Leaving the orchard, the path to the top of the hill met the pathway down through Dawnview Wood where it then carried on towards the estate below, and Sarah's home. My baby-bump unbalanced me as I stumbled on; unease raced my heart. I walked to the oak tree in Dawnview Wood, the twin of the one in front of the house. A sense of déjà-vu threaded its way into my consciousness. A strange breeze carried memories of my brothers: our treks, our happy hunting, our old ways. I glanced around expecting a movement: a boy, a man, a girl, a woman. Tranquillity had vanished, and uncertainty lurked.

My blood ran cold and acid swirled in my stomach. Struggling along the hill, my baby moved appendage-like, obstructing my legs and forcing me to tilt backwards. Sarah whispered to me, her presence skulked close by, ready to materialise from the woods.

'Sarah, where are you? Everyone is worried.'

The long grass crumpled in the winter's cold. My wellingtons thwacked the backs of my legs. The ground did its best to upend me.

'Sarah, go home. Frankie doesn't want you, and I haven't forgiven you for what you did. Go home. Your mother is worried.'

Oaktree House drifted out of sight behind me, beyond the high wall. Clouds dulled the hillside. All around, trees, grass, leaves, and bushes merged into one big obstruction. The dry vegetation rattled its cold bones as I brushed against it, picking my way through the bare, broken bushes, seeking my fear that Sarah had come up here to speak to Frankie.

The place was beautiful on a clear, sunny day when the gifts of spring abound, or when the fullness of summer gave up her bountiful offerings. Then there was joy and thankfulness. I didn't need to be fearful in these woods where I'd spent most of my life. Just because it was dark didn't mean it was different. 'It's just dark,' I repeated prayer-like, as the clouds parted and pale sunlight streamed in droopy rays. Struggling to stay focused, I stepped forward until the looming silhouette of the oak tree towered over me.

Sarah's feet hung limp as they dangled from a sturdy branch. In the distance an owl hooted, closely followed by a fox's call echoing from a field beyond the brow. I had found her. Her hair had fallen forward, shading her pale face. Her naked skin glowed in the silvery light, a ghostly pallor, a cold, empty shell. I touched her naked leg, spongy, smooth, inhuman. She'd stripped herself in the open and arranged her clothes in a neat pile with her shoes on top. Perplexing, bewildering, unnatural.

She fascinated me, this strange Sarah, so different from the Sarah who'd walked beside me. The porcelain mask of her face assessed me as I clasped her soft fingers. She had gone. She had left me because of Frankie. Frankie had wanted me, but she had wanted Frankie. Cold air hit the back of my neck. Did you make her do it, Frankie?

If she'd known he was dead, she wouldn't have joined him, would she? Now poor Sarah would have to endure hell with him. She had opened herself to him, her weakness had cast them into the fires of hell, and they would burn for all eternity.

Back home calls were made to remove her from my land. I prayed that the police would not look too closely around the area. Frankie was just settling in.

Chapter 41

Saturday, 2 January 1971

The first day of the New Year had passed leaving me bereft. Frankie, Sarah and Thora had gone. Money was empty and meaningless when you felt cast adrift in a beautiful ocean.

The watery sun failed to light my bedroom as I huddled under the covers. My arm dropped onto Frankie place. The memory of his warm body taunted me. The fantasy that he loved me played in my mind, and I wanted to stay in that dream.

The curtains were open because I couldn't bear to cut myself off from the world, but now I wanted to fix them so they never opened again. The house was cold, the range neglected, the fires unlit. This mausoleum needed energy and zeal from someone with strength and determination. My baby grumbled and stretched in its womb, and I feared its birth, feared being unable to care for it. Needing the toilet made me leave the warmth of my bed, but I crawled back into my refuge and prayed that time didn't move on to make me face motherhood. Could my brothers help? Could one of them move in with me? Deciding to visit them got me out of bed.

***

My intention to visit Denny and Gerry faded as I drove down the hill. Neither of them had supported my marriage or been to Oaktree house since Thora's funeral. Uncertain of what to do, I abandoned my mission and turned right onto the spine road leading through the estate. As I neared Sarah's home, I changed my mind and turned sharply to head for the library.

My father's arms enclosed me for a while as memories came tantalisingly close. The smell of print, the soft swish of a page turning, the joy of my dad's voice reading to me: excitement, sadness, laughter, as he play-acted the story: enchanting, drawing me into other worlds that existed in better places. I could taste them: cocoa and Christmas wrapping paper flew in from other worlds with their assurances of safety and comfort. My old life beckoned me.

Arriving at my old home, I parked in the lane by the garages. Nothing had changed, yet everything had changed. I was an outsider; the place was my history, not my present. Tears stung as I remembered the first time I'd driven this car. Thora was sitting next to me, already dying. Sarah was sitting in the back, worried about the rifle instead of enjoying the ride. Sarah, taking on the worries of the world and wasting her time on them. Her upbringing, designed to conform to the demands of others.

A vision of her naked feet forced me to stumble out of the car and stagger into the Burchers' back garden. I leant against her back door while Ruby Silver told me to picture what I wanted, what I desired, and focus on it. My necklace sat heavily around my neck as if in support; my earrings caressed my skin, but the awful vision of Sarah's naked body shimmering in the moonlight remained. I didn't mean to hurt her with my words and lack of sympathy. Maybe touching something she cherished would allow me to connect with her. We should have damned Frankie together, consoled each other, and found the strength to dismiss him. Now she has chosen her way, and I had chosen mine.

'Raven. Long time.' Matthew opened the back door. 'Come in. You'll catch your death in this. Though it's not as cold as Ireland.'

The room was a mess: dirty breakfast plates pushed aside, clothes dropped on the chair.

'Mum and Dad have gone to the police. They found a suicide note.' He sat, then laid himself flat on the table, resting his head on his hands. His shoulders shivered and I longed to ease his pain. His fingers scrunched against scratch-marks at his temples.

'Have you come for your books?'

'My books?'

'She left them on her desk. With a note.'

'Oh. Yes.' She had my copy of *Rebecca*, and the thought jarred memories. Laughing, teasing and writing our coded letters, each knowing what the other was thinking. My friend. Long red hair. Green eyes dulled by a lack of confidence.

'You found her. What happened?' Matthew pushed himself up and poured steaming tea into cups.

'Yes.' I stared at my tea unable to look at him. 'I didn't think she'd kill herself.' The words mirrored my guilt.

He picked up his cup and threw it past me. It hit the wall and shattered. Tea exploded in a spray and splashed onto me. I jumped and yelped.

'*Oh-oh-oh* ...' I swiped my hair, my neck, my shoulder as I ran to the sink, where I picked up the dishcloth and soaked it in cold running water. He stood behind me as I dabbed myself, pressing the cold cloth to my burnt skin. There was no defence for what Frankie did, because Frankie chose me, not her, and we both abandoned her. Matthew wanted to hurt me, and I didn't blame him.

'Why did you come here?' He moved closer; his hip touched mine. His breath flowed softly against my neck. I wanted to turn around, to look into his eyes and meet his grief. He leant into me. Our bodies fused as he took the cloth and ran it under the cold tap. He pressed it into my neck. Cold water trickled down the front of my jumper, soaking into the V and running in a shivering stream between my breasts. He watched the water run, his head so close that I inhaled the scent of his hair.

'I need to go ...' I said as dizziness and longing for him engulfed me. The sick feeling that he could replace Frankie didn't cause me revulsion as it should have.

'Don't go.' He pressed again: gentle, rhythmic pressure. A minute ticked by before he sat down at the table. His profile was strong, the straight nose perfect for his face, but his full-fleshed lips had thinned with grief. I remembered the boy he had been: hard, unflinching and cruel to his sister. The skin on his cheeks was pale and mottled from distress. His long brown hair fell either side of his collar in soft tendrils. His shoulders weakened me as they had always done. Their shape, their strength, their maleness. The thought of them close to me punched straight to a spot in my womb. Frankie's baby turned and kicked my ribs.

'Okay. I'll pour you some more tea.' Opening the cupboard, I fetched a cup. 'It's not stewed yet ... maybe I'll make some more.'

'No.' His voice touched something inside of me. My hand jerked, making the teapot lid rattle. 'Just pour it and sit down.' My hands shook as I placed the cup in front of him. He looked up, his face a mixture of the paleness of shock and the blue of helplessness.

'Tell me what happened. Tell me about my sister.'

'She came to see me, the Sunday before Christmas. Told me she was pregnant, by Frankie. He'd told her we'd split up ...'

His head dropped into his hands, and the scrunching of his temples started again. 'Where is the bastard?'

'He's gone away ... with his friends ... France. We weren't married, because he already has a wife. And a child.'

'Oh, for fuck's sake!'

'I'm sorry. I don't know what to say.' I reached for his hand and he squeezed my fingers.

'Tell me why you're here. It's not for the books, is it?'

'To find her, be near her. I don't know where she is. Her body hanging from that rope ...' Tears gushed. Matthew watched but didn't comfort me. I went to the sink and splashed cold water on my face, 'I'm going to her room.'

He followed me upstairs, and we stood for a moment outside her door before he pushed it open. I walked in, but he went into the bathroom. On top of her desk were the pens she'd been using, with some unfinished knitting, a few books, and a note in code: 'Carol. These are yours. I've written a letter to you.'

A pair of daps sat beside the chest of drawers. A vision of us, laughing as we tried on Paula's clothes. Sarah posing. Me drawing a picture, and her hiding it in our secret place, behind the headboard of the bed. She said she loved it and would treasure it forever.

The letter was hidden behind the headboard. In a sealed envelope addressed to me. The toilet flushed, so I slipped it into my waistband as Matthew returned. Sliding into the neatly made bed, I pulled her pillow to my face, immersing myself in her smell. He lay beside me, taking the pillow and placed it under our heads. He turned my face and looked into my eyes as he kissed me. His warmth and the touch released me back into my body. I gasped as my senses jolted back to life and my skin pulsated with the pleasure of his touch. His tears drenched my breasts, and his hands sought my belly, smoothing the swollen mound with reverent strokes. We joined in a place away from our suffering. His passion was my atonement, and the last vestige of decency left me. I was happy to abandon it; to ratify my guilt. We cast ourselves outside of that horrid world and banished ourselves to a twilight place of ghosts and memories, prolonging our agony to satisfy our sin.

He ran a bath as I dressed and made my way downstairs. As I filled the kettle, Sarah's parents returned so I gathered my things and slipped out the back door. They couldn't see our familiarity and guess what we'd done. We must not cause any more pain. I destroyed Frankie with my love, but I wouldn't destroy Matthew. He didn't deserve me.

Chapter 42

Tuesday, 2 February 1971

Spirits walked with me in the early morning and sapped my strength with their demands on my guilty conscience. The year was freeing itself from hibernation. If I could summon the strength to walk in my beloved woods, I would find many buds pushing their way into the light of day. They had more strength than me: they saw a future in their efforts whereas I couldn't look beyond the next minute. The coming spring should have excited me, but it didn't.

Never wanting to leave my bed, I wallowed until twelve unless Perry, or Mr Cutler, came to chop wood or tend the garden. The sight of them toiling on my behalf brought a mixture of resentment and gratitude as I wavered between wanting to be alive and dead. The logs stacked in the kitchen taunted me with the need to either keep warm or freeze to death. If only I could leave this struggle to live, I thought ... but I was weak.

Oh, Frankie, where were you? My despair at killing you knew no end. I wandered around the house, a ghost in residence, with no meaning to my existence. Why did I do it? I asked myself. Why, why, why? I couldn't believe that I could be so cruel and heartless. I thought: I didn't give you time to explain, to say sorry, to make us whole again. I destroyed my life by destroying the one person who gave it meaning. Lonely years of living in this mausoleum stretched before me. Shame would follow me to my grave.

A knocking on the door roused me. I got out of bed and looked outside – a police car. A man in a dark suit took a step back and beckoned me. Opening the door revealed a man in a tweed coat standing stony-faced before me.

'Miss Cage? I'm Detective Inspector Stewart, and this is

Detective Sergeant Harptree.' He indicated the other man, who took out a notebook and pen. 'May we come in?'

They followed me into the sitting room and sat on the green sofa. Their maleness permeated the room, leaving me unsure of my ownership of it. They declined my offer of tea with the shake of commanding heads, as though bestowing salvation from an expected task.

'I can't tell you any more about Sarah Burcher. I found her, that's all.' My breath came gasping, stinging my ribs.

'Sarah?'

'My friend who … died.'

His mouth had a condescending turn. 'We're looking for Frankie Dewberry. Lisa Dewberry, his wife, has contacted us to report him missing.' The word 'wife' forced itself through righteous teeth. 'Did you go through a marriage ceremony with him on nineteen December last?'

'Yes. I know about Lisa. She came here. He wasn't happy …'

'What happened?' He picked at some fluff on razor-sharp trouser creases.

'He had expressly forbidden her to come here. He was livid with me for letting her into "his house", as he called it. He threw us out.'

'Threw you out?'

'Yes. He wouldn't let me back in. I went to Cleave Farm.'

'And why didn't you call us to help you gain access?'

'I … I didn't want to upset him. I thought he would calm down and let me back in.' I shifted uncomfortably under his unsympathetic gaze.

'Mrs Dewberry says she's not heard from him since twenty-seventh of December when she phoned him but he cut her off. Have you seen him since?'

'No.'

'When was the last time you saw him?'

'That was the last time.'

'Where is Cleave Farm?' He stood and walked to the window.

'Half a mile south-west of here. I stayed there, with the Cutlers.'

He looked around to check that Harptree was taking notes. 'So if he was here and you were barred, how come you're here now?'

His gaze took in the opulence of the room and returned to look me up and down, scepticism tightening his mouth.

'Perry – Perry Cutler – told me he'd left, so I came back.'

'And how did he know Mr Dewberry had left?'

'He came here to talk to Frankie, see if he could fetch some things for me. Frankie told him he was going to France on the twenty-ninth. To spend New Year with his friends in Saumur.'

'How was he getting there?'

'Ferry. From Portsmouth. He forgot his passport and didn't have enough petrol to drive back so he phoned Perry to drive down with it. Perry didn't want to, but I persuaded him to go.'

'Do you have contact details for these friends?'

Frankie's address book was in the bureau. 'No. Lisa will, though. He was at uni with them.'

'So you're not expecting him back?' He stood and put his arms behind his back and rocked on his feet.

'No. Not now, after everything that went on. He doesn't want to be with me.' Tears rolled down my cheeks. 'Does Lisa want his things? You can take them if you want.'

'You'll have to ask her that. So it seems he's not missing but has gone to France.'

He looked down at his hands, digesting what I'd said, and I add, 'Lisa has already phoned me, and I've told her that. A week or so ago. She knows he's with his friends on holiday. She's just annoyed with him, that's all. I told her that my friend Sarah killed herself.'

'Oh?' He pulled himself up. 'Why tell Mrs Dewberry that?'

'Sarah is … was … pregnant with Frankie's child. But he left her. Like he left me. Like he left Lisa.'

'So, he's a bigamist who has fled to France leaving yet another woman pregnant.' The detective looked at my abdomen. 'And your baby is his?'

'Yes.' I wrapped my arms around myself.

'It's not surprising he's disappeared. We'll update Mrs Dewberry. Thank you for your help.'

He stiffened as he digested how unsavoury Frankie was. 'If you hear from him, please call this number.' He handed me a card.

As I shut the door, small pains shot through my belly and liquid ran down my legs. Pain stabbed my breath away. More liquid squelched and another pain cramped. I crouched my way to the telephone to call Perry. Frankie's baby was on its way into the world.

Chapter 43

Friday, 7 April 1971

Francine was not a peaceful baby. She veered between howling and grizzling, such was her wrath about entering the world too soon. She rejected the mother who had killed her father and fretted for the comfort she'd had inside me. Pathetic attempts to assure her I was the only parent she needed didn't console her. We endured wandering around our big house and listening to the ghosts of Francine's forbearers. We were the survivors of the family. We had to find the strength to thrive.

Francine whined all day and didn't feed. My breasts were uncomfortable and milk leaked out, spoiling my blouse. She didn't enjoy her bath and was listless. I was so tired and longed for a decent night's sleep as I hadn't slept for more than two or three hours at a time since her birth. As I put her to bed, I noticed that her forehead was damp. The overhead lightbulb had blown, and I couldn't see her clearly in the light from the bedside lamp, so I brought some night-lights upstairs and lit them.

For supper there were eggs and toast, and a piece of apple pie that Sadie has brought over. It was nice of her to call, and we spent a few hours reminiscing about my childhood and how she used to let us play in the garden of the Cleave Inn. She brought Francine a beautiful dress.

At least Francine chased away the ghosts of Frankie and Sarah. There was no space in my head for my wants and desires or anything else except surviving in this monotonous despair. Lighting candles in our room to chase away the gloom reminded of Frankie and that special birthday. Now our bed was a place for tears.

***

The luminous hands on the clock said five thirty. Turning to go back to sleep, I came even more awake with a start. Had Francine been fed during the night? Switching on the bedside lamp, I stumbled out of bed, grabbing my heavy dressing gown. The house was freezing. Lighting more candles, I reached down. She was cold and grey, flopping in my arms. Screaming her name, I rubbed her tiny chest, but she didn't cry. Grabbing one of her blankets as I ran downstairs, I noticed small reddish-purple spots on her chest. Certain she was dead, I jiggled her softly and pressed her to me as I dialled 999 and screamed for help. A woman asked questions, and I tried to answer, but there was no point. She was dead. My precious darling had left me. They were all gone, and I was left alone.

The smell of burning jolted me. Confused, I headed for the kitchen, but nothing was burning there. Thinking that it must be the candles in the bedroom, I rushed upstairs clutching Francine tightly. The room was ablaze; flames leapt to catch the curtains, then spread along the carpet to engulf the bookcase. Dad's books smouldered in black curls of death, red and orange and blue destruction. My heart broke at the sight, so I darted forward to save them but my lungs filled with smoke. Back downstairs, trying to control my hacking cough, I dialled again and spluttered to the operator: 'Oaktree House … Fire …'

There was no point in summoning help. As I dropped the handset, the coiled cord revolved and bumped against the hallstand. Suddenly it became clear to me what I must do. I had to join them now, that was the answer. In the sitting room, I laid Francine in her Moses basket and covered her with blankets. She wasn't to burn, so I took her outside and placed her beneath the oak tree.

Then I returned to my bedroom to welcome the end and make my way to hell.

Chapter 44

Thursday, 6 May 1971

Maytree mental hospital lay to the south of the city. Constructed in the late nineteenth century, the building had the charm of a school toilet block. The construction was designed to portray an obeisance to God and sobriety. The view from my window was of barbed wire atop the perimeter wall, obscuring the countryside – the intention clearly to remind you that you had been deprived of the beauty of life outside your confinement.

Days were spent drugged and apathetic, with no care for food or sanitary tasks. Attempts to bask in my own filth were severely admonished with an increase in various medicines or by being forced into the bath. At least volunteering to use the bathroom meant that I could sit in cold water and attempt to freeze to death. They'd warned me that doing that would force them to remove the privilege of privacy. Allowing me two minutes alone to wash in the yellow, stained bath, using the disgusting red soap, they believed proved adherence to their rules.

Soot seeped in between strands of my hair and fluttered into the air, where it puffed gentle reminders of bad intentions. Of the unforgivable sin of termination. Those smoky wisps of pointing finger-clouds circled to remind me of my sin. Determined to keep my soot-oiled hair, I avoided shampoo and wallowed in the reminder of my failure to complete my task. That Perry had saved me vexed me, but my anger was tempered by Francine's survival.

There was no wish to return home. No wish to live that lonely life without Frankie. He was my dream and vision, and all dreams and the future had been wiped out, erased from my imagination. Sammy and Valerie, or maybe Mother, would care for Francine better than I could. Anyone would do a better job.

I'd failed as a mother – unable to stay awake when my child needed me, and unable to assess that she was sick, not dead.

Doctor Brindleton suggested reconnecting with my life by writing a diary. Start from a time when life was good and chart how it declined. Force myself to accept that I was the author of my destruction. He phoned my mother to ask her to bring in notebooks, but she was too traumatised by events to visit. Then Perry phoned to see how I was, and Brindleton asked him.

Perry sat fidgeting in the visitor's room looking nervously at the locked doors. The sight of him jarred. Numerous drugs had settled within me to normalise and define a new me: a parody of myself, irresponsible and uncensored, released from the confines of sanity. Or insanity.

Perry looked older than his eighteen years. His thinness no longer made him child-like but bestowed the look of an elderly man. Outdoor life had weathered him and vested a toughened skin around his youthful body. The burns he'd sustained gave him the air of a champion. The scars on the left side of his face and head were still raw. I prayed that his hair would grow back. His left hand was bandaged, covering the place where his little finger should be.

My indebtedness to him for saving Francine's life (she also survived her bout of meningitis) sat uncomfortably in me. Being forced to face him was hard, but coping with a visit was a tick on the list paving the path out of here. I'd wavered, thinking that I didn't want a way out, but something in Brindleton's eye made me accept the imposition.

Perry took the notebooks from a large paper bag and placed them on the table – six dark brown books. The smell of leather wafted through the air like expensive perfume. They sat on the table between us, too pristine, too beautiful.

'Do you like them?' he asked.

'Yes.' My answer pleased him, but I didn't want to please him. I wanted to be obnoxious. 'But I can't write in these.' I pushed them away.

'Use them. It's what they're for. I can get you more.' Irritation spiked his words.

'How can I use these for scribbling? It's a waste. Bring me a cheap notepad.'

'Use them because when you write in them you'll remember why you're using them. The doctor says it's important, Carol.'

'Yes … it's kind of you to bring them.'

He sat appraising me and a minute went by. 'Why do you treat me like a … a gofer? After what we've been through.' He looked around. He could walk out at any time, and part of me wished he would.

'It's not that, it's … I can't forget what …'

He reached for my hand. 'Sometimes it's best to forget. You didn't mean to do it. You weren't thinking straight.'

My squeezing his hand made him smile. 'Yes, maybe. Didn't mean to do it. Maybe that can be the truth.'

'But that *is* the truth, isn't it?' His hand felt hot, and I itched to let it go. 'Bad things happen, and we cope as best we can.'

The response of severe panic about the dreadful thing I'd done to Frankie didn't happen. A strange sense of calm surrounded me, and an understanding of why they gave me the drugs. An okay way to watch my life, instead of living it.

'You weren't nice to me when you were with Frankie. It was his influence on you and not who you are. Now you act as though I'm a visitor extending charity to you. We've known each other for years, for heaven's sake. You helped nurse my mother when she was dying.'

'Sorry. The drugs. Feel apart from stuff.' No one must blame darling Frankie for my shortcomings. What I did had united us in a way that couldn't be undone. Staying inside might enable me to avoid him – avoid his impatience and superiority.

Perry sat back, dropped his shoulders and crossed his legs. 'You had a visitor. Matthew Burcher was in your garden. He was pretty agitated. I asked how he got in and he walked me to the gate to show me the lock. It was broken. I reckon he broke it. I've replaced it.'

'Matthew broke into my garden?'

'Reckon so. He was shifty, spooked; something was up with him. Said he'd been to the oak tree where Sarah …'

'No wonder he was spooked, Perry. How would you feel after visiting the place where your sister had killed herself. Remember how you felt when your brother drowned?' Perry's habit of not being able to put himself into other people's shoes irked.

'Anyway, he had a note for you. Was gonna give it to me but changed his mind and rushed off.' Perry caught my disappointment. 'You've not been out with him, have you?'

'What? I love Frankie. Loved. You know that.'

He assessed me before focusing on my raw finger: the skin around the nail was bitten and chewed.

'Anyway, I'll talk to your mum and try to reason with her. She's a bit overwrought, but someone needs to check on what they're doing to you here.'

'Mum hasn't forgiven me for Francine.'

'I'm sure she has. You didn't know she had meningitis.'

'Should have known she was ill, though! Instead I slept, grateful that she was quiet. Grateful. Selfish. She doesn't have to condemn me – I condemn myself.'

'How can you blame yourself for sleeping when you'd no idea she was ill?'

'Because I'm her mother. Don't deserve sympathy. Should be de – …'

Perry considers my words. 'So I risked my life for nothing.'

'No – no, Perry. This place is helping, I think it is. Just … Doctor Brindleton wants me to face failure. How? What I did to Frankie … and Francine …'

He knelt next to me and took my hands, making me worry about hurting the raw patches on his fire-damaged body. Why

182

hadn't I shouted to him that Francine wasn't in the bedroom?

'You're not alone. You have me. I'll get you out of here. You need to be home – and I'll help you. We know what we've done, but he deserved what he got. You know that, don't you, Carol? You must forgive yourself for Frankie as well as Francine. You have nothing to feel guilty about.'

He stared at me in desperation and tightened his grip on my hands, as though pushing his will through my skin.

'Can't …'

'You can and you will. You will come home.'

'Home? Home where? Done so much damage … I won't go to Mother's, won't live away from … him.'

'You can both stay with me … us, on the farm.'

'Want to go home to Oaktree. With Francine. The repairs?'

He returned to his seat. 'Starting soon. The surveyor says there's no structural damage. The builders are quoting this week: three firms for three quotes, for the insurance. It will take several weeks. Then there's the decorating, so maybe a couple of months. You can stay with us. No reason to delay leaving here.'

'Don't know how to thank you. You're so good.'

He blushed and I was aware that there was a way he'd like me to show my gratitude to him.

'You'll be home soon. Here's some post.' He handed over a letter.

'Don't want it. Open it please, Perry.' I handed it back, too tired to deal with it.

He laughed. 'Are you sure? It could be private. It's not a bill. They don't come in thick posh envelopes.'

'Don't have anything private now. It's probably the trust, and you know all about that.'

He pulled out a letter: blue ink-stained, thick cream paper.

'It's from Thwaite & Hamilton.' Perry read; his eyebrows moved up and down as he crinkled his nose. 'Catherine Dewberry wants Francine. She's lodging a claim for custody.'

'She's what?'

'Says you're an unfit mother and you're mentally incapable and unstable.'

'She can't. She can't … *take* Francine. Francine? My daughter. I'm her mother, her MOTHER …'

'Leave it with me. Thwaite will know what to do.'

My soul left my body and the shell crumbled to the floor.

Part 2 - Now

Chapter 45

Oaktree House

Sunday, 3 January 2016

Perry suggests writing a diary as a priority. He thinks the discipline of it, the recording of events, will keep me grounded during the coming months. He remembers that I did this when incarcerated in Maytree Hospital. That I should record the demolition of my home, and life, though, feels like masochism. I scream and shout at the heavens for the disastrous alignment of stars that have occasioned this calamity. But Perry possesses sublime influential powers that ensure his will prevails. I act on his suggestions believing them to be my ideas before realising that they weren't. Possessing such qualities would enable me to rule my world. The ways that others influence us are subtle and many. Love is one such force that seeps into one's conscience. It renders one susceptible to the will of another against one's own better judgement. Hindsight is a wicked torturer.

Perry demands that Frankie is dug up and moved to Cleave Farm. I won't allow it. The demons trapped inside will be released if we open his grave. If Perry insists on moving him, I will confess, now. That's non-negotiable. I reason that if we don't move his body, it proves our innocence: if we had killed and buried him, we would do something to cover it up.

I won't tell Perry the real reason I'll not move Frankie: that I want Frankie found. Time has enabled my decision that this torture must end. Let them hold a funeral and bury him in consecrated ground. If I'm caught and imprisoned, so be it. After all, the crime has imprisoned me all these years anyway. Living in a different prison won't be such a hardship. There; the confession is over and a sense of relief sets me free.

Breakfast is toast made from home-baked bread, spread with Perry's home-made plum jam. Eating it does not help to dispel the unease of last night's nightmare. The same nightmare has haunted me since I stood over Frankie aiming the twelve-bore. His blood flows like a river; the force of it drowns me. The nightmare haunts and taunts me. It will never leave me. His blood drenches my dreams, and I wake to check that the dampness on my skin is not the soaking red metal of death. Heavy rain pounds against the window. I look away and move closer to the fire and pick up my notepad.

Shaking off thoughts of Frankie, I scan the list of packing. The time has come to clear away precious memories. But Frankie steps in to join me; his hovering form lingers behind my shoulder, his breath cools my neck. He oversees the upheaval of my life. We join together to contemplate our dreadful situation. He has aged well, his handsome features barely changed. The essence of him, the verve and joy of him, remains the same.

Francine, my baby, my darling, how I miss you. Maternal instinct dictated that she was in the best place with Frankie's adopted mother Catherine: safe until I could fight for her return. Catherine Dewberry's malicious smile morphs before me like the devil incarnate. She got her way and took my daughter. Her husband facilitated whatever his wife desired, to allow him a peaceful life. And reasoning that at least she'd be cocooned in expensive blankets and chauffeured cars, I relented. But too much money enables dangerous playgrounds. Francine, along with Catherine and Frederick, Celia, and Celia's mother, all died in a helicopter crash in the Alps. My daughter died with

Frankie's lover. Celia may have been holding her on her lap with my one-year-old daughter's arms around her as they hit the earth and travelled to oblivion. Frankie stirs at my side sensing my hatred, but I ignore him. I'll deny him any pleasure he might gain from my jealousy of his tart.

Francine's death put me back in Maytree Hospital for months. A concoction of drugs obliterated my memory of her. For fleeting moments I remember a baby nuzzling at my breast, five toes wriggling in the palm of my hand, and a soft breath escaping her like an angel sighing. That she died with Celia enraged me to the point that I wasted my time cursing her instead of remembering my daughter.

My mother failed to help; her visits were functional and devoid of emotion. She succeeded with four children, whereas I failed with one. Our closeness dissolved as the distance grew between us. She embraced her new life of leisure. The woman she had been, the one who had struggled against death and poverty, became a rich, spoilt dragon. She rewrote her history, deleting her poor ancestry. I hated her for abandoning the home that was such a big part of my identity.

It took a long time to settle into Oaktree House. Mum brought my possessions and put them in the cellar. Pathetic boxes of junk and scruffy clothes so far removed from who I'd become that I couldn't bear to touch them. Maybe I should have reminded her how much she'd doted on Frankie. How impressed she was by his class, his piano playing, and his flirting with her. Perhaps she's guilty of complacency because she failed to acknowledge his flaws. Failed to protect her daughter from the type of man mothers should protect their daughters from. She was angry at my pregnancy, but recognising Frankie's pedigree and place in society, she acquiesced. My elevation out of poverty by marriage struck her as a satisfactory outcome. At least she and Peter helped resolve the bigamy charges and my name-change back to Cage. And she was against Peter spending money on a private investigator to track Frankie down.

Hamilton has instructed architects on the rebuilding of the house. The best position for my new Oaktree is in Appledore Field, where Perry grows lavender. He is not happy about the termination of his lease but agrees, as the compensation is significant. Insisting on the exact place I will live helps restore some of the power I'd lost when the compulsory purchase order dropped through my letter-box. If I can't demand where I will spend the rest of my life, then I will not move at all.

The many decisions that have been taken to facilitate this move overwhelm me. The exhausting process of writing every little thing in lists; lists for packing and storing, for the house-building, for my rooms at Perry's, where I will stay while the new build completes. I wander around unable to relax, my mind whirling as each new tsunami of fear hits it. Even playing my beloved piano with Frankie no longer comforts me. And now a new nightmare assaults me, about the time my dad died. Or maybe it's a reminder of when I first met Perry. Whatever it is leaves dreadful fear lingering, hours after waking. Perhaps it's the young girl inside who's been silent for years. Each day she lifts her head a degree and stamps impotent feet. She forgets that life has put her firmly in her place and that she must accept its boundaries. Each day she tests her strength, and I fear her anger for I suspect that I'll find it hard to control.

Chapter 46

Monday, 4 January 2016

L ily's email tells me how to use Google maps. Hamilton's latest legal executive has opened up a new cyber-world to explore. Poetry and literature are a few taps away. She assists Hamilton with the trust. She's so sweet that I have confided a little about my life. She says to me, 'Don't linger on the past. Let it go. The past doesn't belong in the present. Forget the bad choices you made. Dwelling on them gives them life.'

She's kind but will lose all her compassion when she finds out about Frankie.

Memories creep in and lie hiding in the recesses of my mind, fooling me that they are current, timeless. So many mistakes made when trying to start a new life after Francine's death. Losing the job that Denny and Gerry gave me because of a misunderstanding with the banking. More jobs lost because I couldn't work with silly rules and regulations. Keeping strict hours and performing duties did not fit well with fluctuating mental health. Then Denny married Rosemary Major, my nemesis Sally's older sister. He went into business with Gerry, and they moved their car repair business to Manchester. Samuel qualified as a carpenter and moved with Valerie to Plymouth to renovate holiday homes. The separation from my old life was complete. If Frankie hadn't been close by, I doubt I'd still be here.

As if the turmoil of leaving my home isn't enough of a challenge, on Christmas day Perry has asked me to marry him. His proposal letter sits in my desk drawer. Inside the envelope is an engagement ring, a family heirloom passed down to his dead mother and then to his dead wife. The thought of sliding that ring onto my finger makes me shiver with repulsion. The reasons why he has proposed are uncertain. I'm not young and nubile, or gullible and susceptible, so why he wants to marry me is intriguing. I also consider why I haven't turned him down.

Perry will be in my life much more than he has been through these intervening years. The months until I can settle in my new home are many. Perry says not to think about it too much but to focus on each moment. He will do all in his power to support and protect me. We are both afraid that the emotional upheaval will destabilise me and I'll say something that gives away our part in Frankie's death.

Frankie. My darling, Frankie. Let me walk you back to the orchard so I can sit with you awhile before the bulldozers destroy our garden. Then there will be no more chats in the orchard. Such a pity now that you and I understand each other. We're a couple, aged and comfortable with each other. We sit happily sharing our memories and forgetting our regrets, at peace in the world we've created. You will help me bear the coming anguish that forging relationships with strangers will bring. Play the piano, Frankie. Play something soothing as I watch the damp winter leaves pile high against the hedge and swirl in the breeze.

The dull winter sun sits behind a foggy mist and struggles to burn through. A man is approaching. It's not Perry. Panic floods me. Pulling out my phone, I frantically press his number. He answers just as the man reaches me.

'Perry. Erik Schmidt is here.'

'On my way. Don't close the call. Keep the phone in your hand and scream if he comes too close.'

Erik Schmidt stands in my orchard. There's nowhere to hide.

Chapter 47

Monday, 4 January 2016

Schmidt's wrinkled face oozes unpleasantness. The same sneer lurks at the corners of his mouth; the same dead reptile eyes stare out. Shock renders me speechless. The tension in my feet unbalances me. The back gate is too far; he will catch me. We assess one another. A swirl of dead leaves rustles along the ground, caught by the strengthening wind. The acidic smell of lemons stings my nostrils.

'Hello, Carol.' He smirks. 'You look worn out. Life has not treated you well, considering.' He turns about, indicating with his hands my home, gardens, the extent of my land.

'I thought you were in prison.' My words struggle through trembling lips.

'Oh, the years! They have gone!' He throws his arms wide and circles the air, then adds, 'Whoosh!'

'Yes. Um, I didn't think they would …' Don't provoke him. Look for words of pacification.

'Let me out? That's not nice.' He looks left towards the house and tips his head, assessing it.

'I ... I have to go. I have a cake in the oven. Goodbye.'

He jumps forward and stands three feet from me. 'Don't you want to know why I'm here, Carol?' His voice is a hoarse whisper; his penetrating eyes force me to look away.

'No. Goodbye, Erik.' I take a few steps.

'But you will be very interested in what I have to say.'

'No. I won't. Please go.' My hand barely grips my mobile.

'Oh, Carol! You need to know why I came to see you. I came because I need somewhere to live, and I will be living *here*.'

Drawing in a startled breath, I choke on some spit. 'You … what …?'

'Yes. And I need money, and you have plenty.'

My mouth works. Panic hip-hops through my chest as I clear saliva from my throat - get away from him; get away. Heart racing, breathing raspy gasps. He was in the lane the day Frankie died. Perry saw his car. He knows. He reaches for me and I screech and jump, clenching my fist.

'Ah, Carol, you want to fight, eh?' His cough morphs into a high-pitched manic sing-song laugh. 'You're a fighter, yes? Frankie wanted you to be a fighter. He would have liked that. But he got a nag. Do you nag him still? Is there no peace for him? Where did you put him?' He walks around me in a circle. 'Where shall we find him, eh? Should we tell the police what happened that Christmas, eh, Carol? Should they be digging here? Should they be digging there?'

He points to a place the other side of Dawnview Wood. I breathe a sigh of relief. He's stabbing in the dark.

'You find that amusing?' He comes closer. I move my mobile into my left hand and clench my right fist, ready.

'Please go, Erik. I'm going to walk away and if you follow me, if you touch me …'

He throws his head back and cackles. 'I *will* leave you, Carol. Perhaps you've had enough of me today. You've had a shock. It's a shock for me, too. It's a long time since I see this place. It's a long time since Frankie. Many years locked up on the say-so of silly girls. You never visited me, Carol. No visits to your teacher to thank him for his help. Yes, it's a long time, but then it's no time. You remember it all, don't you? But we must forget yesterday. Goodbye, Carol. Goodbye for now. I'll call again tomorrow. I'll look forward to it. I hope you look forward to it, too. And I hope you remember Frankie. I hope you remember you're guilty – because you are guilty, Carol. Guilty of seducing men without a thought about their feelings. You're a bitch and a whore.'

He turns and walks back towards the driveway. A vehicle

rumbles along the lane and squeals to a halt. A door slams and Perry shouts. Running after him because Perry will have a gun, I pray, 'Please don't kill Schmidt. We can't bury another body.' At the edge of the driveway, Perry is aiming at Schmidt, who has raised his hands.

'Carol, tell him not to be stupid, eh. Tell him one murder is enough.'

'Stop talking rubbish, Schmidt. You're frightening her.' Perry pulls the gun into his shoulder. 'Now get off this land and don't come back.'

'Don't threaten me.' Schmidt laughs again in his sing-song, manic way. 'You would kill me and bury me here? You are stupid, Perry. Like you always were.'

'I'm warning you, Schmidt. Don't come here again or I'll feed you to the pigs.'

'Ah! Is that what you did with Frankie, eh?' He turns to look at me. 'Did the pigs like your lover, Carol? Did they eat every bit of him? Even those special parts you liked so much?'

Schmidt's manic booming follows me as I stumble and weave to the house. My boots slip on the moss-covered path, and then, at last, I'm through the back gate. I collapse on the sofa in the orangery. An overload of adrenaline and lack of oxygen flips my heart. Straining to hear the boom-crack of a shot, I close my eyes then dive under a rug.

Chapter 48

Monday, 4 January 2016

The sound of a key in the lock rouses me. Perry walks into the orangery and turns to look back out into the garden. His demeanour is confident, and after a cursory glance he sits in his usual place on the sofa opposite me. He has not been in the main part of the house since that day. The day of the fire. He has duplicate keys for every lock here but keeps them hidden away at Cleave Farm.

'We won't see him again.' He leans back; his hand touches the left side of his face and rubs his hairline.

'He will come back, Perry. What's to stop him? He said he wants money and to … to live here.'

'He won't be back.'

'What if he comes back tonight? What if he breaks in?' Perry doesn't answer. He rubs his chin, ignoring my distress. 'What are we going to do? He knows something.'

Perry laughs. 'He doesn't know anything. He's bluffing. He knows Frankie went missing. That's all. Suspicion.'

'But he was here. That day …'

'Just told him about the inquest. He didn't know about it. Took the wind out of his sails.'

'Oh, you would have thought …' The newspaper reports flash into my mind. 'Posh boy disappears and kills himself in the River Loire.' 'Bigamist drowns in a French beauty spot.'

Perry had gone back a few months later to leave Frankie's clothes and wallet next to the river near Ben's holiday château. We never expected that the conclusions drawn would finalise Frankie's disappearance. But his parents wanted him laid to rest. Lisa wanted widowhood, not desertion. Money talks its way to the solutions it requires.

Perry rests back and closes his eyes. He's tired. The scars on the left side of his face have faded, but their outlines remain a permanent reminder of the tragedy. His hair is long on top; it covers the burns around his scalp and left ear, but not those around his left eye. He has scars on his body that I've not seen. My stomach lurches; it often does, so near to his deformities. My selfish determination to die meant that I didn't notice he was searching for Francine. He almost sacrificed his life on a fool's errand.

'Besides, if he had seen something he would have used it already. Used it to get out of prison, get a shorter sentence ... something.' He rubs his hands and shakes them. He's making sense, but I can't relax. 'Why don't you make us some coffee? And what about a piece of cake?'

I nod. My kitchen is a welcome refuge.

***

We settle with coffee and cake. Every thought about Schmidt is batted away and replaced with a picture of a rose. Roses are today's flowers. Perry gets impatient when I cannot control my emotions, so flowers are my new anti-meltdown weapon. 'I'm getting on with the sorting and packing. If you could hire a skip for me ...'

'No need. I'll send a couple of lads over with the flat-bed. When's best?'

'Any time tomorrow.'

'Tomorrow at ten.' He puts his plate back on the coffee table and sits back.

'Thank you.' Perry has taken care of me over the years – those day-to-day necessities that Hamilton's, and the trust, can't supply. He's driven me to medical appointments, garden centres and, with his late wife, Laura, clothes shopping. He stays close to me without invading my space; he's a satellite orbiting my world, always ready to catch me if I fall. It can't be solely because of the terms of the trust.

Now I shop on the internet, and I get the feeling he misses our trips, although he never says so. We still go to the garden centre for plants, and to the doctors. When I told him how Lily helps me with the internet, he frowned and changed the subject. He likes to be my guardian and my jailor; he likes to monitor my mental state to ensure that I keep our wickedness locked away.

Focusing back on the packing to be done tomorrow, I draw on all my resolve to deal with the next task. Frankie's clothes, clothes that comforted me in my darkest hours, will be packed next. Denim with his smell of musk. His record player and records will still take pride of place in my new house. Rubbing the red skin on a finger, I wring my hands with the stress of it. Then it hits me: Perry wasn't surprised to see Schmidt. 'You knew he was out of prison, didn't you?'

'Yes.' He fidgets and looks away.

'You should have told me.'

'There was no point in worrying you.' He pours coffee. 'Anyway, you have secrets. What happened between you and Schmidt?'

'Nothing.'

'Nothing? I doubt that. He's a paedophile. You went to his school. He used to come here to see Thora for some reason. Did you find out what was going on between them?'

'No.' I'm not used to all this in-depth talking. We've never talked about anything too personal before. Lately, though, we have had long conversations about too many things I don't like. I hate it. I want him to go.

'You should tell me. I need ammunition to get rid of him. But I doubt he'll come back anyway.'

Schmidt mustn't come back. 'I'll keep a gun by the front door.'

'Not a good idea, Carol. You're so jittery, you may use it.' He cuts a chunk of cake and puts it in his mouth. His hands are dirty. He should wash them or he'll get a stomach upset. I've washed my hands several times since he got here. A crumb is on the edge of his lip, and I want to brush it off.

'Tell me about Schmidt.'

'Nothing to tell. He enticed me into his house by offering me Art and English lessons. I went a few times, got suspicious and stopped.' My hands shake so I put my fork down to press them together, trying to blank the images of what happened. 'He didn't touch me. He was just creepy.'

'He didn't touch you?'

'No. He moved on to another girl.'

'What happened to her?'

'I don't know.' I shrug, 'She had an older brother. Maybe he dealt with Schmidt.' Frankie was all-consuming back then. I didn't tell the Headteacher about Schmidt, and Perry mustn't know about my apathy. 'Do you want more cake?' Standing dissipates my irritation with this long conversation.

'Sit down, Carol. Please.' Perry places his elbows on his knees and presses his fingers together. 'I'm sorry I didn't tell you. I didn't think he'd come here. If I'd thought that he'd ...'

'Well, you weren't to know. Anyway, thank you for your help with him.'

He narrows his eyes. 'There you go again – treating me like a stranger.'

'I'm sorry. I don't mean to ... It's just ... I'm not used to ... this.' I wave my hands at us.

'We've had plenty of coffee and cake over the years.' A piece of cake drops onto my lap and I jump to reach for a napkin. Perry sighs; irritation jiggles his breath. 'I enjoy seeing more of you. You know that, don't you? And you moving in while the new house is built is good. We should've got to know each other better before ...' He stands then kneels in front of me, 'Have you thought about my proposal?'

The action startles me. His body is too close. Heat and the smell of open fields rise from him. Perry never smells of anything other than fresh air, not the sweat of a working man, not aftershave. His eye twitches.

'I'm flattered that you've asked me ...'

'Please, Carol. Don't turn me down for any reason other than you do not –'

'I'm not turning you down.'

'You're not?'

'No. I'm accepting your offer.'

'Oh ... Can I kiss you?' He moves closer.

'Well ... you'd better. If we're getting married, we should ...'

He leans into me, his hips against my knees. A memory of the time he pinned me down and grabbed my breast surfaces, but I bat it away, replacing it with a picture of a rose. We were just kids. He saved my life.

Our kiss is different from the ones in my youth, those with Frankie and Matthew. Strangeness mingles with warmth and the pressure of unknown flesh. The kiss is what it is, and it fits who we are now.

As we part, Perry smiles and pulls me to my feet and kisses me again, crushing me to him. Just as I cannot bear it anymore, he breaks away. He looks like the cat with the cream, all smiles. Not knowing whether to worry that he wants more from me at this very moment, I take a small step back. Flattery has long since passed me by, and maturity does not incite the passion that used to flow through my veins. Comfort and acceptance are poor cousins of lust and craving.

'Small steps,' he says, sensing my discomfort, and squeezes my hand before sitting down. Breathing a sigh of relief that he is sensitive, I say, 'This will work, Perry. Getting married will be good.'

'Yes. I've always loved you, Carol. You've not felt the same about me, but I hope you will love me.' The vulnerability on his face is refreshing, something he's not shown in years. Not since I was in Maytree. He continues, 'You know how I loved Laura.

These last five years since she went ... You don't replace her, and I don't replace Frankie. I'm happy you've found, um, something for me.'

'Oh, Perry, you're so ...' I take his hands. 'I hope I can be strong. I'm a good housekeeper ... and gardener ... and I can write you poetry.' If I wish for it, it will come true.

'I don't want a housekeeper or a gardener, but please write me poetry.' As I kiss his lips, the stirring of passion moves in my belly. I'm dizzy at my sudden change in demeanour, and the forwardness of it makes mé panic. But then adrenaline mixes with an emerging lust that I'd thought had long since disappeared.

After a while, we part and return to our chairs, to relax in the glow of our new intimacy. My heart pounds with the excitement of this change. That my long-forgotten passion would stir and release itself amazes me. This could work. Like Ruby Silver says: if you want something enough, it will happen. Perry and I will be very happy, I decide as I stroke Frankie's necklace.

'Let's have some more coffee.'

I jump up. 'Of course – where are my manners!'

'No need to jump, precious, at least not yet. Wait until we're married.' Perry grins, but something in his eyes tells me he's not joking. It's been a long time since I've felt this energised. Are these reawakened feelings meant for him? Does passion fit any available man?

My thoughts shift and reality bangs in. I killed a man, and we buried him. Our union will not be one of lovers, but of criminals covering their backs. Praying to Ruby Silver won't change a thing.

Perry asks me to fetch his mother's ring and places it on my finger. He wants us to go to the registry office tomorrow and fix the date – life strides onward regardless of my hesitancy. He will ensure that work starts on my new Oaktree House immediately. I will not live at Cleave Farm when we are married, so if he wants to marry me he must ensure the house is built without delay. I'm not deluded. He doesn't love me. He wants to keep a close eye on me and being married may give him some proctection when we are prosecuted. And it may protect me.

Chapter 49

Saturday, 20 February 2016

Perry talks about his dead wife Laura lately. She slips into our conversations unbidden, like a saint to be admired and loathed simultaneously for her sainthood. Laura this, Laura that – and a sense that he is nervous about marrying me. The effect, though annoying, is endearing, too, as he recognises her supportive qualities and other wifely benefits. She never told him she was ill; just soldiered on, afraid to make a tough time worse when the farm was struggling. Then he discovered that she had an insurance policy he didn't know about, providing the extra cash he needed to expand his business. Even in death, she took care of him yet he fails to visit her grave.

It was Francine's birthday a few weeks ago, on the third. On that day I was ill with panic. Perry comforted me, but by the end of the day, he had complete command of my fragile state. He persuaded me to book our registry office marriage, my judgment having deserted me. His triumphant grin haunts me. He dismissed my assertion that I would not marry before I could move into the new Oaktree House. We are to be married on Tuesday, the nineteenth of April, at two. The date races towards me like an appointment for an unpleasant medical procedure.

There's an article online from the local newspaper: the human cost of compulsory purchase. The feature includes a description of me, by 'villagers' who 'know her as a recluse, sheltered by her money'. I'm 'not seen about much and never join in with local events'. A journalist has discovered my link with 'the socialite' Izzy Dewberry-Newberry.

The invasion of my privacy is as astounding as it is distressing and brought on a panic attack. People who know nothing of me allude to suppositions they deem to be true. It says Izzy's father was the philandering young playboy Frankie Dewberry. He lived for a short time in the soon-to-be-demolished Oaktree House during the seventies. He 'disappeared' and was later presumed drowned in the River Loire. An inquest decided it was an accident, although there was a suggestion of suicide.

The rest of the article concentrates on Izzy and her drunken antics. Now in her early forties, it seems she never grew up. She's had three husbands but no children, and plenty of close relationships with women. The wording suggests she's a lesbian when you could just as reasonably conclude that she doesn't trust men as fathers to her children.

If I were fifteen again and met Frankie in this enlightened age, would I still make him the centre of my universe? Passion and lust are hard to ignore. Those feelings are the central force in the survival of the human race, why humans set about seducing, trapping and manipulating a mate. Young women today make sexual desire fit in with their other hopes and dreams. 'Life is for living to the full, not restricting yourself', is the mantra.

Emailing the link to Hamilton for him to check for any libel, I say a prayer to Lily, who has taught me about the internet. Learning these things is easy using online guides aimed at the elderly, LOL. It's easy for me to sort things with Hamilton through my email account. Lily has suggested I get an e-reader, and one is in the post to me.

Google maps are a revelation. The Google van has not entered the lane to my house, but I can travel along the main road. I click along towards Cleave Farm and back again. Back to the Cleave Inn on the main road, and then through the village to the Oaktree Inn. Spying on houses and driveways is a revelation. We have internet shopping, saviour of the housebound and anxiety-ridden recluses. The world is ours at the touch of a button. Before I click out, an email slips into my account. Lily reminds me that they will start to strip the house for all re-useable items, from floorboards to roof tiles. The foundations and new road are already laid for the new Oaktree and they will need the materials soon. I reply, 'Not yet. I need more time.' She replies, 'They are demolishing it on 9 May and it's best that all is stripped at least a week before.' I don't bother to reply. Nothing I say can change anything.

Perry has an idea to soften my move to the farm. Move into my new rooms now, while I still have access to my home, and then I can always move back here for a few days if I'm anxious. That way I can return should I need to. It's about feeling in control. He has Googled it. It's a way of avoiding the finality of a last-minute move, which could be too shocking. The idea makes sense, so I agree. Now the move is this weekend. There's little time to enjoy my home, or many nights left to sleep in the room where I conceived Francine. Perry says my sentimentality hinders my ability to move on and adjust. It's true, but he doesn't understand that sentimentality underpins my life and that without it I'm nothing.

Today he will move some furniture and books from my study, along with Frankie's record player and records. The piano Frankie plays at night to lull me to sleep is going.

Two scruffy men arrive in the flat-bed truck with scruffy, old-fashioned blankets. The strong wind promises rain, but they assure me they have tarpaulins. Retreating to the kitchen, I nurse a cup of coffee until they leave. Watching my precious things being manhandled is a step too far.

The phone rings and Perry apologises, saying that they have dropped Frankie's record player. He muses that he is sure to find someone who restores these old things. He thinks it's a bad idea to bring my things back even though I cry. He won't budge. There will not be an 'in the meantime' escape. Perry has taken over, and I've allowed him to. My study is empty. There's no computer. How silly of me not to realise it would go.

Perry wraps his persuasiveness about my move in concern for my depression. When I protest, he suggests he should call my doctor. Although he sounds concerned, a threat that I must obey him hangs in the air. I have no choice. Where else can I go? He never intended for me to have a staggered move. This is my last day, but at least for a few months, I can visit and pack before the demolition starts, although there will be workmen here to strip out the fixtures and fittings.

He makes an appointment with my doctor and will drive me there. Anti-depressants will help me cope. If he is to be my husband, I must allow him to take care of me. He wants me to remove Frankie's necklace and earrings, but I won't. Those adornments are part of who I am.

Back in my bed, under the covers, I hold my breath until dizziness makes me gasp. I can regulate my breath. It's one of a few things left that I can control.

Chapter 50

Friday, 4 March 2016

That Christmas in 1970, when Frankie was unwell and wanted to be on his own, Perry's house was my refuge. It had warmth, with friendly fires and Elsie's homemade cushions and rugs. Now the house has been completely modernised, with oak doors and floors heated underneath. It's doubled in size. Solar panels sit on the roof and the barn, as well as rows of them in one of the fields with the poly-tunnels. The furnishing is cold, in flat greens and browns, all glass, chrome, straight lines. The cushions on the sofa are so perfect I daren't touch them.

My new rooms are on the first floor at the back of the old part of the house. They afford me some privacy and quiet. Frankie's piano has to stay in the small downstairs reception room. When Perry is out, I take comfort in stroking the keys that Frankie once stroked.

On the other side of the farmyard, the converted barn houses offices and facilities for the staff. Although it's a fair step away, I hate that it's there. Perry's dogs are in kennels at the back of the barn, and the cats live in another barn over the ridge. Pets are not allowed in the farmhouse, nor is comfort from tokens of sentimentality. The noise of the working farm and the busyness of the many people disturb me, so I avoid the rooms at the front of the house. But Perry insists that I meet key personnel. Louise, his secretary, and Emily, who runs the lavender side of the business. Trying to be polite is stressful. My social skills have been lost over the years and this foreign place seems to require a different language.

The view from the large windows in my study and bedroom is over farmland and not of the working areas of the farm. A heavy shower washes away the bright sunshine as if reflecting my mood. Raindrops like spiky rods pierce the grass, leaving shards scattered on the land.

The bedroom opposite mine belonged to Simon when he was alive. Behind the locked door, the room is probably exactly as it was. When I was seven, I lay in his bed with that nasty bump on my head. My search for the angels to take me to heaven, where my dad was, had failed.

Adjusting to this new space is daunting. Curling up on the floor and wrapping my arms around myself doesn't protect me from these weird surroundings. *The girl* inside wriggles like a worm on a hook. Diazepam will sort me out, but I'd better not mix them with my new anti-depressant prescription.

***

Walking back home each day gives me breathing space and time for calm although the house is a mess. No carpets or doors. At my request the floorboards downstairs have been left. A team of men work with logistical efficiency to reclaim anything of value. They are upstairs today and every hammer blow and creaking of wood panelling reminds me that I'm on borrowed time. My labelling, packing and arranging collection for onward transfer to the storage unit must be hurried. How strange that in my lists I had not synchronised a diary to tell me that this house would become inhabitable so quickly. Maybe Perry was being kind to get me out of here so quickly. But I doubt it.

Finishing the books is the task for today. Then Thora's study. Unused, but cleaned quarterly on a rota with the rest of the house, it holds an air of reverence. Or it did until the stripping out started. Perry asked why I had not emptied the room before. I said it would be sacrilege to do such a thing, which was beyond his comprehension. There was comfort in the room as she left it. He forgets that she was Frankie's mother and Francine's grandmother. The room represents a dynasty. Hamilton has written to the hospital to see if the medical tomes belonging to Thora's father could be of use.

The books finished, Perry sends men to collect them. Hamilton has arranged for a valuer to come tomorrow for a final check. We must ensure that valuable items are kept safe. That so much of my house will be in my new home is reassuring. They will take the roof tiles soon.

Dust flies everywhere and the air carries germs and bugs that will damage my lungs. Old housekeeping ledgers and anything else unimportant goes into black rubbish sacks. A sense that I am rummaging through confidential items assails me. Photos drop into a box. The deep drawer at the bottom of the desk is full of letters and diaries. The letters are in three batches tied with ribbons. The first is a correspondence between Thora and her mother, Cynthia. Most are from when her mother was in Paris, and tell of the delights there. A few are from holidays and some from her mother's friends.

The next batch is a correspondence between Thora and her father, Russell. He spent time training in London and Belfast. Thora's schoolgirl writing is precise, in the way a child tries to impress its father.

The last batch is different. Lavender envelopes tied with lavender ribbon. They must be love letters. Should I read them? Why not? Thora's dead and her friend, probably, also. Glancing through the first, I skip to the signature. Frankie. Thora's in love with a man called Frankie. How odd. That's a chilling similarity between us. Did this man let her down? Was the animosity she had towards my Frankie based on her relationship with this Frankie? The envelopes have not gone through the mail. No clues as to who this man is.

'We can still meet Wednesdays my love. Do not think I will desert you or betray you. You are the love of my life.'

I read the next one, also dated November 1961.

'I thank you for your kindness. It will be hard for everyone in these early days. Without your love, my life would be worthless. Our love will fortify us and keep us strong. I thank God for you. Without you, I would not exist, but you know that. You saved me. Your ministrations keep me from Hell.'

Ah, a patient! That's why they were hand-delivered. Should I destroy them? They could tarnish Thora's good name. They must burn, so I take them to the fireplace.

The struck match bursts into flame. It seems too final, too harsh, as though I'm killing a living thing. Best put them in my handbag, along with Thora's diaries.

The room is almost clear, just a few newspapers left. I gather them up and drop them in front of the fire. Why keep all these? The adverts are nostalgic and funny. One was from late 1950. Frankie was born in February 1950. I remember his lie that he was nineteen when we met but he had turned twenty. There's a piece about Professor Frederick Dewberry, Frankie's 'father'. He was a lead clinician at Maytree Hospital and was taking a post in London to head a new initiative. A research unit was looking into ways to cure mental health conditions without drugs.

The next newspaper carries a short report on Perry's brother Simon's death. He fell in the lake while fishing on Chewton Lake and his brother was unable to pull him out. It had been a sunny day that had unexpectedly turned to heavy rain. They had taken their bikes unbeknown to their parents. A tragic accident. October thirty-first 1961. Halloween. Perry was eight and Simon twelve. I'd first met Perry the following April just before my eighth birthday. I can't burn these, so I place them in my bag and throw the rest into the fire.

Chapter 51

Tuesday, 8 March 2016

As soon as Perry leaves for work I make my way back home. The heavy frost is blasted by freezing rain that threatens to annihilate me. Having access to the house for only a few more weeks is like walking towards a cliff edge. There's nothing to do but stumble on to meet the day when barbed wire fences will restrain me. Perry had threatened to send a couple of men to load everything and take it to the storage unit. He backed down at my fury. His predisposition to take control and decide what my best interests are unnerves me. Telling him not to do that is tiresome and leaves me uneasy. Homelessness and marriage loom before me like devilish teases about unknown tortures to come. He will choose his battles strategically in our war. He is learning which battles to don his armour for, and which he will win bare-handed. Already there is a shift between us that allows his armour to become increasingly redundant.

As I cut across the lane, a Peugeot with French number plates approaches and stops next to me. A man winds down the window, letting in the rain. His weathered skin is tanned deep into its pores. Thick, short-cut grey hair lies silkily above a lean face. The foreigner looks at me, searching my face. I turn away at the intimacy, but recognition dawns. A strange shaking goes through me. It's Matthew. He's grinning as he motions me to him.

'Hi, Raven. Is it you? Except Raven is not … um … Long time, no see. Where are you heading? I'll give you a lift.'

'No … thanks. I'm going to Oaktree.'

He gets out of the car and embraces me, kissing me on both cheeks. 'Good to see you. How are you, Carol?' He touches the damp hair curling on my shoulder.

'Fine. I'm fine …' The nearness of him unnerves me, so I step

209

back. He appraises my silver hair with fascination.

'Good. How are things? What've you been up to?'

'Nothing. Still here, still …' I shrug my shoulders. What to say to this stranger who meant so much to me a lifetime ago; who still invades my dreams uninvited? Worlds slide apart and I'm falling into a dark crevasse without handholds. 'I'm in the middle of moving.'

'Moving?'

'Yes, Oaktree House is being demolished. It's being stripped out as we speak.'

'Demolished? Oh, is that because of the ring road? It's a nightmare driving through town at the moment. Can't believe it, after all those years of them threatening to build it.' A shadow crosses his face as he looks towards my home. 'So they're coming all the way up here? When will they start?'

'May, at the earliest, but we'll see.'

'Oh.' His eyes fix towards Oaktree. 'Will it affect much of your land?

'The house and all the land to Dawnview Lane … and the orchard … but not Dawnview Wood, where Sarah …' I study his profile then fixate on his shoulders. Their shape stirs my belly.

'Where will you go?'

He doesn't look at me, and his voice carries a lack of interest: something distracts him. 'I'm building a replacement house the other side of Cleave Farm.'

'Oh? Near Perry's place?'

'We're getting married.' The words tumble out and surprise me as if I'd not thought to speak of it. Matthew turns, his attention caught.

'You're marrying Perry?' His confusion verges on distress. He lifts his arm to reach out to me, then lets it fall back to his side. 'Why?'

'Why not?' How dare he jolt back into my life and question me.

'Sorry, that's rude. I didn't mean it like that. I meant ... well ... congratulations. When's the happy day?' His eyes have left me again and are scanning around, seeking something he fails to find.

'Nineteenth of April at the registry office. You can't come. Just two witnesses and us.'

He turns back, registering my curtness.

'I won't be here anyway. I'm only staying a few days. Chrissie's sold our old house. She inherited it from Mum, oh, must be twenty years ago. She's moving to Chewton Magna. We've been clearing the place out. Not had time to sort it all, so I've got a car-ful to take back.' He walks toward the hedgerow and looks again towards Oaktree. His focus on it is unnerving unless he's searching for Sarah's oak tree and has forgotten where it is.

'Perry said you'd moved to France after Sarah ... You didn't stay in Ireland.'

'Ireland? No. Too remote for me. But the hotel did well as an artists' retreat so I made quite a bit when I sold it. I went to France on holiday and met up with that friend of Frankie's ... Ben something ... He invited me to his château. Turned out that the campsite next door was for sale, so I bought it. Done well for myself. It's a goldmine. Best place in the world – and I've been around a bit. Made enough to travel all over, but nothing beats home. France, I mean, not here. Going back tomorrow. Was at a loose end and thought I'd drive around our old stomping ground. It's been years.' His words trail off as he turns back to me. We stand apart, the past filling the gulf between us. 'Sorry to hear about Sammy's passing.'

'Oh, how did you know?'

'Julie told Chrissie. She's doing well. Partner in a law firm, and four children.'

'You have four grandchildren?'

'Not Chrissie – your niece, Julie.' His thinks I'm ignorant,

211

which I am. My whole family are unknown.

'I didn't know they kept in touch.'

'I think everyone does, on Facebook and whatever. Chrissie signed me up and I looked at it for all of one day.' He chuckles.

A car engine sounds along the lane. I struggle to take my eyes away from Mathew's smile and the engorged vein in his still-youthful neck. He has a slim, muscular frame and looks as strong as ever. Deep inside my Matthew must lurk ready for me to release him. As he talks, he communicates invisible channels of energy, igniting long-forgotten yearnings. Places exist beyond my present confinement that are preferable.

The engine slows and stops a short distance behind me. Matthew stares intently at it. 'I recognise that guy from somewhere.'

'Who?' Turning, I see that it's Schmidt's car. 'Oh, God!'

'What's wrong? Here let me ...' He takes my elbow to steady me, and we both look at Schmidt as he stares back at us. 'Is that the teacher ... the paedo, Schmidt?'

Matthew runs towards the car. Schmidt jumps, recognition dawning. He guns the engine and heads towards us along the narrow lane. Matthew pulls at the car door.

'Matthew!' I run towards him as he falls. Schmidt races away.

'When did that bastard get out. Ow, my knees ...' He stands and rubs at the wet earth on his trousers.

'Not long ago. Don't rub it, you'll make it worse.'

'Does he still have that house?' Matthew rubs the outside of his thighs and grimaces in pain.

'Don't know.' The thought that he could be living not far from the end of the lane is nauseating.

'Could go along and check. Smack him in the face as a welcome home present.'

'Matthew you can't, you –'

'Why not?'

'But why would you? He never did anything to you, did he?'

The look in Matthew's eyes speaks of more than a passing interest in thumping a paedophile. 'I could hit him for *you.*'

'For me? Why would you do that?'

'So I'm right then? He did something to you?'

'No, he didn't ... so don't. I'd better go.' My fingers press against my temples to keep out unwanted images.

'I'll give you a lift. Don't say no, because you're too shaken up. Get in.' He opens the passenger door and stands erect, waiting for me to acquiescence.

Here's another man telling me what I should do with the absolute conviction that he knows best. He's like Perry. The illusion that something was simmering between us ceases. I hesitate to think that I should obey him; that I should allow some primaeval conditioning to dictate to me. Pushing through the hedgerow, I walk away. Matthew's eyes bore into my back the whole walk home.

Chapter 52

Tuesday, 19 April 2016

Rays from low sunshine illuminate my shaking hands, as the list of things to do trembles in them. The restless night vanishes into the cold morning as my pen flows across the paper. Our wedding day is here. The air tastes different, and sunbeams wave through the sky on a jagged course. They sense they may shine on a travesty: a quiet, registry-office event with two witnesses, Louise and Hamilton. Noting my thoughts in my diary, I ignore *the girl* inside who whispers at me to run away.

Perry's son, Timothy, won't be returning from the Philippines. His wife and children don't want to travel. I haven't told Denny and Rosemary, or Gerry. They live in Manchester and have made a fortune from their car repair franchise business. Valerie, Samuel's widow, is in a nursing home. I've no idea where any of my nephews and nieces live. They've all abandoned me. I ponder joining Facebook but can't see the point. They're not part of my life. Their occasional visits to Oaktree had arisen from a sense of duty rather than kinship. Relatives are names and dates in my birthday book. Reminders to post obligatory cards with obligatory cheques.

Thoughts of Matthew continue to disturb. He has metamorphosed back from an irritating stranger to a lost lover. His eyes are at my back constantly since I walked away from him. Reminders of our past, of Sarah, of Frankie, that whole other world, consume my daydreams. The timing of his return is causing no end of confusion. Two souls meeting again doesn't happen without reason; the stars map our destinies. Why was he driving along at the very time I was crossing the road? His face muddles with Sarah's. The past threatens the peace of this day and casts shadows over any happiness my medication has induced.

My low-heeled shoes remind me that I mustn't stand taller than Perry. He has mentioned several times about me not wearing heels. I rarely do anyway; they're not conducive to farm life, or any other comfortable life. My dress, of pale rose-pink satin and lace, hangs on the full-length mirror. This afternoon it will turn me into a bride. An innocent, who in times gone by would have subjected herself to her husband's demands. There will be none of that in our marriage. Perry will adjust to my behaviour; he has no choice. We've been sleeping together since the day I bumped into Matthew. It's been an unsatisfying yet compulsive experience. Unable to reject him, I allow him to use me. He fails to recognise my lack of interest, continuing through the motions in spite of me. Thoughts of Laura distract me during sex. She must have been very undemanding, for Perry knows nothing of the female form. He avoids touching any flesh that's not directly required in the process. Should I blame her for not teaching him, or is there a reason why she didn't? I didn't have to tell Frankie, or Matthew, how to make love.

The sense of unease settles and won't go even though I resolve to be positive, at least for today. Perry is short-tempered, demanding to have his way over the simplest of things. Frankie may have been a philanderer, but he was never vicious or nasty. Frankie teased but backed down to keep the peace. That was his seduction technique, but at least he acknowledged my place in our relationship.

Perry has spent years looking after me, and I, a prisoner of my own making, have been extremely grateful to him. He professes to have loved me all this time and yet sabotages his altruism. He reacts with frustration and impatience to any different viewpoints. Trusting him is the only way for our relationship to develop so I accede, to avoid confrontation. It seems to work. Tempering my views to fit with his is the least a wife can do.

Today we join in matrimony, and that commitment has a fatal quality to it. Divorce is a possibility should our marriage fail, but I am not a quitter anymore. My resolve to greet the world head-on will not allow for escape plans that are not conducive to a happy-ever-after. I check that I have taken my pills.

If Perry doesn't settle, a failed marriage will be better than life with a turbulent child. I've lived alone for ages and can do so again, as *the girl* reminds me. Perhaps he resents that I hold the key to his freedom. For years he held the key to mine as I languished on the edge of sanity in Oaktree House. The discovery of Frankie's body slips ever nearer, sealing our fate. Insisting that he killed Frankie is an option for me; after all, I was heavily pregnant at the time. It's pre-wedding nerves, although I didn't have any nerves when marrying Frankie.

My disposition toward Frankie is changing. Moving house, away from him and his imminent discovery, has affected my emotions. Reading my recent notes, I have compartmentalised him in a way I had not done before. Frankie fits into boxes, he's this, and he's that. He's no longer all-consuming. Is that because I have slept with Perry? Or because I'm forcing him away in preparation for when they find him? Am I distancing myself from him to avoid pain? Ruby Silver does not answer. I already know that one should not trust such a transitory emotion as desire. It puffs up big and then disappears like smoke on the wind.

Maybe I don't have a sixth sense and don't understand men, but positive choices are the way forward. Being in love and building a home together is my uppermost desire. Visualise it, and it will come true.

My dress slips over my head, but the vision is of someone unrecognisable – a strange creature wrapped in finery concealing a sham of a woman. The heavens shift and the earth spins on its axis as if the end of my life nears. Alarmed, I pull off the dress and hang it back on the mirror to obscure my reflection. Its purpose will last long enough this afternoon when we will stand before witnesses and declare our love aloud. It's such an indecent act.

Moving here, to Perry's farm, with the ghosts of his mother, father, and drowned brother is repulsive. A condition of our marriage was that we would move into the newly built Oaktree House before the ceremony. Perry has overruled that, but I will not live here any longer than necessary. He was not pleased but relented when I became hysterical. Hysteria is the one weapon he is unable to compete with, although I fear he will act against me if I continue to use it. When we're married, he may plan to have me committed. A madwoman's testimony against her husband will be questionable. Hamilton will keep a close eye on any attempt to have me sectioned. Although once found guilty of my sins, he will have little cause to help me as the trust becomes invalid. Better not dwell on this, though, as my plan to end my life will rise to the surface. I'm trying to live outside those negative thoughts.

Living with all these people milling about is loathsome. They're meant to keep away from the farmhouse and stay near the converted barn, but they wander everywhere. Perry can't ensure they keep away, because they are working. Agitation forces me downstairs to look out of the window for him. He's talking to the woman, Emily, who manages the lavender production, which is moving along the ridge to make way for our house. She's an expert on the growing and selling of lavender and Perry speaks her name in reverent tones. She stands too close and giggles, touching her hair. Willing a stray lock into place behind a little ear, she tips her grinning face to one side. Her flirtatiousness is not surprising. He's a catch, and the thought that he might leave me for her is uncomfortable. She should dress in a more feminine way, though, if she wishes to entice him.

At last he walks away, but she stops him and says something, then awkwardly kisses his cheek. Perhaps she'll take her shirt off in case he's in any doubt of her intentions towards him. I should take a diazepam. I need all the help I can get to become Mrs Cutler later today.

Chapter 53

Monday, 9 May 2016

On the twenty-fifth, it will be my birthday. My dad sings to me as I check that the plan for my new garden is the same as my old garden. It's a strange time in one's life to move house.

The road construction equipment bursts into life. Dust, dirt and unrest fill the air. Furtive eyes dart about familiar surroundings, fearing that those too will disappear. The air churns, and wildlife moves itself to seek new holes and nests. Disruption, with long travel delays, is reported in the press.

The noise of machinery reminds me that Frankie's grave is on borrowed time. The graveside bench is stored ready for my new garden. Fretting, and wandering the corridors out of sight of the windows, helps to pass the time. Or curling myself into a ball on the landing carpet. Diazepam will help. Must order some more online. It's amazing what you can get. Luckily, Louise deals with the post and passes packages directly to me.

It's been five years since my old Ford broke down and I visited the village. My hairdresser visits me to cut and colour my hair when I can be bothered with the fuss of it. Keeping it long makes it easy to manage, and dying it silver is no longer required. I send an email to Lily asking for a new car. Thora had the foresight to recognise that a mother needs a car, so there should not be a problem with the trust. It will be nice to drive again, have the freedom to come and go and not feel so claustrophobic. The thought of freedom is more enticing than the reality of it, though. Lily will arrange for a car, one that reminds me of the seventies. *The girl* gets excited at this.

Chapter 54

Monday, 30 May 2016

Dreams about the past have been plentiful recently. The day after Mother's birthday party back in 1970 was this morning's memory. Frankie had a split eyebrow that healed with a tiny silver scar where his eyebrow refused to grow. Mother was angry at Denny, and Mario was angry with Frankie. It's doubtful whether Frankie paid Mario for our meal, although it didn't appear to affect their friendship. Mario still joined us that summer to play his acoustic guitar so beautifully. If only Sarah had been stronger and had not felt so intimidated by Ben. She would have made a good partner for Mario. He liked women with some weight on them. He would have been good for her, and she would not have left us.

The buzz of the doorbell startles me. I call Perry on my new mobile phone. Lily helped me choose it. She calls it a 'smartphone' and has taught me how to use it.

'Someone has rung the doorbell,' I hiss when Perry answers.

'They probably want the office. Have you asked who it is?'

'No.' The intercom was installed so I didn't have to face people who make this mistake, and yet I fail to use it. 'Should I?'

'Yes.' He doesn't disguise his impatience. He never does anymore. 'Or I can phone Louise and check with her.'

'No. I can manage.' I don't want Louise involved. She already takes control and thinks herself indispensable.

'And don't disconnect.' He raises his voice as I drop the phone from my ear and make my way downstairs. 'Who is it?'

'Miss Cage? It's the police.'

Perry hisses at me to stall them as I freeze. They will say they have found Frankie. We must not say anything. Let them do their forensics. Chances are they will mess it up and we will be okay.

'Miss Cage, can you open the door please.' My fate has arrived.

'Just finding the key.' Taking a deep breath and fixing a smile, I open the door.

'Hello. Sorry about that. I don't like opening the door when I'm on my own.'

'Hello, Miss Cage. I'm Detective Sergeant Rose, and this is Detective Constable Harptree from Chewton CID.'

They hold out wallets with pictures and badges, but fear makes me blind. The name Harptree rings a bell. There was a Harptree investigating Frankie's disappearance, but this man is in his thirties.

The woman smiles. 'Can we come in?' Nodding, I lead them into the sitting room and motion for them to sit.

'Miss ... um, Cage, is it?' She places her hands on the hem of her skirt and pulls it down to her knees.

'It's Mrs Cutler. Carol. Perry and I married at Easter. Would you like tea? Or coffee. What about coffee? I've been practising making lattes.'

'No thank you, Carol. We're fine. Is Mr Cutler – Perry – available?'

'He's on his way. I called him ...' Don't speak, don't say anything.

'Good.' She tugs at her skirt again. 'Has your husband always lived here?' She waves a hand around.

'Yes. This farm was his father's and his father's father's, and was in the family even before then I believe. Why?'

'Just confirming. And you have lived in Oaktree House ever since, um, Thora Kent died? She left you her property in 1970, is that correct?'

'Yes.' She's working up to say that they have found him. My sweaty hands pulse.

'And the council purchased Oaktree House and grounds for the ring road?'

'Yes, the house, but not all of the grounds. Just a strip to widen the road.'

Perry walks in. 'Hello. Perry Cutler.' He puts his hand out, and they shake. The woman tells him who they are and asks him to sit, but he declines and stands next to my chair.

'Last Friday, during the demolition of the Oaktree estate, two skeletons were uncovered.'

I gasp. I can't help it. She said two. I grip my hands to stop them from shaking. She expects us to comment. Perry asks, 'What do you mean? Two skeletons?' He shifts his weight onto his other leg and says, 'I don't understand …'

'We believe they are those of a child and an adult.'

My head spins, so I bend forward. Perry kneels, takes my hand, and asks, 'Do you mean there's a cemetery on the grounds, an extension from the church over the road or something?'

'Oh. Do you have any details about a graveyard?' She looks from me to Perry and back to Harptree, unsure of herself.

'I don't, but that's very odd. Two skeletons. Whereabouts were they?'

She flicks through her notes, 'In the orchard, about ten metres from the boundary wall that runs around the house.'

Darkness descends as I pass out, and then Perry is saying, '… no, she's fine. She needs to lie down. Now, unless there's anything else?'

'What happened?' I struggle to sit up.

'Sit still.' He pushes my shoulders to the back of the chair before sitting on the padded arm.

'Bodies … somewhere, um … where did you say?' I ask.

The woman looks up from writing on her notepad. 'In the orchard, just outside the walled garden. Are you okay?'

'Yes. But … there can't, there couldn't, how long? How long have they been there?'

'We're not sure.'

'But I've lived in that house since 1970. So they must be from before that?'

DC Harptree turns a page in his notebook but doesn't speak. DS Rose says, 'We estimate about the late 60s or early 70s. Clothing and other indications. I can't say more at the moment until forensics give us more information. As soon as we have that, we'll come back and talk to you again. For the moment we're asking what you know, as they are on your land.'

She looks at me, then Perry, 'Can you tell us anything at all, anything you remember? People reported missing in the area at that time?'

'Well, I don't know anything.' I say, but Perry interrupts.

'We've just said we don't. We can't help you. My wife's not well and –'

DS Rose raises a hand. 'Mr Cutler, we need to establish any facts. We will take statements from you when we have the results of our preliminary investigations. They are on Mrs Cutler's land, so we expect you to help in any way you can. You will remember that a young boy went missing in late 1969.'

'Well …' he starts to reply, but I take his hand and cut in. 'I don't feel too good, Perry. I need to lie down.'

'Okay.' The female officer looks at each of us in turn, not convinced we're innocent. 'We'll come back when we have more information. In the meantime, if you would both cast your minds back for anything you might remember. Here's my card. Leave a message anytime if I'm not available.'

'I'll see you out.' They follow Perry to the front door.

A dead child buried with Frankie. They will think I killed it too. The thought of a dead child buried in the orchard chills my bones. All those times I sat and talked to Frankie I was talking to a child as well. Who would kill a child? But of course: Schmidt. Was that why he was always coming to the house? Maybe they will reason that he killed them both.

Chapter 55

Wednesday, 8 June 2016

The police are taking their time examining the site. I watch them from Symes field, taking care they don't spot my binoculars. They'll arrest us soon, and it will be a relief for this guilt to end. There will be no new Oaktree House, and the legacy of Thora's family will die. My full confession could end Perry's involvement. Planning is all it will take. They won't know that I was seven months pregnant because they won't be able to establish exactly when Frankie died. Besides, pregnancy doesn't hamper a woman in a rage. I'm sure such a woman could find the strength to bury a body if necessity demanded it. The stress brought on my early labour, so it will make sense that I did it all. That will release Perry from his obligation to me. A suspended sentence for knowing what happened may be the worst he'll get, with luck and a good solicitor. It depends on my word, and our word is all the police will have. My farewell letter sits in the top drawer of my desk, along with a bottle of pills. I contemplate my final walk to Sarah's oak tree with a sense of relief. *The girl* inside doesn't stir, not wishing me to cut short her wrath before she can find appeasement.

***

They have removed the oak tree at the front of Oaktree House. Its twin behind the house in Dawnview Wood, near the path leading to the council estate, remains. Sarah's hanging tree stands strong as a lasting tribute. The road will not extend to Dawnview Lane, the point where the land slopes and begins its long decline to the estate. That is where I shall join her, although hanging is not for me. Living from day to day is a duty to perform in the meantime.

This time I'm ready when they knock on the door.

The police settle on the sofa as Perry hurries in. The same Detective Sergeant Rose sits in the same chair, pulling her skirt over her knees, but this time a different police officer joins her. Both are wearing plain clothes, emphasising the seriousness of the situation. He introduces himself as Detective Inspector Philpot. He has the colour of someone just back from a hot climate, a dry sunburn, with sand ingrained in his skin. The area around his eyes is pink from wearing sunglasses.

'Mr and Mrs Cutler ...' DI Philpot checks that he has our full attention as Perry sits on the arm of my chair. 'We're here to talk to you again about the bodies found in your orchard.'

'Was Oaktree House built on a cemetery? Have you checked the church records for the child?' I ask.

'Yes. May I call you Carol? We have confirmed that your house isn't built on a cemetery.' DS Rose writes something on her notepad as he continues: 'The clothing and other items suggest a date around 1970. Around the time your husband, or rather, boyfriend, went missing.'

Perry interrupts. 'If you mean Frankie Dewberry, he was not Carol's husband. He was a bigamist, and the marriage wasn't legal.' An edge to his voice makes the DS raise her eyebrows. Philpot turns to me.

'So, Carol, how did you feel at the time when you found out Frankie was already married. That you had been, how should I put it ... deceived?'

Perry cuts in: 'What has that to do with anything? How d'you think she felt?'

'Please answer the question, Carol.' The policeman sets his jaw; his dark eyes stark in his pink skin.

I cannot answer, so Perry does. 'Well, there's no need is there? Frankie Dewberry killed himself in France, as you should know. So what has he to do with this?'

A look of uncertainty crosses Philpot's face. He looks at Rose, then back at me, and says, 'If you would just answer the question, Carol.'

'Well, I wasn't happy.' Perry shifts but doesn't speak.

'Before you went through the illegal marriage ceremony, you lived in one of the council houses on the estate?' I nod. 'Explain to me why you were living in Oaktree House when Mr Dewberry disappeared? I believe his birth mother had already died by then, but he didn't inherit it?'

'No. Although she was his birth mother. He lived in London with his father and adoptive mother.' I look at DS Rose. 'You know that already.'

'I need to check the facts for myself.' The man has tinged pink in embarrassment. He hasn't read our file. Oh God, we must have a file. My stomach turns to water.

'So tell me, so that we are clear: what happened to the house when Thora Kent died?'

'It was left to Francine, our daughter, in trust. Frankie lived in London. He only stayed here because Thora was ill. Oaktree House was never his home. I moved in before Thora died, to nurse her. We got married, except we weren't married …' I feel dizzy saying so much.

DS Rose scribbles quickly. Philpot asks, 'Then what happened?'

Perry says, 'Frankie's wife, Lisa, turned up with their daughter. Frankie threw her, and Carol, out of the house. Next thing, he was gone on holiday to France, so Carol moved back in. That was the last we saw of him.'

'He had another child? How old?' Philpot stares at me.

'She was a baby that Christmas, two months or so. Isabella.'

'Isabella Dewberry?'

'Yes,' says Perry, 'I expect you've heard of her, Izzy Dewberry-Newberry. She's the granddaughter of the eminent psychiatrist Sir Frederick Dewberry, who was Frankie's father.

Lisa's father was Sir Francis Wolverton. Lisa married Vincent Newberry, of the Newberry clothing dynasty, after Frankie was declared dead.'

'Oh. I've heard of her.' The policeman stops to consider this. The newspapers are full of the comings and goings of Izzy.

Perry continues, 'Frankie lived in London. He only spent a small part of 1970 here, on and off from Easter to the Christmas. He was going home to his wife and daughter most weekends, unbeknown to Carol. And spending time in student digs with a friend – I think his name was Ben.

'So he didn't live here?' Philpot asks.

'Hardly. The only reason he kept coming here was that he thought he had a chance of persuading Doctor Kent to change her mind and leave Oaktree Estate to him. It didn't work. And, of course, he was using Carol for the same reason.'

Can they leave now? Much more of this and I'll vomit. But Perry is revelling in it. He squeezes my shoulder in jubilation, as though he's stonewalled them.

Philpot rubs his chin. 'But the last time Frankie was seen was at Oaktree House, so he was living there then.'

'If you can call that living somewhere.' Perry's irritation is apparent. 'He went to France from there that Christmas. That was the last time we saw him. Sir Frederick Dewberry spent hundreds trying to trace him. The trail went cold in France. They believed he killed himself, as he was often depressed, apparently. Some mental condition causing highs and lows.'

I flinch at the unkind description, and Rose cuts in, 'Yes … we have checked the missing person report filed at the time.'

Philpot contemplates this before he asks, 'Frankie wore a ring on his middle finger, right hand. Can you confirm that, Carol?'

My heart races; they have found Frankie's ring. 'I don't remember a ring.'

Rose hands him some papers and points. He glances and says, 'Lisa Dewberry's missing person's report at the time states that he did. Gold sovereign ring on the right middle finger.' He gives the report back to Rose. Opening a case, he pulls out a small plastic bag.

'We recovered a ring from the skeleton. Is this Frankie's, Carol?'

Plastic stretches around the ring, giving it a shimmering appearance. The compulsion to look away is strong, so I breathe in deeply. Long-suppressed memories flood back. Laughter, and a caressing hand on my breast: his ghostly touch runs down my back.

'It could be his ring. He was wearing one on our wedding day. It was years ago.' He loved that ring, the weight of it, the expense of it.

'Can you remember this sovereign?'

'Is that a sovereign? I don't know anything about men's jewellery. Whether that's the same one I couldn't say.'

My fingers clutch the heart on my necklace as he says, 'Do you want a closer look at it?'

Recoiling at the thought that he'll take it out of the bag, I sit back in my chair. 'No … Thank you.'

He puts the bag back in the briefcase. The memory of a raised arm, an axe falling, and a chunking sound brings up bile.

'Lisa Dewberry says it's his ring.'

Perry says, 'Well then why are you asking Carol? Lisa was his wife, so she would know.'

'But Carol was also living as his wife.'

'She wasn't his wife. We have established that.'

'What I'm saying, Mr Cutler – Perry – is that Carol knew him well enough to know what his ring looked like.'

'Did she? She knew him for nine months. She didn't know what his wedding ring looked like and he had one of those I expect. He didn't wear that while with her, or she wouldn't have married him. Are you telling us the body is Frankie Dewberry?'

'Well, we haven't established that …'

'So you're asking Carol to identify a ring that may not have belonged to Frankie, who may not be the body you have found. Isn't it best you ask questions when you know what to ask instead of upsetting my wife?'

Philpot's cheeks flush, and he fumbles with the catch on his briefcase. DS Rose is checking back through her notes as Philpot continues.

'We have an update for you on the child. It's a boy aged about eight to ten. A nine-year-old boy went missing in 1969, a few weeks before Christmas. Do either of you remember?'

We say no together, but I remember the bloody school sock lying under the door of the cellar. It was from the same school uniform Perry wore. Perry places his hand on my shoulder. Philpot looks to me. 'You must have read about it in the papers.'

'I didn't read the papers. My mother certainly wouldn't have scared me with the news.'

'And what about you, Perry?'

'No.'

'So you're both sure you do not remember anything about a missing boy at the time?'

We both say no again.

The policeman looks at Perry, 'I'm surprised you don't remember because the missing boy attended Chewton Manor, which was your school.'

'As you can see, I live miles from the school. I did board, but in '69 I was doing A levels in an area apart from the main school and had stopped boarding. If he was nine, and I was seventeen, I wouldn't have known him. News like that was kept from children back then. The school wouldn't advertise the fact.'

'No, I suppose not. Though you were hardly a child.'

He looks back at me, and I want to correct him, as Perry was very child-like, his short, thin frame devoid of manly features.

The inspector pulls out his wallet. 'Well, that's all for now. Here's my card. Get in touch if you remember anything.'

They both stand and adjust bags and notepads. I can't breathe. 'We'll be back when we have more information.'

Philpot follows Rose to the front door, stops and turns. He gives a short nod, and they leave. As soon as the door closes, I collapse onto the chair, too shocked to cry. We were expecting this, but nothing could have prepared me for the reality of it. Perry sits on the arm and pulls me into his arms.

'I can't go, Perry. I can't go to the station, and they're bound to need statements at some stage.'

'It will be hard, but you must. Shall I ring Doctor Hughes and get something to help you?'

'I don't think anything will work. Oh, what am I going to *do*?'

'Stop worrying. They're trying to scare us.' He pats my hand and pushes a stray hair off my face. 'They need to look at someone else. You know who.'

'Who?'

'Schmidt, of course. There's a dead child, so who else.'

'But ... do you think he's capable of killing ...'

'Of course he is. We all are. *You* ...' He smiles apologetically. 'You know what I mean: given the right circumstances, we're all capable. It has to be Schmidt. I was hoping they were coming today to tell us they'd linked him to the case. Or better still, that they'd arrested him.'

I bury my head in my hands. 'But what proof will they have after all these years? What proof of anything?'

'There must be something.'

If there is something, I'm sure Perry will find it.

Chapter 56

Monday, 13 June 2016

I'm dreaming about a boy from school, his face a familiar landscape of skin and bone. My subconscious feels a deep intimacy. His eyes hover near me. I look down to the stubble on his chin, which is that of a man in his twenties, established and set deep into his pores. He seems to ebb and flows around me as his body metamorphoses on my skin. Sex transmits from his developed chest to my breasts. His legs are long and lean and rub against mine from hip to ankle in an impossible manner. He sits on an invisible chair. My dream-self closes in, and I slide and slip over him, daring to sit on his lap, daring to touch his throbbing body. The air is filled with static from our mutual attraction. Although unable to breathe, I stretch out my arms to take his face in my hands and exhale into his mouth.

At last, he's here, my love, my man, my lost prince.

Pulling him near, I taste his sweet dry apple breath as I kiss his lips. My soul feels a great release, a lifting, and joy soars through me. A rhythmic beat emanates from him as I place my hand on his arm, but the pulsating is mine. It courses through my veins from my heart to fingertips, exuding a palpable heat. It spreads an unstoppable flowering into my brain. I sigh, moan and turn in my bed, restless from the restrictions of my dreamy imagination. My body, the captive of my nocturnal yearnings.

Now he drifts away; his spirit softened into dust and white light. Desperate to hold him to me, I draw in a deep breath, filling my lungs to breaking point. Then, like a kettle reaching the boil, the air escapes, hissing its way up through my throat. It bursts with a guttural, high-pitched scream, and I awake to find my nose bleeding.

Lying back, I consider allowing the blood to choke me. Let it fill my throat and put an end to my miserable life. But I stretch over and grab some tissues and wad them up my nostril. I am not in Frankie's bed, but I have the life and death of him inside me. Deep in my belly where sometimes he stays calm, and other times he stirs until I try to vomit him out. But I could vomit until my stomach burst, and he would remain. He torments *the girl* inside, prodding her with his charm and reminding her of his duplicity.

My dream had been about another youth. Boys from my past were nobodies. Why would such a male invade my dream, an imposter steal my desire? It must be a case of simple crossed wires. But this dream-lover was not some boy-child I'd dismissed as being of no consequence. Turning, I groan and hide my head under my pillow. It was Matthew. I had forgotten those images. Him running wild with my brothers. The man next door who possessed the looks of my best friend but none of the self-doubt. A version of Sarah I could truly love.

***

We are eating lamb chops, broccoli and mash when Perry tells me he's been talking to Arthur Smith, owner of the estate agency. Arthur had mentioned that a guy called Matthew Burcher had phoned to ask him to look for a house in the village. He'd recognised the name, and did Perry know him? It turns out Arthur knew Matthew's father from when he worked at Cleave Farm. Matthew had specified that he wanted to live in Oaktree Cleave, rent or buy.

So Matthew is coming home. He'll be here and not just in my dreams. The coincidence with last night's dream is uncanny. Has Ruby Silver worked her magic? But Matthew returning now is useless. If only I hadn't panicked into marriage. Has Matthew been thinking about me since our meeting? Has he come to rescue me and make up for lost time? There is time for us to be together now they've taken Frankie from me. Having an affair holds a certain allure.

Chapter 57

Thursday, 16 June 2016

They have identified Frankie. The boy is the one who went missing from Perry's school in December 1969. Fear tastes like metal-coated pears in the back of my throat. A sense of not quite waking up, as though the dawn is reluctant to drag itself into the morning.

Yesterday we went to the police station. DC Harptree and his colleague took my statement while Perry was with DS Rose. They told me there was a glove in Frankie's pocket, part of a school uniform. They were fishing for information, so I stopped listening. Then they told me Frankie had been decapitated. Smiles crossed their lips, and they noted my shock. They asked how it made me feel knowing that had been done to him. I told them I had nothing to say about it and breathed a sigh of relief. They don't have a clue about what happened. Frankie's skeleton must have broken up under the weight of the earth – how inept they are. They wouldn't catch me out. My darling went into his grave intact. Imagine picking up a severed head! Even Perry would have baulked at that, and he certainly would have complained. A seven-months pregnant woman couldn't do that: wield an axe and commit such a heinous crime. It was hard not to enlighten them about what exactly happened.

Perry said, 'Fine; I didn't tell them that you killed him,' when I enquired how it went. We didn't talk about the decapitation or the glove. It's best not to know how it got into Frankie's pocket. Perry may have accidentally buried his glove, so he'll have to do the explaining if they find his DNA on it. But it's the type sold by general school uniform outfitters and worn by thousands of boys. Schmidt must have left it somewhere, and it somehow got picked up by Frankie or Perry.

We told them about Schmidt to connect him to the boy. They were very interested in my account of his 'private' tuition of me. They're going to interview Christine Allbright to see what happened to her. It's not easy remembering that I didn't help her – but then she had an older brother with a nasty temper. My threat to tell others could have put Schmidt off his predatory ways. It's doubtful, though. Urges always have to be satisfied, as he continued to demonstrate, and spent years in prison as punishment.

Perry told them about Schmidt's many visits to Oaktree House. We did a good job of informing them that he was a regular visitor to Thora and Frankie. Implicating that Frankie had any relationship with Schmidt makes me nauseous, though.

Going to court and standing in the witness box terrifies me. How will I be strong enough? They don't know that Perry went to France on Frankie's passport, and they'll be unable to trace how Frankie came back into the country. The inquest had concluded that Frankie death was an accident: Perry had placed a set of Frankie's clothes, his watch, and wallet, at the edge of the fast-flowing Loire. The place was not far from Ben's family château. Finding him buried at Oaktree will tell them that he didn't die in France. They asked questions about how his things got there as though we knew about it. We said nothing, other than ask his friends who went to France with him. We're keeping our fingers crossed that they don't check the records for Perry visiting France, or that those records won't exist anymore.

They will speak to everyone who stayed with us that August, except Celia, of course, because that witch is dead. I do not want to meet these people but will have to if there is a court case. What will they tell the police about me? That I was the best hostess, or that I was a low-class pretender who tried to stifle her lover's artistic talent?

We will keep saying that we don't know anything. They have nothing to go on and won't know what questions to ask. We pray the forensic evidence is weak and insufficient. Perry destroyed the axe, hosed down Frankie's blood, and washed it into the soil. The garden was unrecognisable, changed to separate areas, my secret gardens within gardens. Hopefully the diggers have churned it over. The glove in Frankie's pocket was soaking wet with washing liquid.

It will be impossible for them to pin down an exact time or place. They have nothing to support any supposition they might make. When Frankie returned from France will elude them, as there is no return journey. We hope the whole thing will be too complex, a nightmare to investigate. Schmidt is the easy option for them; the child compounds his guilt. He's evil and should be in prison. The fact that he did not kill Frankie is irrelevant. I must stop thinking about it now, or I'll go completely insane. Of course, I know that Perry killed the boy. How else would he know exactly where that grave was? I'm sure by the way Perry is with me that he doesn't like women. We are to be tolerated.

Chapter 58

Sunday, 19 June 2016

Izzy Dewberry-Newberry is making waves in the news about how maligned her father was. She's given an interview outlining the many police procedural failures in the investigation of Frankie's disappearance. She is seeking redress, not for any compensation, but so 'no one has to go through her pain'. She has stopped falling out of nightclubs in various states of inebriation and has separated from her latest squeeze – such is her distress about the father she never knew. The fuss has incited reporters to phone or arrive at the farm shouting their wish for his 'second wife's input'. This has not improved Perry's humour towards me. We'll be happy when she has his body and the high-profile funeral she craves. If I had the strength, I would meet with her and tell her exactly who her father was. Instead, I have written a letter she can have when I'm dead. The outside world is a terrifying place, and I don't want to go there.

Perry arrives home as our meal is ready. He looks tired as he goes to the sink and washes his hands. Why can't he wash off the mess before returning? There are plenty of washing areas on the farm.

As he slumps into his chair, I say, 'Hope you're hungry. There's enough for four.'

He sighs. 'Not really. I want this business finished.'

'I'm praying that they've enough on Schmidt. Everyone knows he's a paedophile. There must be plenty of evidence to get him for that lad. And he was hanging around here all the time.'

'Yes, he was …' Perry picks up his knife and taps the table.

As I put his food in front of him, something in his manner jars a memory. The recollection crushes me. 'Oh Perry … I've just remembered … oh, how could I forget …' I hurry to the door.

'Calm down. What are you talking about?' Perry follows me.
'The letter, *the letter*.'
'What letter?'
'The one Thora wrote when she was on one of her cruises. Asking me to abort Francine and keep away from Frankie, or something. Oh, I can't remember. She said Frankie had some information on Schmidt from her files and was going to blackmail him, or her. I don't know why she would say such an awful thing about Frankie.'
Perry raises an eyebrow, 'Tell me you still have this letter.'
'I do. It's in my box of poetry. Files on Schmidt and others are locked in the filing cabinet in the storage unit. Not the actual hospital files, Thora didn't have those. She did studies on types of deviancy. She told me to destroy them, but I didn't. They were confidential and to touch them would have somehow contaminated me. I didn't read them ... well, I glanced at them, years ago. The keys are here.'
A vision of the cellar room below the kitchen spins in and out of my mind. That room had the sock stuck beneath the door. When I cleared it out, there were two locked filing cabinets and an empty desk. Perry's men moved the lot into the storage unit. Sickness fills my stomach. I swallow it back as I head to my room to find Thora's letter.
As he reads, a smile spreads across his face. 'Good girl. This letter may mean our troubles are over.'
'What will you do with it?'
'You're going to give me the keys to the storage unit and the keys to the cabinets, and I'm going to take them and this letter to the police. The police will be able to put two and two together to make four. Frankie ended up in a grave next to a child probably killed by Schmidt. There's evidence that Frankie blackmailed Schmidt. What would your conclusion be?
'Schmidt will tell them we murdered Frankie.'
'Yes, he will. But who are they going to believe?'

'Is it enough to make them believe that Schmidt killed Frankie?' I sit and put my head down to my knees.

'Well, my precious Carol, it's a damning insight into the sick minds of two people. I'll take a copy first, then be off.' He kisses the top of my head and leaves.

Sliding to the floor, I pray that this will work, while admonishing myself for making public Frankie's frailties. Attributing evil acts to those who are evil, though, is easy. What does the injustice of that matter? We must punish all evil in whatever way we can.

Chapter 59

Wednesday, 22 June 2016

Quaking in the early morning light, I am neither awake nor asleep as my dream surrounds me. My eldest brother, Gerry, turns the key in the ignition of the Ford Popular. The engine sparks into life and hums throatily. He looks at us and says, '*That's* what you want to hear,' and we all grin and clap. Sammy says, 'Well done, mate,' and Denny says, 'Wow, that's amazing.'

We open the doors. Denny wants to sit in the front, but I get there first, so he tweaks my hair and says, 'Okay, just cos you're a girl.' He pokes my ribs before getting in the back. Gerry guns the engine and pulls out of Cleave Farm, turning onto the top lane. We're flying along at forty, too fast for the narrow, winding road. I check my watch and see it's milking time. Mr Cutler will be herding the cows around the next bend. The car speeds onward and they come into view: Friesians fill the lane. We plough into them, tumbling into a whirlpool of black, white, and the deep red of blood. Tilly, the Collie, flies towards me and hits the windscreen. There's a loud crack-wallop, and burst veins shoot blood in fountains.

Waking, but reluctant to lose the dream, I let it play on. Tilly lies still, blood staining the white fur around her leg. It oozes in a halo around her neck as the gunshot penetrates. Mr Cutler breaks open the twelve-bore and removes the orange BB cartridge. He pats my shoulder, 'It's for the best, Carol. It's for the best.' He lifts her and throws her onto the trailer as though she were a bale of hay. Perry will have to bury her next to Spike and Juno.

Shuddering, I reach for my glass of water. Those long-forgotten memories jag at tears in the back of my eyes. I swallow, trying to hold on to the vision of my brothers and Tilly, that feeling of life and vitality mixed with death and reality. Memories of my youth and my family are a strong presence today.

Meanwhile, dreams of Frankie have ceased since they found the bodies. Frankie has gone.

There's a Frankie-shaped void inside me. Perry should fill that void, but he doesn't have the temperament of a true lover. He hovers around love unable to commit to the all-consuming passion he fears may destroy him. A state which, by its nature, will leave him in a compliant position. He is not strong enough to be my equal. I feel it in his fists, his voice, and his inability to control himself. He wavers between despising me and tolerating me. I'm a punishment he takes to entitle him to a maid and a whore. I irritate him with my anxiety attacks because I can't control them; he doesn't understand that they have their own life. They flourish amid his aggression.

The girl inside favours Matthew. Foisting upon him the same ability that Frankie had to consume me diverts my frustration. That I should be independent and not yearn for another union crosses my mind; but I dismiss this: loneliness and failure will not be my epitaph. The longing to be a soulmate is powerful. If I wish for it, it will come true. There must be some point to our existence before we pass from this world of suffering into oblivion.

***

We invited Matthew for a meal last night. We celebrated that Schmidt had been arrested, amusing Matthew with our relief. That Perry had invited him surprised me. Later it became apparent that they had met last week at the Oaktree Inn. They had discussed their various commercial projects and had come up with a business idea. Last night's meal was not a social occasion, as I had supposed, but an opportunity to debate the plan for a camping site. Yurts and glamping are the new 'in' thing. The pair's enthusiastic chatter fizzed around our wineglasses: Perry had the land and Matthew had the business knowledge and spare cash. They brushed aside my negativity about their plans. Failing to influence them, but succeeding in irritating them, I retired early. They cannot start this partnership. Matthew will be here regularly, reminding me of our past and paths not taken. At least they didn't talk about Frankie.

***

The recent turmoil in my life is causing problems with my rationality. The past is a cruel torturer when one is forced to confront it in such a harsh way. Nowhere to run and hide. Nowhere to compartmentalise former mistakes and rationalise them as the innocent transgressions of a foolish girl. Breathing exercises fail as the overwhelming guilt of what my hands and my mind have accomplished allows me no reprieve. I feel that *the girl* inside has risen from her box. She breathes in the same air and starves me of oxygen.

A memory floods back as I take one of my pills. Waves of dizziness come, as forgotten memories of Sarah's betrayal flow like sewage. Unpleasant fumes stir in my nostrils. Sarah recorded everything in her diaries: trivialities written to validate her existence. Nothing much happened to her, yet she recorded the empty days of her life as if they were worthy of regard. There would be a record of Frankie's meetings with Schmidt if she witnessed them. If she was capable of betraying me, then she was capable of recording that Frankie was less than perfect. She could do what I had been incapable of doing.

Matthew will have those diaries and must be persuaded to hand them in. It's doubtful that her parents would have destroyed them. They kept her room intact as a memorial despite the shame her suicide brought on them. It wasn't general knowledge she that was pregnant, which saved them from total humiliation. Her diary for 1970 must be given to the police. It will assist my freedom and help atone for her infidelity with Frankie.

Perry has become increasingly agitated. Late into the night, he talks on in a pitiful attempt to rewrite the history of Frankie's demise. That he was forced to do it; that the terms of the trust weren't a consideration. His regretful involvement and subsequent criminalisation are resulting in sleepless nights and an inability to have a satisfactory life. All his actions are misguided by some unknown feeling toward me that he cannot recount. Tiredness and regret for his stupidity are the reasons he lashes out. That we may be absolved from Frankie's death does nothing to diminish his viciousness, and his controlling behaviour escalates.

My thoughts to turn to Matthew.

Matthew must be my new soulmate.

The girl inside agrees.

Chapter 60

Monday, 27 June 2016

The roads are a mess of traffic lights and one-way systems. Driving along the lane and then across the ring road to reach Matthew's house takes all my determination. The journey must be made, as my need to see Matthew consumes me. There's no reason for arriving at his house unannounced.

'Oh. Carol. Hi. I wasn't expecting you.' Matthew looks annoyed.

'Sorry for calling in but I was driving around and –'

'No problem. Come in.'

Matthew's house is so like Perry's that I shiver. The 'cottage' is a large detached five-bedroom house. He's renting it until he can buy it. The owner is dying in a nursing home. With his death imminent, his children want to sell as soon as he draws his last breath. The callousness of their behaviour is shocking. Matthew takes the view that bricks and mortar shouldn't hold sentimental value.

A glimpse into the front living room shows that it's under renovation. Matthew walks into the rear, which opens up into a large kitchen-diner. There's a conservatory at the back letting light flood through. The garden is massive, full of mature trees and shrubs. Matthew notes my excitement at the sight and promises me a tour later. He appreciates that I've spent half my life gardening but am unable to do so now. The colour scheme is cream, with odd walls and furnishings in red and orange to add warmth. The kitchen is utilitarian, all clean lines and stainless steel. The renovation has removed all warmth, though: no signs of a woman's touch, no hand cream by the sink, no plants on the windowsill.

He picks up the kettle and says, 'I'm about to make tea. D'you want some? Sit down.'

'Yes, please.'

He makes the tea and brings it to the sofa. There's no subtle way to ask him this, so I blurt out as I sit down, 'I've come about Sarah's diary.'

'Oh.' Matthew is suitably startled. 'What diary?'

'She kept diaries for every year. I'm hoping your parents kept them and that you or Chrissie has them now.'

'No idea. I have some stuff upstairs.' He smiles and cocks his head to one side, confused amusement pulling his forehead. 'Why?' His hand rests on his thigh. I want to put my hand over it, connect us.

'Because there may be information in the one dated 1970, about Frankie ... and Schmidt.'

'Schmidt? What does he have to do with Sarah? You're not saying he ... touched her or something?"

'No, of course not. It's just Frankie was – well, I denied this to myself at the time, but Frankie was blackmailing Schmidt, and Sarah would have witnessed it. The pair meeting up, or whatever was going on. She would have written about it.'

'You sound quite sure.'

'I am. I liked to think Frankie was perfect but he wasn't.' My heart doesn't lurch at my betrayal like it used to. My body doesn't sweat and quiver as I speak of him. It hasn't for some time now, and the freedom from it strengthens me.

'I don't know if I can read her diary.' He wrinkles his nose in distaste.

'But you must. The police need the information to catch Frankie's killer. Schmidt.'

'Schmidt? You think Schmidt killed Frankie?'

'Yes. I'm sure he did. I have a letter from Thora warning me about Frankie blackmailing him. That's a good enough motive for the police to consider the possibility. Would you like me to read it for you if you don't think –'

'What? No!' Matthew jumps up and paces, balling his fists.

'Oh, I'm sorry. I didn't think.' I go to him and place my hands on his shoulders. 'It's so important that I overlooked how it might affect you. But Matthew, the police should know.' I squeeze his shoulders, willing him to calm down. 'Why not just hand it to the police to save yourself the distress?'

He stills. 'Sorry, Carol, but you need to go.'

His voice is firm. He follows me as I grab my bag and make my way out. At the threshold I turn once more. 'Please, Matthew, let the police have that diary. Don't let Schmidt get away with murder. You owe it to Sarah.'

Turning the ignition, I pray that he's convinced. Matthew hates Schmidt, and if there is anything in her diary, he'll enjoy putting a stake into Schmidt's coffin.

Chapter 61

Wednesday, 29 June 2016

P erry knocks on my study door and requests that I come to the sitting room. As I go downstairs, I hear voices and am startled to see that the police are here. They are grim-faced and ask me to sit down before they speak. Then DS Rose tells us Schmidt is dead. He's been murdered by a man who has a ten-year-old son. He swears that Schmidt confessed to murdering the boy found with Frankie. But not Frankie. There will be an inquiry into what happened, and heads will roll, she assures us. That he will not be tried and convicted is a blow. A guilty verdict would resolve this.

She tells us about the new evidence. Christine Allbright's witness statement outlines Schmidt's conduct. And Matthew had given them Sarah's diary, with information about where and when Frankie and Schmidt met and what they were doing and saying, and about Frankie blackmailing Schmidt. The sock they found in one of Thora's filing cabinets belonged to the boy, as did the glove in Frankie's pocket. Perry asked if there was any DNA and they declined to answer, but in a way that suggested there wasn't.

Perry asks if they are convinced that Schmidt murdered Frankie and they say they haven't discounted it. If they know what Frankie was blackmailing Schmidt about, they're not saying. But then they trip up and say they're sure Frankie blackmailed Schmidt about the murder of the boy. We don't ask if they have established a timeline. We don't press them; they may realise that there are holes in their investigation.

As soon as they leave, I collapse onto the sofa, but Perry assures me that Schmidt's death is the best outcome for us. He can't protest his innocence. I'm nervous about the many loose ends, though. If the police step back and think logically about it, they may not come to the same conclusion. But Perry is having none of my doubts.

'Carol, now they've established when all this happened, the thing always in your favour is that Frankie was decapitated. They won't consider that you had the strength to do that while heavily pregnant. Or in your weakened state after giving birth. I found it hard to accept at the time – what you had done, how you had destroyed him.'

His words sting. 'What do you mean decapitated Frankie, destroyed Frankie? I didn't ... I don't know what you mean.'

He eyes darken into pinpricks, he pulls himself up and grabs my arm, and shouts, 'Don't try to get out of it this late in the day. What you did was sinful. Disgusting. Why don't you take a tablet and lie down? I'm going back to work.' His fingers dig into my flesh leaving more bruises as he pushes me away from him. The coffee table holds well as I crash onto it, but the corner knocks the breath out of me. A sharp pain radiates in my lower ribs.

With that, he storms out, leaving me on the floor. My brain fugs as I try to recall what happened. The memory of what I did when killing Frankie is locked in a box that's buried deep in my soul. My culpability will destroy me if it pushes its way into my consciousness. *The girl* inside knows the full horror, but I won't ask her. I won't let her tell me that I decapitated Frankie.

Pain consumes me and I breathe raggedly. Uncertain of how to sit, there's no choice but to hobble to my mobile. Who to tell? No one to confide in; no one to help me. Reluctantly, I phone Perry. He'll be very pleased that he has to take me to the hospital.

Chapter 62

Wednesday, 27 July 2016

My fractured ribs are healing. I'm proud of myself for convincing the medical staff that I fell onto our coffee table on my own. It seems they consider domestic violence when a husband brings his wife in for treatment late at night. Especially if both parties give slightly different versions of what happened. Perry's near miss at being branded a wife-beater has not stopped his abuse, though. His fear of my implicating him in Frankie's murder had always been my protector. Now we're virtually in the clear and married, he trusts that he is free to do as he wishes. He tells me that Laura's mother reminded her that just because she didn't say 'obey' in her wedding vows, it's implied. Marriage appears to give women a smokescreen of independence. The situation is intolerable, and I must work my way out of it.

The internet holds many self-defence tactics, and I intend to deploy some soon. My ribs are the last straw. He tells me it was my fault for speaking as I did. That I cause his bad humour because I am *me* is unpalatable. In my frustration I think of ways to kill him. But that will not do. I will not go to prison for him, so I must stop obsessing about the various ways a man can die on a farm.

My soul yearns for love, but I must focus on staying sane today. The radiant sunshine helps lift my spirits. Matthew draws me to him, and I ache to see him now Perry is showing his true colours. His simmering impatience and surliness have undertones of real violence. Perry doesn't like me interfering in his business plans with Matthew. He says that I may be rich but so is he, and he can do as he wishes, marriage or not.

Driving my new car across the temporary road to the village,

I wonder why Matthew has invited me to his house on my own. And why I haven't told Perry. Parking outside Cherry Tree Cottage, I check the time. The painkillers won't kick in for another hour, and when they start to work I'll feel sick. Then it will be time to return home before I get too fuzzy-headed.

'Carol. Thanks for coming. Go straight through.'

We drink coffee from over-sized orange cups and saucers, sitting on the large red comfortable couch. After placing my cup down on the oak coffee table, I lean back carefully, in the superfluity of deep cushions. Our legs are inches apart, and the thought that, but for a coverlet, we could be in bed sends a thrill through me. Matthew is a handsome man. Age has not diminished his allure. A buzz of maleness emanates from him. Does he feel what I feel? My skirt slides up over ten-denier stockings, exposing a few inches of thigh. Has he noticed that my legs are still toned and unblemished, a fitting testament to an active life in my home and garden? Sex with Perry has stopped due to my rib fracture, and I'm not sure it will resume.

Giving the police Thora's letter, coupled with Schmidt's death, has released a weight from my shoulders. Not having to lie anymore, I can relax into myself. No longer living with concealed guilt restricting every waking moment, my innermost feelings long for the freedom of expression. Opening up about aspects of my life is a new concept. Perhaps it's the effect of a cocktail of medication, but this urge to unburden itches like a scab loosening from my soul. I can be whatever I want to be now.

Matthew is enquiring about the time Frankie left me, or rather after Schmidt killed him. My new liberty encases me with a cosy fuzziness as we discuss this. Frankie's body is safe and Schmidt is presumed guilty of his murder. Perry and I are free. Perry has warned Matthew not to talk to me about the bodies. Perry continues to control what I do and who should say what to me and when.

'Did you have any idea that Frankie had come back?'

'Come back?'

'Yes. You said he went to France, but he was in your orchard, so he came back.'

'Obviously. But I don't know when. I was staying with Perry's family when Francine was born.'

'Oh, do you know exactly when he died?'

'No, I don't. I was staying with Perry that Christmas, and again when Francine was born for a few weeks.' His questioning is disconcerting. 'Why do you ask?'

'No reason. Curiosity to know the grisly facts, I suppose. Wondered if the police have any more details.' He laughs and moves the biscuit tin in front of me. 'How's Perry?'

'Fine.' My mobile buzzes so I drop my bag on the floor, out of the way.

'I'm quite surprised about Perry. He's not the old goat I'd thought he was.' Matthew takes a sip and winces before putting his cup down. 'Your set-up at Cleave Farm is impressive. Perry's foresight to move into the organic business was inspired. And who'd have thought lavender would be so profitable? Thank you again for the wonderful meal. You certainly know how to cook, Carol.'

Has he forgotten about the fingertip bruises he saw on my arm? A lucrative business idea trumps any qualms about a business partner's penchant for abusing his wife. He continues: 'So what do you think about the campsite?'

'Perry hasn't mentioned it again. You're still going ahead with it?'

'Well, yes, of course we are. I thought you would know.'

'Perry doesn't tell me what I don't need to know.'

Matthew looks perplexed at my irritation. He picks up his cup and sips, 'Well, it's a great money-spinner. I've finished working on the business plan; I'll print a copy for you to take.'

'Why not email it to him?' Is this the reason he asked me here? Matthew laughs. 'Of course. I forget about technology. We didn't have wifi and what have you on the campsite. It was a real 'get away from it all' place,' He fetches a pad and pen. 'Jot your email addresses down.'

As I write, I say, 'Not thinking about retiring then? You must be nearing seventy.'

'A few years yet, thanks very much. Don't think I'll ever retire. Been too active all my life. Can't see myself sitting around doing nothing.'

'Why did you leave France then? You said it was your home.'

He flinches, and a fleeting grimace of trepidation passes across his face. 'Sometimes life's a bitch.' He smiles and says, 'Excuse my French.'

'Oh, what happened?' As I sit up I draw in a deep breath and hold it to override the pain.

'Nothing in particular. Apart from my relationship of twenty-five years breaking down.'

'Sorry to hear that.'

'Don't be. We wanted different things; she wanted me to sell the campsite and retire. I didn't. Then, when she left, it turned out the campsite lost its appeal. But it was too late for her. She'd 'moved on', as they say. So I thought I'd see out my days near Chrissie. D'you want a biscuit?'

'No thanks.'

'I wanted to ask you something,' His glance jars me and tells me that I won't like whatever it is. 'Will you take me to where Sarah died? I've forgotten where the tree is.'

'I … you can't access it from this side, with all the building going on, and …' Surely he doesn't need me. The next time I go there I don't intend to come back. My ribs are hurting so I shift in discomfort, then I remember he knows the field and the way to the oak tree as well as anyone. It's an excuse to be with me.

'Are you okay? You look like you're in pain.'

I want to tell him that Perry broke my ribs but can't see that it will change anything. 'Yes, just a bit of cramp. Drive to the other end, where Schmidt used to live, and head up along the top lane, then right into Dawnview Lane. You shouldn't have a problem.'

'Oh.' He's disappointed by my answer. 'Yes, of course. I'd forgotten. Will you come with me? Only I can't go on my own.'

His gaze holds mine intently, stopping me from looking away. I struggle to hide my dread, but he would expect me to show emotion, so I cry.

'I'm so sorry, Carol,' He wipes away a tear, his fingers sending shockwaves across my cheek, 'That was tactless of me. Forgive me.'

'Nothing to forgive. She's ... was ... your sister ...'

'And she was your friend.'

'You know that's not entirely true, Matthew. We weren't friends. Not when she –'

'What do you mean? I thought she wrote in her diary that you two made up.'

'No; although she did come to see me about a week or so before ... It was a long time ago. I can't remember much, except that Frankie came between us.'

Matthew looks confused. 'Oh, I must have read that wrong.' He's hurt, and I feel the need to reassure him.

'Things weren't good between us, but I'm sure we would have become friends again. Our friendship was more than a quarrel over Frankie.'

He ponders this. 'I'm sure you would. And now we know Frankie didn't leave.'

The conversation is unnerving. 'I'd better go.'

'Go? You've only just got here. I'm sorry if I made you uncomfortable. Me and my big mouth. It must have been a massive shock for you when they found those bodies.'

Why is he saying this again? We already went through it when he came around for dinner. I say nothing, so he says, 'There I go again. Sorry. At least they got that bastard Schmidt. Who'd have thought it, eh?' He drains his coffee. 'Two bodies buried in your orchard. Who'd have thought Frankie had been blackmailing Schmidt, no wonder he was never short of money. Wonder who else he was cadging off? Thora, no doubt.'

'I have to go.' Nausea starts up, or it may be Matthew upsetting me. I must leave before drowsiness stops me driving.

'Don't go. I'll shut up. Come and see upstairs. I need your help with the soft furnishings. I'm hopeless. They need a woman's eye. What d'you say?' He walks to the stairs, so I follow.

'Oh, I don't … well, I suppose ... But it will all be ordered online. I don't go to shops.'

'Yes, that's fine. Perry told me you didn't travel too far from home. Just popping in here a second.' He slips into the bathroom. That Perry has been talking to him about me and my problems wounded me. How dare he. Now I've been cast as a freak.

Ahead is what looks like the main bedroom at the front of the house, so I take a step towards it. Something catches my eye inside a smaller bedroom to my left. I push the door and take a few steps, before sinking to my knees. Cardboard boxes with the name ' Philip's Store' on the sides sit against the wall. Musty air and dry dust float out as I pull a flap, knowing what I'll find. Sarah's diaries, her posters, her hairbrush, all packed up. An open time-bomb waiting to be ignited. There's a note in code with a translation written underneath, each letter in my handwriting. Back in Sarah's bedroom, she floats towards me with her pouting face, dismayed by my reluctance to do what she wants. She tightens her cardigan, arms across her chest. The small swell of her belly crushes me.

'Oh God, I'm sorry – I forgot.' He kneels to tuck the cardboard flap back in. My legs are like jelly. His arms snake around me as he attempts to steady me, but my dead weight unbalances him. We fall to the carpet. A deafening wailing noise fills the air but is muffled when he smothers my face with his shoulder. As I move to catch my breath, he cups my face then puts his lips on mine. We melt together, hot tears mingling. But this time his hands don't seek my body; this time we are no longer young and pliable and full of rampant hormones. The disappointment as he pulls away shoots a dagger through my heart. I'm repulsive. Age and realism stunt us so that passion no longer flows uninhibited. Turning to my side, I pull my knees to my chest to relieve the pain in my ribs. A chasm of emptiness tempts me to freefall into it. He sits, and I lie, while the boxes containing Sarah's past wait with their toxic contents, a reminder of past times and past mistakes.

'Sorry,' he says. 'Arthritis in my knees.'

'Are you okay?'

'Yes, if I can get up.' He winces, so I get up and offer my hand. He gets to his knees and struggles up. 'Very sexy, don't you think? I didn't stop because I didn't want to. Don't think that. You're married, Carol, and this, us – well, it's not on, is it?'

'No. You're right. We can't. I'm sorry for kissing you back. That was wrong of me.'

'Don't be like that. If I'd thought for one moment you and I stood a chance, I would have returned before now.'

'But you didn't, so let's forget it.' I lean over and flick through a box of Sarah's clothes; the material itches my fingers. 'Gosh, these take me back. I can see her knitting this cardigan. And this bag. She took it apple-scrumping one day … the day we first met Thora.'

'Do you want any of this?' His hand shifts through the items.

'No. Of course not. Why would I?'

'Oh, I don't know. Memories. Good times.'

Does he think that's funny? Perhaps I'm too dismissive of Sarah's friendship. 'Maybe I'll take some of our letters,' As I reach for the other box he jumps, then gets down on his knees quickly, gasps and pulls it away from me. 'Oh, sorry, when you asked if I wanted anything, I presumed…'

'Just remembered I hadn't checked everything in here.'
'Oh. I don't think her other diaries show me in a bad light.'
'I'm sure they don't. Anyway, best I keep them safe.'
'She wrote everything down, however boring. I couldn't be bothered until the time I was sectioned. Are you okay?'
He's ghostly pale as he slides along on his knees and then lets out a yelp. He winces and shifts his weight as he sorts through the box. Picking up some paperwork, he says, 'I'll just put this away,' and limps out of the room.
I follow him into a bedroom that's set up as a study. I wonder what he's holding. A diary? A letter? There's no chance of finding out. At least not today.
'I'd better go. I'll look at the soft furnishings another time. Or email me a list of what you need and the colours you want and I'll get some ideas.'
'What? Yes – sorry. Sometimes she … gets to me when I least expect it. I'll see you out. Sorry, for everything.'
A sad old man stands before me and all the magic he'd possessed flies away like the puffed-up sentiment it is.
'I'm sorry too,' I say as I walk away.

Chapter 63

Thursday, 4 August 2016

The decapitation of Frankie itches at my brain. In my struggle to accept my violence, I must have ignored and forgotten my evil actions to allow myself a reasonable existence. The devil is close on my heels, waiting for a confession so that society can slaughter me.

Driving calms my nerves, so I set off for the village in my new Mini. The road stretches for miles, bringing with it the temptation to drive anywhere. Escape, flee, run, the words curl around my tongue like enticing morsels I want to devour.

The symptoms of a crisis flow through my arms to the steering wheel. It's as though there's something in the air trying to contact me, trying to get a message through. Maybe Ruby Silver has noticed that I sway from her mantra of visualising my future to attain it. The persuasions of Lily and her doctrines focused on the here and now are more likeable.

The noticeboard outside the village shop displays a newspaper headline. Nervously I leave my car and buy a paper, ignoring the glances of strangers.

There's a piece about the murders and Schmidt. The police are not pursuing anyone in the matter of Frankie's death. They have wound the case up and breathed a sigh of relief that further man-hours aren't required. That must have been why they called the other day, although I refused to speak to them. Perry could deal with them.

Last week a few online newspaper reports disturbed me. They said Frankie's body had suffered several axe wounds and was completely destroyed. But how can that be? I remember putting the gun down and taking the axe. My anger was frightening and uncontrollable. But it's a blur. His blood flowed across the path and into the edge of the lawn. I remember that blood; it still flows through my dreams.

Something is odd about this newspaper report shaking in my hands. Schmidt was there that day, Perry saw him. Supposing *he* decapitated Frankie. Schmidt could have done it while I was semi-conscious in the front garden. I have no idea how long I was in the garden before Perry arrived, maybe an hour. Perry must know more than me, but I cannot ask him. He believes I chopped off Frankie's head. Maybe I did chop off his head. I wanted to hurt him in a way that showed how much he had hurt me. But what if Schmidt killed him? He could have followed me and struck while Frankie was incapacitated. Maybe I'm not so evil after all. Schmidt was there. Perry saw his car. He wouldn't have liked Frankie's evil blackmailing. Frankie, who wanted to get money without doing anything more strenuous than demand it. It would mean that the charge was correct and he was guilty and I am innocent. Except I buried the body – but then I needed to keep my Frankie safe. If only I could remember and be sure of my sins.

We all paid for the emotions Frankie stirred in us. Some of us had seen the error of our idolising, and our love had turned into hate. He incited the kind of hatred that invades souls and claims your sanity. No one hated Frankie more than I as he brought the axe down on his leg. Frankie was a betrayer of women, yet his evil seed produced two daughters. The gods must be laughing.

Not wanting to go home, I pull into the car park of the Cleave Inn and switch off the engine. Perry has just recovered from another bout of gastroenteritis. He can't understand why he keeps getting sick and says it reminds him of the time just before Laura died when he'd had the same thing for months. I do what I can for him, but he's best left alone as I don't want to catch it. Luckily, unlike years ago, he has the staff to run around after him.

It's eleven thirty on a Tuesday morning. All around is quiet – a pair of magpies squabble in the grass. A car sweeps past then parks near the side entrance, the one used by the proprietors. A tall, thin man wearing a grey knitted waistcoat gets out and offloads a wheelchair. He takes it to the passenger side and helps an old woman transfer into it. It's Sadie, the owner of the pub. Lovely Sadie, who used to let us play in the pub garden, use the swing, pinch crisps and lemonade from the patrons. She brought stews to me after Francine was born. She sat with me and helped me knit a matinee jacket – a sweet woman. She signed the trust for Thora and was the only friend of Thora's I knew.

Opening the car door, I call her name. She turns, a huge smile bursts onto her face and she shouts, 'Carol!' with obvious delight. I go to her.

'Come here,' Sadie says and opens her arms to take me in a hug. As I bend to hug her, I cry. The scent of her perfume holds the smell of better days.

'Oh, Carol, how are you, my darling? I followed all the newspaper reports. I knew it wasn't you, didn't I, Steven? Told everyone you couldn't be a killer. Proved right, wasn't I!'

'Oh, Sadie.' I try to control my emotions. The papers haven't been kind; no smoke without fire. Steven looks unsure.

'What's wrong, my luvvie? And what have you done to your arm?'

'Oh, I've broken it. It's almost healed now. This brace supports it as it aches so much. Perry did it, I mean he got it for me ... off the net.'

'The net? Oh, the computer. Come in and have a chat. Steven, get me in and put the kettle on.'

'I'm sure Carol has better things to do.'

Astounded by his presumptuousness, I say, 'I would love to have a chat, Sadie.'

'There you go, Steven. Now, take me in then get a move on.'

We enter a room at the back. It's large and has a dining table, a settee and a television. Steven pushes Sadie to the table and secures the brake before casting a disapproving look and leaving.

'Here, sit down.' Sadie points at the chair next to her then lays her hand on my face. 'So lovely. You're lucky to catch us at a quiet time. My grandchildren, Steven's children, run the pub, but they've gone on holiday somewhere – um, Spain or Italy … doesn't matter. Taken my great-grandchildren with them. Steven is running the show for them. He took over from us in the late 90s or sometime. Doesn't matter when things happen, does it, because they happen if you remember when or not.' She laughs at her failing memory and pats my hand resting on the table. Steven enters carrying a tray loaded with the tea paraphernalia and places it down.

'Thank you, Steven.' He turns to leave, but Sadie shouts after him, 'Steven bring me that tin … you know the one. The one with Sheila's photos in.'

'Congratulations on your wedding. Have you seen many photos of Perry as a boy, because we have some? Sheila, my daughter, died last week, or sometime, doesn't matter, she's dead, and we found this tin with the photos. Sheila was sweet on Perry's brother Simon. Did you know Simon?'

'No, I didn't. He was already dead when I first met Perry.'

'Oh? Let me see – Perry would have been, um, and Simon was, can't remember when he died … no, Simon was older, at secondary school, I think … doesn't matter – he died.'

Steven comes back with a biscuit tin and places it on the table. 'Will you want anything else?'

'Just lunch in an hour will be fine,' Sadie says dismissively. I admire her strength. Why can't I speak up like that? She whispers, 'It's my weekly trip here. The only time I get let out of the care home. He's a bit moody about it.' She chuckles as she lifts the teapot but can't manage it, so I take it. She grabs the tin. 'Anyway, let me show you these.'

She rummages through the pile of old photos. 'Here we go, there's Perry with William, um, Mr Cutler. And there's Simon and William, with my daughter, Sheila. These were taken the

Easter before Simon died. And there's Perry and Simon with their mum and dad; Sheila took that one. You can see Perry takes after his mum, but Simon is his father's boy. And here's one with Matthew – Matthew Burcher.

'I didn't know Matthew knew Simon.'

'Oh yes. The Burchers moved to the housing estate sometime, um, well, it was after Simon died ... Mr Burcher got a job at the tobacco factory, but before that he was a farm hand on Cleave Farm. You've forgotten he was there that day you ran away from home and got caught up with the cows at milking time.'

Taking the photos, I study them. The picture of a young Matthew stirs long forgotten memories. Simon reminds me of someone, but who evades me. He's the image of his father. Why had I not seen photos of Simon? There must be some about the farmhouse. Sheila has the same gentle face as Sadie.

'Why don't I remember Steven and Sheila when they were young?' I ask.

'Boarding school. We sent them away. I was against it but their father, well ... But they're a few years older than you anyway. Sheila was sixty-eight or -nine or something this year ... Doesn't matter – she's dead.'

She hands me more photos. 'And here's one of Simon. Strange to think he would be dead not long after. Drowned, in the lake. He wasn't a strong swimmer, not like Perry. Perry tried to save him of course, but, well, he wasn't strong enough ... doesn't matter ... they were kids. How did Perry cope with, you know, his brother drowning in front of him? I wonder. Not being able to help. How do you get over something like that? Eh? Must haunt you for the rest of your life. Something so terrible happening.'

'Yes, I suppose it did. I mean, it does. But he doesn't talk about it.'

'No, well, stiff upper lip and all that. His mother never took to anyone being, what's the word, can't think, doesn't matter ...

ah, I know: *emotional*, yes, that'll do, or sensitive. Gosh, I remember all the big words today.' She laughs then sips her tea before continuing.

'Shouldn't laugh ... doesn't matter. Sheila was heart-broken. She spent all her school holidays mooning after him. Went to that farm every chance she got, right from, oh, about age six, I suppose. Loved Simon from the day she met him.'

Sadie rummages some more.

'And here's one of William alone. Sheila was trying to make him pose. Look at that grin. He was a lovely man, but his wife, well, she was a different story. Never understood why she became so bitter. She was nice when they first married.'

Taking it, my blood runs cold as his features hit home. It can't be, can it? The stance, the cheekbones, the impish grin. Perry is nothing like him, but then Perry takes after his mother. The photo confuses me. He's Mr Cutler and yet a different Mr Cutler. Not the plump, huffing-puffing, curt man I remembered. This William Cutler is young, without a hat and with hair. Blond hair. Slim and attractive, in a way I had never noticed as a child growing up. The photo is a revelation. But what difference can it make now, after all this time?

Sadie notices my attention to it.

'Good looking, eh? Pity I didn't marry him. But you got his son, eh?' She winks at me then chuckles, 'Well, Frankie took to Elsie, and I lost out.'

I laugh at her confusion. 'What've I said now?' She chuckles and pats my arm.

'You said "Frankie" instead of "William". Frankie was my hus – ... boyfriend.'

'Oh. Well, it's not wrong, but it's confusing. I always thought it a bit funny that Thora's nephew, um, son was named Frankie, and William's nickname was Frankie. Especially when I caught the two of them ... anyway, it's a long time ago ... doesn't matter. And she told me she was raped when she was away somewhere.

Did she tell you? 'Suppose it doesn't matter who knows now, everyone's dead.'

Shivers flow through me as the truth hits. Thora and William; or rather, Thora and 'Frankie'. Is that why Frankie was called Frankie?

'Oh, have I said something out of turn? You're very pale. It was probably nothing. After all, they were good neighbours for years. He signed the trust the same as I did. Doesn't matter now, does it if they liked each other? I'm sure nothing happened between them. Elsie would have had something to say about that, I can tell you. If she had known anything was going on between them, well, we would all know about it. There would have been hell.'

'I'm sure, Sadie. Yes, she told me about the rape. Can I borrow these ... to show Perry?'

She hesitates, so I say, 'Oh, don't worry, I'll bring them back. I won't forget, I promise.'

'Well, yes, I suppose, but don't lose the ones with Sheila. You can keep the ones without Sheila. She only kept them because she'd a crush on Simon.'

'Well, then, I'll take the ones without Sheila – thank you. I expect Perry will only be interested in his family anyway. Thank you, Sadie.'

I snap my bag closed.

Chapter 64

Thursday, 4 August 2016

Simon's bedroom door key will be in Perry's study but the spare key to his study will be in his office in the converted barn. The ground floor, containing Perry's office, is accessed by many workers. They use the kitchen, toilets and shower room. There's a restroom and workers sit about drinking tea or coffee at all hours of the day and night depending on what's being harvested, loaded or delivered. When I try the door, his office is locked.

'Hello, Mrs Cutler.'

Jumping, I clasp my chest. 'Hello … um, Louise.' Perry's secretary gives me the creeps.

'Did you want something?'

'No, I … well, I've lost a key and Perry won't be happy. I'm supposed to start cleaning out one of the rooms in the farmhouse. But I can't find the key, and I thought there'd be a spare in his office.'

'Oh,' she says, and she weighs up whether she should help me. 'I'm not allowed to give out keys, as they're spares and if they go missing he'll have a fit … I mean he won't be … you know.' She flushes at her disrespect.

'Yes, my husband can be rather ... um, *sharp*,' I say, and raise my eyebrows in a conspiratorial way to reassure her. 'I have a way. If you open the door and bring back the key straightaway? I won't be able to lock up when I finish so I'll tell him I lost the key then. At least I will have started to clear the room, whereas now when he comes back, I won't have.' I try to look downcast.

'Okay, I can't see any harm. Which one is it?'

'It's labelled "Simon's room".'

She fetches it then follows me. I search for something bright and breezy to say but daren't speak in case she notices my nervousness.

'This is it. Thank you, Louise.' She opens the door. 'You don't fancy giving me a hand, do you?' I push the door open and let her have a glimpse of the contents.

She sniffs the dusty air. 'No, sorry, I must get on,' and scuttles away.

It's always the quickest way to get rid of someone, to suggest they help you with some work. Shutting the door, I look around at the abandoned boxes and rubbish. Everything is where I remembered. The bed is against the wall still covered by the blue candlewick bedspread I'd burrowed under to stop the sick, dizzy feeling after bashing my forehead. That day when I was seven resounds throughout my life. Trying to find my dead father in the lightning storm, meeting Perry, discovering this place, and nearly getting killed; some days are indelibly stamped in your memory, and I often wonder what life would have been if I hadn't taken the decisions I did on that day. Or the decisions I made the day I first walked into Oaktree House.

Sitting on the bed, I remember Perry taking a book from the bookcase and hiding it in his waistband. It may have been a diary. Perry has never been a 'book person'. He's an outdoor type, a gardener, a farmer.

Something about Sadie's photos hinted at a truth I had not seen before. Something at the edge of my memory floats like a black ghost. The harder I try to capture the thought, the more it slips away. Something compelled me to come here. That Perry could return and find me here frightens me. Perhaps the feeling is caused by the many chemicals I take to keep me sane. Visiting Sadie was an eye-opener into the dynamics of this family. That Mr Cutler, or should I call him Frankie, may have been having an affair with Thora is a revelation. Secrets swirl temptingly in the atmosphere.

Simon's room holds twelve years of his life. Perry tried to

save him from drowning but couldn't. Chills run up my spine as a real fear of Perry grows. What if he didn't try to save him? What if he was glad his brother died? What if he walks in and catches me? Fear spikes, and it demands respect.

The room is no longer a shrine. Where are the clues that will reinforce my sixth sense that his death wasn't an accident? What if his mother had discovered the truth that I'm suspecting? What if Simon was going to share a dark family secret with her – the sharing of which could have been more destructive for his mother then her son's death had been. A dead son and brother, or a destroyed marriage with your parents separating? Depends on whose viewpoint you look from, and who the truth would hurt the most.

Sarah and I hid our letters and secrets on the back of the bed headboard. Grabbing it with both hands, it shifts away from the wall sending pain through my shoulder and arm. Another tug and it moves six inches. A book is taped to the back, set inside a recess. It falls easily into my hands: a diary. The sound of voices prompts me to slip it into my waistband as my stomach turns to water. There are other secrets here. Fear must be ignored if I'm to find them.

Chapter 65

Monday, 15 August 2016

Matthew and Perry have gone to look at the campsite. They will call it 'Raven's Retreat'. Matthew winked when announcing the name; Perry has no idea of its meaning. They plan to open soon. The heated yurts have no seasonal limits and will be booked up until Christmas.

The pub in the hamlet of South Chewton is a mile's walk away. It's noted as a 'short ramble through dales of lush vegetation, complete with an excellent variety of England's many species of tree and shrubs'. They plan a fishing lake. I pray this project fails. Perry will put up 'no entry' signs but people will consider themselves temporary owners and will take little notice of boundaries. The paying of money implies entitlement. My complaint that strangers will wander across my land falls on deaf ears.

That they are getting on so well is a source of irritation, but their absence has enabled me to search the farm. The loft has yielded a set of letters from Thora to 'Frankie'. That he never destroyed them highlights his arrogance and reminds me of another arrogant man. Leaving something so incriminating tells of a sense of immunity from embarrassment or fear of discovery. Were they hidden when Elsie was alive? Maybe he sought some solace from them after Thora's death. Who am I to judge another's feelings when I have irrational ones myself? Maybe we all need an unattainable lover to keep us tortured but alive. Waiting for that exquisite moment when our heart's delight comes to us and completes us. That we will never be complete leaves us with the desire to keep hold of the dream. Reality is such a let-down.

While rummaging, I notice insurance papers for Laura. Her

insurance was not a surprise to Perry as he had taken it out three years before she died. Why lie about that? She died of an infection of her leg leading to sepsis. She delayed in getting help and then it was too late. Why didn't Perry take more care of her?

The diaries and letters, along with the newspaper cuttings, have shown me a new reality. The events at the time of Simon's death are clearer. Family life would not have been easy if they knew of the secret affair. That's why Simon died, I'm sure. The entries in his diary dated 1961 are clear:

I don't know what to do about the witch. I have tried to forget what I saw, but the image won't leave me. I can't sleep. Should I tell Perry? Should I tell Mum? I hate you, Father, for doing this to us! Why! Why! Why! She's just an old witch, and I hate her. HATE HATE HATE.

Then another:

Now I know about them it's so easy to spot the signs – the looks that passed between them when she brought the pie yesterday. He was gone for hours to replace a lightbulb. Does Mum know? Something passed through her eyes when she remarked he'd been a long time fixing the bulb. She turned away as he shrugged. How dare he hurt my mum. How dare he!

A few days later:

I have to tell Perry, but it will break his heart. He loves Mum dearly. I can't tell him. He mustn't know.

And:

I went to the witch's house today. She had a visitor. A young boy called Frankie. He's a bit younger than me I think. He was

268

in the garden, on the swing. He reminded me of me. The witch
came out to call him in for lunch, and my father appeared. They
stood together watching the boy then Father pushed him, making
him laugh. Made me sick.
  Father said he would tell me to come and cut the grass for
her. I'm not going to do that, and he can thrash me as much as
he wants. I will ask to board at school full time. Mum will let me,
if I say I need to for my studies. Mum mustn't find out the boy is
at the witch's in case she goes there. She'll see that he looks like
me. He looks more like me then Perry does. Perry looks like Mum.
They have the same black hair. I don't think Mum is my mum or
I would have black hair as well. I hate them all.

Simon's pain makes me cry. Betrayal attacks his sense of
home and security. He is floundering in the waters of teenage
hormones mixed with the reality of adult cruelty. He is finding
out that the only person you can rely on is yourself, and he is not
coping well with this truth. The last entry reads:
  I must tell Perry even though he's too young to understand. I
can't keep this to myself. Or better still I will tell Mum as she
needs to know. Or I will go to the witch and kill her. She deserves
to die for what she is doing to us.

He is beside himself with rage now, with no idea of which
way to turn. A few days later, he was dead. Mr Cutler, Frankie,
was having an affair with Thora. The photos confirm it. My
Frankie is the image of Mr Cutler. If he knew who his father was,
I'm sure Frankie would have told me. Thora invented the rape to
cover her duplicity. Perry knew I'm sure, and he would have
stopped Simon from telling their mother. Perry would not want
his mum upset and have their lives destroyed. She was probably
keeping knowledge of the affair to herself, but if Simon shouted
it from the rooftops, then she would have to address it. That
would have devastated them.

Someone is shouting and banging on the door.

'Mrs Cutler. Carol. Come quickly. Perry's had an accident and the ambulance is on its way.'

It's Louise. Grabbing my bag, we run and get into the jeep. 'They're in Spring Field. Matthew is with him, and a couple of the lads have gone along the top lane to show the ambulance where to go. Perry fell awkwardly from the tractor and lost consciousness, but he's regained it now.' She puts her foot down and we fly across the field.

'How do you know this?' I ask.

'Matthew phoned me. Are you okay?'

'Yes, of course.' Why didn't Matthew phone *me*? 'He's not badly hurt, is he?'

'I'm sure he'll be fine.' She pats my leg and I turn away to hide my disappointment.

Chapter 66

Tuesday, 16 August 2016

Perry stayed in hospital last night due to a concussion. He has broken a bone in his right forearm, but it should heal without complications. He's not happy that they have put on a cast. Luckily, he's left-handed. Matthew tells me how he fell off the tractor, but I tell him to shut up. He assures me he's not offended by my reluctance to know the details. Perry's still alive is all I need to know. He should be discharged later today, all being well for him. Not for me.

There is time to search through the loft and Simon's room again. Many assumptions about Perry's family tempt me to conclusions. I must take care to reach the correct ones. That Mr Cutler is Frankie's father is almost certain, but more proof will not harm.

The TV news tells me horror stories about killings and bombings, so I turn it off and take my sandwich upstairs to my study. As I finish eating, the front door bangs open, so I go and look down the stairs. Perry is heading for the kitchen, shouting my name. Fear freezes me, as I'm sure I put Simon's diary on the kitchen table before I made my lunch. As I stumble down the stairs, Matthew walks in through the open front door.

'Hi, Carol.'

'What are you doing here?'

'Nice to see you, too. Dropping Perry back. As soon as he gets changed, we're heading over to the site to check the plans.'

As we walk into the kitchen, Perry is standing transfixed, Simon's diary in his good hand. He looks up at me. This is not going to be pleasant, but I decide to speak first.

'Hi. You're back. I didn't expect you. You should have phoned …'

'Why bother you? You couldn't pick me up.'

'No, but I would have prepared lunch or something. So, you're okay …?'

'Not waiting until they could be bothered to discharge me.' He flicks through the pages in his hand.

'It's Simon's diary, isn't it? I haven't read it. Well, only the first pages. But when I realised what it was …'

'Where did you find it?'

'In Simon's room. Thought I'd clean it. You know how I hate dirt anywhere.' He regards me with horror pinching face.

'Don't go in there again. Get Matthew a coffee while I get changed.' He walks out with the diary, and a stream of cold air follows in his wake.

'Is something up?' Matthew looks worried. Perry has mostly hidden his contempt for me from others, but the pain has loosened the mask he wears to keep up the appearance of a loving husband.

'Nothing different from normal. Tea or coffee?'

'Whatever you want. You're going to be okay, aren't you?'

'Why wouldn't I be?' I turn and stare at him. 'He's got a broken arm so I should be fine for a while. Unless he forgets and uses it to hit me, but at least it may hurt him more than it hurts me.'

'Carol …' Matthew sits at the table floundering for words, then whispers: 'I don't know why you stay with him.'

'Nor do I. But he is my husband. He didn't force me to marry him.'

'But he shouldn't treat you like this.'

'Are you going to stop him?' I pour boiling water over instant coffee.

'No. Of course not. It's not down to me …'

'Are you going to stop working with him? Making money with him?'

'No … I can't. Everything's in place. The finance, the

partnership …'

'Exactly, Matthew.' Placing his coffee in front of him, I turn and walk out. 'See you later. Milk's in the fridge. You may have to go upstairs and help him when he realises he can't change his pants.'

Fear runs through my blood as always, but now the icy coldness has a tinge of fire. The loneliness of an empty house, with its creaking rooms and breathless air, I've accepted. The whispering coldness of my lover's eyes as he leaves my bed is a repeating dream I've tolerated. The four-in-the-morning night sweats when the devil visits, I've endured. Give me these things over marriage any day. I've learnt to fight my internal demons alone, but the external ones are perpetual. And the ones that come from a spouse – well there's no suitable rational response. Only the default of 'kill or be killed'. And I hope that I don't have to implement that one.

Chapter 67

Thursday, 25 August 2016

It's a day for celebration, and the air feels alive and fresh. Perry sits beside me as I drive us towards the lakes. His arm is still in plaster, and the bruising on his head and leg has turned all colours of the rainbow. My role as chauffeur both irritates and pleases him. He hates having to rely on me but loves to ridicule my driving. I'm allowed to drive him all the way to Chewton Upton today, as Matthew and Louise are busy.

Driving always gives me a buzz. The thrill and the freedom; the control it imparts; the independence gained. Holding power in my hands is exhilarating: the power to kill or be killed, stemming from the slightest error of judgement. There's a reason for my good spirits, for I've made a decision. A decision that makes me happy and, for once in a very long time, makes me feel that I'm in control of my life. The simplicity of the decision astounds me, and I wonder why I'd not thought of it before. Positive energy floods me; I'm reborn. My years as a prisoner, confined to a life locked inside my head, are at an end.

Until today, I've been unable to stand up and shout out, 'I have been wronged, and I have done wrong,' and let the world judge me. For if I had not allowed Frankie to crush me, then I would have retained my independence. Then used my intellect to mitigate my shortcomings.

A gospel reading comes to mind: 'The truth will make you free …'

As a child, I questioned how something intangible could impact something tangible. Lately, I've discovered a truth. A truth that broke the invisible chains binding me – and now my new life beckons. The truth has set me free. The answer was within my grasp all along.

Happily driving towards the lakes, the sun shines, trees sway, and ahead we will see the beautiful expanse of sparkling blue water, a breathing body of birds and fish and sailors. A part of heaven here on earth. To take certain steps on my journey requires answers to difficult questions. Perry needs to answer questions even though he wants to forget. Forgetting the past will have to wait awhile. Drawing upon my shallow reserves of bravery, it's time to clear the air. If he truly loves me, Perry will appreciate that I need to do this to ratify my decision.

A shudder of nerves and exhilaration rises as I begin. 'Schmidt didn't kill Frankie.'

Perry turns from gazing at the scenery.

'Don't be stupid, Carol. He was the only one who could have killed him. Or did you spend these last months convincing me that you couldn't have done it to see if I'd fall for the lie? Are you saying that it was you who chopped off his head while seven months pregnant? Why are you dragging this up again, for God's sake?'

'I still feel that he didn't, even though I convinced myself that he must have. Or that child. That child was a boy. Schmidt liked girls.'

'You need to stop this now. You're a bloody lunatic.'

'It seems so wrong, him killing a boy. He never went near boys.'

Perry turns, and I glance around. His gaze unnerves me.

'What does it matter? Girls, boys, it's all the same. He liked children. It's all done and dusted. Schmidt is dead. We're free. *You're* free. You don't have to worry about this anymore. You're free of that bloody Frankie.' His angry words are measured.

'But I *was* free. I was free when Frankie was alive and when Frankie died. I was already free, Perry.'

'What are you on about? Schmidt killed Frankie. If he didn't kill Frankie, then you did. I can't believe anything you say. We've been living in hell for years because of this. Because of

275

what Schmidt did, or you did. Frankly, I don't bloody care anymore – except for my part in this sorry mess. Covering up for you was not the best decision I've made.'

'But you didn't cover up for me, did you?'

'What the fuck is wrong with you, woman? Have you gone insane?'

He's angry now. I need to calm him. 'No … I'm sorry, Perry. Maybe it's all these drugs I take.' I pause. 'This is a huge change for me.

I have appeased him, but I have planted a seed that tells him I don't believe Schmidt did it. He could see that the mess Frankie's body was in must have taken some real force and energy, much more than I had at the time. He has registered my words and no amount of backtracking will stop it growing. He'll be assessing this. How long am I safe as his wife now? How long before he understands that I've worked out who killed Frankie?

'You need to stop thinking about it. Let it go. We have a life together now. Maybe go abroad for a holiday. Matthew knows some great places in France.' He rubs my leg. 'And if you feel you need something, counselling or anything … well, we can get you whatever, the best money can buy.'

'Thank you, Perry. You're so kind to me. You have always been kind to me. Watching over me, protecting me from other men, keeping me locked away in Oaktree House.'

His head snaps around. 'Now what are you saying? I never kept you locked away. You kept yourself locked away. It was you who didn't want to venture out into the world. You who didn't seek help. Don't fucking start blaming me for your insanity. I *helped* you.'

'Oh yes, Perry. You have always helped me. But as my keeper.'

'Your keeper?'

'Yes, my keeper.'

'Right! That's it! I've had enough of this. Pull over now. I'll call someone to drive me the rest of the way. You need to take

some diazepam or something. I'm going to phone your doctor.
You're going into a mental crisis again. You need help, Carol.
I'll get you help.'

'Okay, Perry. I'll pull into the lay-by on the other side of the
lake where there's plenty of room. I don't want to make any
uncomfortable moves at the moment. Is that okay?'

'Fine. Just calm down.' He fumbles for his phone but can't
locate it.

'I'm fine, Perry. I couldn't be happier. For once in my life I'm
in control.' Perry grunts so I continue. 'Do you want to know
why I said Schmidt didn't kill Frankie?' He says nothing. 'I'll
tell you, so you understand my reasoning.'

'Go on then, but watch the road.'

'Well, as we know, Frankie was chopped up … decapitated,
and there must have been a lot of blood.'

'Yes, there was.'

'Yes … exactly. You cleared it up. I didn't see the state of the
garden. That always niggled me; the fact that the garden was
soaked for days, and not just where Frankie had been lying. So
much blood to clean up, and yet *I* wasn't covered in blood.'

'What do you mean?'

'If I had decapitated Frankie and chopped him up, I would
have been soaked in his blood. But I wasn't. I was seven months'
pregnant, and you never thought it odd at the time.'

'For fuck's sake! I don't have a bloody clue what I was
thinking at the time. Apart from keeping us out of prison. What
does that prove? That I didn't think about how much blood there
was or wasn't? I was eighteen!'

'It proves you knew I didn't kill Frankie.'

'You're mad. You did kill Frankie. You know you did. I'm
just humouring you by pretending to agree that Schmidt did.
Schmidt just killed the kiddie.'

'I didn't kill Frankie. He was alive when I left him. Yes, I was
responsible for him chopping into his leg. And I abandoned him.

But he was alive. I thought he'd bled and died from that wound. But he didn't, did he?'

'Then Schmidt killed Frankie. He'd reason to, that's for sure; Frankie was blackmailing him about the kiddies, the paedo thing. He wanted him dead; he'd motive. Anyway, one of you did, and I no longer give a fuck which one of you it was.'

'When you saw the garden, the carnage, you didn't ask me how I did it. You would have rationalised that a heavily pregnant woman with hardly any blood on her couldn't have repeatedly lifted an axe and chopped up … um …. But you didn't need to figure that out because *you* killed Frankie. If Schmidt had killed him, you would have called the police. There would have been proof. But you didn't. You let me believe I had killed him because it suited you.'

Perry is silent. Fear of what he'll do flows through me. I'm not safe with him. I'm dead if I return to our empty house. He's planning to kill me now, but I continue.

'And you had a motive.' Ahead is the lake, where the water laps next to the road. 'You killed him to stop him from ruining your life.'

'I'm not capable of killing anyone. You know that, Carol.' His clenched fist betrays the tension in him, white knuckles like a skeleton's bones.

'Ah, but you are. You killed your brother, too. So you have killed both of your brothers.'

'*What!* What do you mean, *both* brothers?' Perry turns again to look at me. He's going to hit me or grab me. We have reached the lake road, where there's no barrier separating us from the water. I estimate we're a few minutes away from the place in the road where I have decided we will die. I can accelerate if I need to.

'I read Simon's diary. I also found letters written by your father. Your father was Frankie's father. He was sleeping with Thora, having an affair. Did you sneak about and watch them,

Perry? Did you see them together in Thora's bed like Simon says you did?'

The air between us quivers with violent waves of hatred that fill me with dread and resign me to my fate. He has not reacted, for fear of us crashing. Perry will not chance any damage to a single hair on his head.

'Your brother's diaries told me all I needed to know about you. You liked to torture small animals. Did you get pleasure from that? Or was it, as I suspect, that you felt nothing? You feel nothing for anyone or anything; you have no soul. Was that why Simon was afraid of you? Was that why you drowned him? Or was it because he was going to tell your mother about Thora? And then another brother arrives to interfere with your inheritance. Did Frankie want money from your father? Did he blackmail him?'

Perry sits in stunned silence, his arm resting on his chest. My knowledge breaks his hold on me. He cannot control me any more now that I know his secrets. But there's no way he'll relinquish his power, so he will have to kill me.

'You miserable fucking bitch. I'll have you committed forever for this. Spreading lies about my family. How dare you. You're just a common slut from the council estate. A dragged-up madam who dares to put on airs and graces. Stop right now! Stop!' He throws his arm and smacks the back of his hand into my face. My nose bleeds. I taste metal at the back of my mouth.

'Oh, we're going home, Perry. We've just arrived.' I press his seat belt release as I floor the accelerator and head off the road into the lake. We fly for a moment, suspended in time until the deep water rushes to meet us. In our remaining seconds, I scream, 'I'll see you in hell, Perry.'

Chapter 68

Monday, 19 September 2016

My psychiatrists insinuate that I'm a victim of others: manipulated by their egos and desires. I'm not sure of that. I have needs of my own; my ego demands its own pleasures. Perhaps I have confused my wants with my needs. Don't we live in a world with ways to facilitate your choices? Who can say which of us makes the righteous ones?

This time, my hospital stay is not at Maytree but an ordinary hospital for sane people. Initially I was comatose in the intensive care unit, but now I languish in the hive of activity and never-ending light that is a hospital ward. My spinal cord is intact but compromised. Breaking bones in your neck and spine doesn't necessarily leave you paralysed. My surgical and ongoing care has been, and is, excellent. It's as well they do not realise they're saving the life of a killer.

Perry is dead, so at least he'll not be able to break any more of my bones. I should feel something about this – guilt for his murder; grief about his loss. But there's nothing but relief now the stress of living with him has gone. I will not return to Cleave Farm because it is not my home and will stink of him.

My consultant asked me why my rib and arm have healing fractures and how I had acquired them. My story about attempting to ride a horse fell apart upon deeper probing. Admitting to being a victim of spousal abuse is like releasing a dirty secret to the world. Your compliance makes you an accomplice and robs you of your dignity. They had records of my broken bones, the bash to my head when I tripped in the garden, and the burns to my hand when I misjudged the pan of boiling water. All this, coupled with the fact that he caused the accident when he lost his temper and hit me in the face. No wonder I lost control and drove into the lake.

Yesterday, the two sixteen-year-old boys who braved the cold water to save me came to visit. The local newspaper wanted a photo. The dynamic duo are being put forward for bravery awards. One of them was excited, but the other was quiet and barely spoke as he slouched into his hoodie. His shaking hands and nervously tapping foot, along with his reluctance to speak, made me feel sorry for him. Neither had seen a dead body before. To see one that had smashed through a windscreen had been a fascinating horror for them.

Killing Perry should incite panic attacks in me. But the fact that I am a murderer and have taken a life seems to create no further impact on my mental health. It's as though I have already spent my life paying for my sins and have completed my penance. Or it may be that morphine, sleeping tablets and anti-depressants have neutralised my guilt receptors. Years of various mind-numbing medications have to bring some positive benefits.

Today Matthew will take me home. Not to Oaktree House, though, as I cannot physically cope there. He wants me to move in with him. His front sitting room has been converted into a bedroom. My wheelchair can move around the ground floor and out into the garden. The utility room is now a shower room. He has declined my offer to pay for the expense, and I'm a little uneasy as to why he has gone out of his way to accommodate me. That I can communicate with anyone at any time, thanks to the internet and my smartphone, helps to convince me I will be fine there. Without those, I would not move in. There is no way I am going to become a prisoner again.

The business survived, with Matthew and Louise running things until I regained consciousness. I've confirmed them as managers long term. Louise has been a godsend, and I have forgiven her for any designs she may have had on my husband. She'd better not transfer her desire to Matthew.

Matthew arrives on the dot of visiting hours every day even

though they do not keep the timings strict. I must confess my sins to him. Surviving death has made me strong. I appreciate that God, or the devil, has spared me to allow me to atone for my sins before my final goodbye.

He kisses my cheek and asks how I am before settling onto the chair. As usual, he has brought us giant takeaway lattes and chocolate shortbread. He picks up his cup and salutes, 'Cheers,' with a nod of the head before saying, 'Guess what? Louise and Emily got married last weekend. They kept that a secret didn't they! Nice that they can make things legal after all these years.'

'Louise and Emily? You mean a joint wedding?'

'Louise and Emily got married. To each other. You look pale. Are you okay?'

'Yes. I'm fine. It's a bit of a, um, shock. I didn't know they were ... together.'

'You didn't know? I'm not sure how you could have missed it.'

'I don't get involved with the staff. I wouldn't be interested in their, um ... relationship.' I was sure Emily was flirting with Parry that day. Why did I not see that she wasn't?

Matthew picks up his coffee, puzzled at my response. 'Anyway, everything is going well. Nothing bad to report. Your solicitor wants to see you, but I told him you're not well enough yet.'

'Don't do that, Matthew.'

He jumps at my anger and sloshes his drink. 'Do what?'

'Speak for me. What you should have done is ask him to call my mobile and ask me. I'm fed up with men talking around me, over me, without me, as though I'm invisible.'

'We're not all like Perry,' he says, but sees that I'm not convinced. 'Sorry ... I was just looking out for you. I thought –'

'But you don't *have* to think, do you? If I'm too unwell to deal with Hamilton, I can tell him myself and arrange things myself. And yes, you're doing what Perry did – and guess what happened to him.'

Matthew looks around to see if anyone has heard me. 'That's not funny, Carol.'

'It wasn't meant to be. He started small, you know. He didn't wade in, guns blazing, in the beginning, or he would have frightened me off. You know Perry abused me, and you were appalled when I told you the full extent of it, yet here you are at the thin edge of the wedge, doing the same thing.'

'That's unfair. I'm taking care of you, saving you the stress of things.'

He's offended, but I don't care. I'm no longer in the mood for pussyfooting around. 'I know you have good intentions but what you are doing is taking my power and control away. That was fine when I was in a coma, but it's not the case now. If we are to live together, you must stop "taking care" of my life for me.' Before he replies, I add, 'I have something important to tell you before I move into your home. You may change your mind when you hear it.' My coffee is hot, but I sip it anyway while I drum up the courage. 'Perry and I killed Frankie.'

'What?' He puts his shortbread back on the paper serviette on the bedside chest.

'And I killed Perry.'

His head snaps around to look at me. 'Are you feeling all right? You are pale. Shall I call a nurse?'

'I'm fine. I needed to tell you. I couldn't hold onto it any longer. Perry and I shared our secret all this time, and now he's dead there's no one to …' Shrugging, I pick up my shortbread and eat. Matthew watches me; his foot taps nervously on the floor as he considers what to say.

'Schmidt killed Frankie. The police had plenty of evidence, and he'd be convicted if he'd lived.' His look is challenging, as though he dares me to contradict him. 'Are you saying the pair of you killed the boy as well?'

He's sitting so far forward on his chair that I think he may slip off.

'No. Perry killed the boy. I have evidence. Schmidt liked girls. He would never touch a boy.'

Matthew sits back, repulsed, and his arm knocks his coffee, but it doesn't fall. 'Let's not talk about this here. Wait until you get home.'

'You don't mind taking in a killer?'

'You're not a killer. You're just mixed up. Your skull has a tiny fracture, and they warned that you might have memory loss. You need to forget these strange thoughts and rest.'

'Will you tell my doctor?'

'No.' His reply is quick, although I know he suspects some truth in my confession.

'Are you sure you want me to move in?'

'Of course I do. You can't move into Oaktree on your own.'

'I have enough money to hire nurses, whoever I need.'

'It's not the same. You need to feel safe. You need someone to take proper care of you. Have you read the dreadful newspaper stories? Carers stealing money, leaving the disabled sitting in their excrement, starving? Anyway, you'll still have nursing care, but under my supervision.'

I don't argue the point. He takes my hand and strokes it just as my consultant arrives to cast a judgmental eye over our affectionate behaviour. He will think I deserved Perry's abuse as I'm a flirt, and that a firm hand is therefore needed to keep me in line. He'll have no problem discharging me.

The girl inside has settled down in her box and rests peacefully.

Chapter 69

Friday, 21 October 2016

Perry's estate is proving problematic as his will doesn't leave everything to me. Hamilton is arranging for the trust to buy a big part of his land so that his other benefactors, and the taxman, can have their cut. We will obtain it cheaply, as the trust owns many access roads and a stream that cuts through Perry's land. This restricts or denies access to any potential new owner and makes the property worthless. I do not want the land sold for housing, so have told Hamilton to do whatever is necessary. I need a different solicitor to deal with my inheritance as it conflicts with the trust.

The business has to close, since it is not a viable proposition, for the same reasons of access. The business is not free to cross my land. Afterwards, though, I will start it up again and employ the same people to do the same as they were doing. It's a shame to see it go to waste. I've offered an experienced organic farmer the manager's role, and Emily will run the lavender side again. Unfortunately for Matthew, the yurt business has died a death through my lack of interest. He's strangely uninterested in it himself and didn't push for his investment cash back. Nevertheless, I've refunded him.

***

Matthew and I went to the Oaktree Inn for our usual Friday night meal. I'd discovered that my initial nerves about going to this new place are banished now that we have been here many times. The place is old-fashioned and boring; filled with middle-class oldies. I conclude that people are not having as much fun as I'd imagined. They eat, staring at anything other than their companions, then order more wine. Perhaps I have not missed out on much over the years I'd locked myself away from civilisation. I'd been spared a bored spouse and an expensive alcohol bill.

It rained hard today, and I wanted to say *let's not go* but didn't want to annoy him. People leave me alone now they've had their fill of newspaper reports of my terrible accident. Strangers are sorry for my loss; I'm repeatedly assured.

The rain stops by the time we pull back onto the drive. While I wait for my bones to adjust to standing, I think about my other house, almost completed, less than a mile away. I can move in soon.

Hobbling across the threshold on one crutch, the failings in our relationship that I'd noticed hit through once again. The physical gap between us, the tapping fingers, the willingness to please at the moment but not in the long term. There is no long term. No plans, no holidays, no meeting of the family, no future. That I ignore these facts intrigues me. I'm a glutton for punishment and deserving of derision. He has acknowledged that I am a killer, albeit justified. He will throw me out as soon as it seems respectable. The impulse to run and hide surges and I beat it down with my sense of respect for the hospitality he's extended to me.

He has opened a bottle of wine by the time I walk into the sitting room. As soon as I can stop these painkillers, I'll be joining him. I've developed a taste for the few small glasses of excellent French wine I've had. The television is on and he finds a film, so we settle back. He pours himself another large glass. The action triggers the insight that he has been drinking excessively. He has to abstain because he drives, so he starts knocking it back when we return. Perhaps he drinks to make the evenings and nights with me more bearable. I glance at him as he raises his glass to his lips, and as if he knows what I'm thinking, he says, 'Cheers,' and winks. He pours a half glass and hands it to me, saying, 'It won't harm.'

'Perry was a beer drinker.' I take a sip. 'Not that he got too

drunk. He stayed just sober enough to know what he was doing ...
Sorry – I don't know why I said that.'

'You don't have to worry. Talk about him. Tell me anything
you want. It's the best thing to do to recover from the shock of
death.'

'I don't know if that's true.' I swallow a mouthful. This will
help me sleep.

'You need to talk about them. The dead. You talked about
your dad a lot according to Sarah's diary.'

'Did I? I don't remember.' I must find her diary and read it.
There must be a way of getting the key to his study.

'And none worse than sudden death. When your dad killed
himself, I couldn't understand it: that someone could do that
deliberately. But I was only, what, ten? So long ago. But the
shock that went through your mother, your brothers. They were
right to protect you from it at the time, don't you think?'

My glass drops from my hand, the red wine spills over my
dress and cascades to the floor.

'My God. They never told you? Please, don't tell me you
didn't know. Oh, Carol, I'm so sorry.'

His hands wave around me, then there's pressure as the side
of my face is pressed into his shoulder.

'Sammy said they would tell you when you were older. God,
I can't believe they kept it from you. Why would they do that?
Why, when ... when ... well, when this can happen, has
happened.'

He pulls me in tighter, and I yelp as pain shoots through my
shoulders and spine. There is a large red stain on his cream carpet.

'You need to get some paper towel and soak that up," I say.
"And water, I think, to stop it from setting. And then, or is it
white wine, put white wine on it before –'

'Stop fussing.'

'But you have to act fast or it will be ruined.'

He pulls me gently to my feet and leads me out of the room.

We reach his bedroom and walk until my leg hits the bed.

'Sleep here tonight.'

He pulls my jumper over my head; the resulting pain flows and is comforting in its normality. His hands hesitate in front of my bra. 'I'll leave you; I'll go downstairs for a bit. Sort that wine stain out.'

Sitting on the bed, shimmying out of my clothes, I pull my legs up and carefully shuffle my bottom until I can slide naked under the duvet. I'll need the toilet and water for my painkillers. It will be too hot in here later, but I'll leave when I'm woken by the usual night terrors. The gates of hell often open to lure me into the deep darkness of the night.

He gets into bed and I stiffen, expecting more talking, more apologies, more confirmation that I am a bit player in my own life. Other people know more about who I am, where I am, why I am. They know what's best for me and I should accept that to keep the status quo.

His breathing is steady. He's not asleep. Maybe we will lie awake all night, side by side, unable to cross the gulf between us. My father killed himself. I toy with the words, considering again if, on some deeper level, I knew; that the truth had been festering away like an abscess.

'How?'

'He hanged himself.'

'Mum said he had a heart attack.'

'She was protecting you. I'm sorry …'

'Don't. Don't tell me.'

'I could have checked, Carol, sounded you out. I feel for you ...'

'But you don't love me.'

He turns and tries to snake his arm around my stiff body, before leaving it crooked above my head.

'No. I don't think I do. I thought I might. Especially remembering how we were when … when Sarah died.'

Relief sits between us. We don't love each other. We can stop now.

This last week we had stumbled through awkward sex that I hadn't felt physically well enough for but was afraid of losing him. Losing him meant losing my last tie to my past and history. Without him, there was no one left, and I'd be truly alone. It was a miracle that he'd come back into my life. Now I need to keep him as a friend.

'Why did you come back? You love France. Why move back?'

'Chrissie and the children.'

'You never see them.' He takes an exasperated breath and removes his arm. 'Well, I've been busy: your recovery, renovating this house.'

It's not true. He doesn't phone them. They have never visited. 'I forgot. I'm selfish taking all your time.'

'What's that supposed to mean?'

'Sorry – I didn't mean it like that. I'm grateful to you. You know that, Matthew. I wouldn't be this fit and healthy if it wasn't for you.'

'And that's saying something.' He laughs and touches my cheek and we laugh together, enjoying some common ground, relieving the tension. He has changed the subject. Before I can ask him when he will see Chrissie, he says, 'Don't let what happened with your dad set you back, Carol. You're doing so well. I would hate to have done anything to hurt you. Please say you'll be okay. Please say you forgive me.'

He's crying. I turn and take him in my arms as his body quakes with giant sobs. Minutes pass, my shoulder is hot and wet; the weight of him aching my ribs. I decide to go home. The new Oaktree House may not be home yet, but, like the time after Frankie died, it won't take long to settle. I want it enough to make it happen.

Chapter 70

Monday, 7 November 2016

Autumn comforts with its colours and fullness. The promise of warm fires and family gatherings enter everyone's thoughts. Matthew comes back swearing about the bloody 'C' word; that it's too soon, for Christ's sake. The Christmas build-up has started. I'm looking forward to moving out and going home – a New Year in the new Oaktree House. It will be mine alone, my home and my refuge, just like before. There will be no history and no ghosts living there. Lily has arranged for a comprehensive clean. The garden is laid out to my plans, right down to the new orchard with the bench in remembrance of Frankie. The sun will rise and set at different points, but the garden has a more southerly aspect. New shrubs will fill the borders.

Matthew doesn't know I'm leaving. The void between us gapes wide after his tactless words about my father's death. No one who loves someone would have done that. Besides, no matter how much I'd wanted us to be a couple, there's no chemistry. He's pleasant and affectionate, and we have a short history that bonds us, but passion eludes us. His kindness for taking me in requires that I release him from any further obligation towards me.

The wheelchair is long gone, and I can manage with one crutch. My bones have healed, and my physiotherapy is working. What the human body can repair is amazing. Peak fitness is good for the body and the mind. Gardening, baking and cleaning the house will be my daily routine once again. My legs are strong and I want to drive, but Matthew has taken the garage keys with him to Cleave Farm.

The flowers I've gathered for my father's grave are wilting

on the draining board, so I put them in fresh water. The cemetery sits on the outskirts, high above the city. We shall go there tomorrow.

The day stretches ahead devoid of medication. My doctor says I cannot have any more opiates and must rely on aspirin or paracetamol. Matthew is here so often that he could intercept deliveries from any online ordering, and start conversations about package contents that I'd rather not have. The frustration is too much; there must be a spare set of garage keys somewhere.

Matthew's bedroom is tidy: the quilt pulled back to air the bed and a small window open. Keys aren't in the obvious places. In the bedroom-cum-office at the back, I glance around the pale oak furniture. The desk drawers are locked, but a cupboard door catches my eye. It's ajar.

Packed on the shelves are boxes of Sarah's things. My skin crawls as bad memories return. I wish I hadn't seen them. Keeping my thoughts away from those old times helps me stay sane. Now light shines onto those feelings once again. My fingers touch her cardigan, then the white stretchy bag. She walks away from me complaining that I will shoot her with Mr Cutler's rifle. Thora's car backfires as it drives into view. A taste of bark and sour apples catches in the back of my throat. An autumn breeze has a chill edging its sunlit warmth. The past slides into view, and I'm back where it began, where life unravelled. If we hadn't gone scrumping that day; if Thora's car hadn't broken down. If I hadn't met Frankie. If I had been older and Matthew had asked me out on a date after Paula died.

A tsunami of failures swirls as I drop carefully to my knees. All the mistakes, the bad choices, bad hormones and bad decisions. One disaster after another. Crawling, I edge towards the door but don't have the strength, so I lie exhausted next to the desk chair. There's nothing to be done as I slip into my comfort-blanket of dejection and nestle in its familiar comfort.

A key is stuck under the seat of the chair. It glints at me like a hidden jewel. Why hide a key there? Before I pull it off, I check for a roll of tape so I can stick it back there when I've finished. It slides easily into the lock of the desk and turns to release the drawers – chequebook stubs, accounts books, invoices, bank and credit card statements. Matthew is reassuringly wealthy and boring. A pile of paperwork written in French, stamped with official ink from town hall offices. His old passports, euros, and ticket stubs tied in elastic bands. In the bottom drawer is a locked metal box, the sort for keeping important paperwork fire-safe, yet his passport and cash lie loose in the other drawers. The key is in the corner of the drawer. I unlock the box.

Sarah's diaries are inside, along with several letters addressed to Matthew. At the bottom is one addressed to me. It has zigzag lines around the edges of the envelope, our code for top-secret and urgent. We used curvy lines for notes about boys and circles for anything else.

The opened letter has its flap pushed back in. I don't remember it – have I simply forgotten what she wrote? And why keep it? We always destroyed all our letters to shreds after reading, as if they contained State secrets and not our girlish observations on life. A feeling of dread makes my heart flutter, and I take a breath, debating whether I should read it.

Sarah's bedroom comes flooding back. That day after her death. The day I sought solace in the familiarity of her room when my world had imploded. A letter slid into my waistband and forgotten. Passion for Matthew erasing all thought of it. Is this the same letter? Pulling it out, her words speak to me; her truth flows into me.

My world crashes as the entire foundation of my life crumbles away. The floor rushes up to meet me and sends a crack-thud through my left shoulder. It shudders through my arm and chest, stopping and restarting my heart.

The shattering truth explodes and opens blood vessels, making me dizzy. A blinding light shines into the recesses of my mind. This old piece of paper from that other world, that other continent, sits like gelignite on the floor. Dare to move. Dare to allow time to tick on. Stay here, in this spot, forever. Stop my thoughts from injuring me with their kaleidoscope of knowledge.

What is the point of knowing this truth when it cannot change what's happened? Too much of my life has gone. That this letter could have saved me from a miserable life cannot be contemplated. Dare not be contemplated.

Sarah, my friend, my confidant, would not write this if it were not true. That she did for our friendship, for our sisterhood, makes me feel small and unworthy. I did not extend any consideration towards her. I hated her for what she did to me in stealing Frankie.

What gave Matthew the right to deny me the truth? And to continue to deny me when he knows how my part in Frankie's death has restricted my life and doomed me to be an outcast. How dare he keep this from me? Here I am again, unable to function. That I have taken the blame for other people's deceitfulness and secrets, rankles. And that Matthew knew the truth but was happy for me to believe a lie.

This is why he keeps on about how brutal Perry was. How he deserved everything he got. How I should get a medal for getting rid of him. Why he keeps me focused on Perry's guilt; why he's now sure that Perry killed Frankie.

As I gather up the papers, some photos slide out of an envelope. Turning one this way and that, I try to make out what the subject is. I flick to the next. These are polaroids of a naked girl. I have been staring at a close-up of her genitals. The girl is Sarah.

Shuffling along to the bathroom, I vomit as soon as the toilet seat is up. Those photos are of Frankie's bedroom, but my Frankie couldn't have taken those. He knows girls like to keep their mystique and privacy. When he asked to take a photo of me topless for a keepsake I'd told him not to be silly. If he wanted to see my breasts, he could see them any day in the flesh. Sarah in her weakened state allowed him to overrule and undermine her sense of dignity. She was a fool, after all. There is a limit to the degree you allow men to walk over you. That limit had announced itself to me with fatal consequences. The problem is, what should be done to settle old scores and attain fairness? No one but me will benefit from the comfort of justice. No one will bother on my behalf. I must rest and decide what to do. I must not act in haste and ruin my life again.

Chapter 71

Friday, 25 November 2016

In Matthew's study, I search for Sarah's diary for 1970. Her words had helped the police to charge Schmidt, but now I'm sure Matthew did not give the whole of her diary to them. The pages after mid-December have been torn out. Matthew has used me. He didn't return home to be near Chrissie. He did not refurbish his house at great expense out of any sense of love or compassion for me. He's not comforting a woman deserving of love and affection. I'm a scapegoat, a stooge, a convenience to ease his life and sense of family honour.

A reason to mitigate my rage eludes me as I pace the floor. Blood vessels will burst if I don't calm down. A way to avenge the damage he has done to me thrusts itself towards my hands; I wring and clench them in a symphony of frustration. The only answer is destruction. The only resolution is annihilation. It's time to end it all. This time I'll do something better than I did with Perry. This time I'll make sure we both go. For now, diazepam will calm me enough until I form a plan. My secret stash must be used.

Chapter 72

Monday, 28 November 2016

Waking from a heavy sleep that has lasted most of the weekend, the sixteen-year-old girl inside me is emerging. She pushes, pulls, and stamps her feet in a tantrum. She frets and tells tales of unfairness and injustice. People fail to perform the necessary kindnesses; to provide the support that will ease her life. She curses the world and blames it for her situation while seeking absolution from her sins. She hides from the truth and shrinks from blame. It's painful to ignore her as she blasphemes and cajoles me, seeking my favour and cursing my indifference. She seeps from the box deep inside me; the fight to control her zaps my strength.

She will never leave me. She demands obedience and is canny and persuasive. Vindication that she is winning comes when the sweet taste of her proposition for vengeance flows like nectar through my brain. So I take up arms, unable to resist as she whispers seductively in my ear. Separation is not an option for us; we can only live a short time apart, but in the end we will die together. For we both know that if you want something badly enough you have to focus on making it happen.

Once again I read Sarah's coded letter. Why did she use such simple code? Matthew read it easily then kept it from me. Matthew ruined my life. *The girl*, boxed-in and stifled, becomes distressed at this injustice. She punches my heart and restricts my lungs. She demands retribution and honesty. Her relentlessness stops me from sleeping, and I meander through his home like a zombie.

Matthew has noticed how withdrawn I've become, but unlike Perry, he's afraid to call my doctor. My blaming my inability to perform any duties on exhaustion and withdrawal from painkillers seems to placate him. *The girl* will have none of my resistance. Her anger reaches a crescendo as she whooshes in like a banshee until I give in and fetch the twelve-bore.

Matthew is at the farm and will return soon. When he does, he will head straight to the kitchen and switch on the kettle. Opening the door to my room, I sit and wait, the loaded gun heavy across my lap. *The Girl* is happier now, although she prods me to ensure complete conformity to her will.

She tells the truth. He could have told me. He had plenty of time to tell me. He felt that the truth was his to keep and not to share. I would have kept it secret. I know how to keep a secret. What made him think he was the master of my sanity? What gave him the right to deny me the secret justice I would gain and deserve?

Tyres crunch on the drive. He's back. I follow him to the kitchen and stand against the island. The loaded gun clicks shut, and I test its weight against my shoulder. This is going to hurt, but not for long.

'Hi, Carol … What are you doing?'

'I found the letter. Sarah's letter. You should have given it to me. And photos of her naked. You're sick.'

'Hang on. Wait a minute. I didn't take those. What do you take me for? You know me. I would never –'

'I don't know you at all, though, do I. What man would let his … friend … the woman he now lives with, has made love to, think she had killed someone? Let her live for years with guilt. Let her ruin her life locking herself away …'

'Oh no … no, no, it wasn't like that. I didn't know that. How was I supposed to know you thought you'd killed him?

He takes a step towards me, but I pull the gun up and aim, so he steps back.

'That letter was mine. You should have given it to me. You had no right to keep it from me. At least you could have given it to me when they found Frankie. You could have told me the truth then.' His chest sits in my sights as I lift the gun and pull back my shoulders, balancing, my feet apart.

'Carol. Please don't. I would have told you if I had to. Please believe me. That's why I came back after they found him. I would never have let you go to prison ...'

'Go to prison? I've been in prison all my life. I thought I'd killed him! Then I convinced myself that Schmidt had killed him. Then that Perry had killed him.'

'You thought Perry killed him? Is that why ...?'

'Yes! I killed Perry because I thought that. Not because he abused me. I thought I deserved his abuse because I thought I'd helped Frankie's killer. I maimed him, leaving him ready for his real killer to take advantage. The thought that he killed Frankie – have you any idea what my life has been like? And you came back here cosying up to us. That's what you were doing, isn't it? The Yurt business was just an excuse. Pretending you had feelings for me when you were perverting the course of justice.'

'Don't take that high-and-mighty line when you were happy to see Schmidt go down for it. You made sure you did everything you could. And so did I. I gave the police Sarah's diary with details of Frankie and Schmidt, their meetings, money changing hands. I had to read that sick bollocks.'

'And the photos?'

'Frankie got Sarah drunk and took those. Sold them to Schmidt.'

'Then why do you have them? Why haven't you destroyed them?' The gun is heavy. I lower it to rest my elbow on my hip.

'Destroy them? They were evidence. Just in case, but God knows I couldn't hand them to the police. Schmidt taunted me with them, so I got them back. Went to his house and beat the shit out of him. Nearly killed the bastard. It was in the papers. They never found his assailant, because they didn't look too hard for a nonce-beater.'

For a moment I see the concerned brother, the hero, the man

who should have put everything right.

But then he says, 'Have you any idea what *my* life has been like?' And I remember his stories of his wealth from the campsite, the travel around the world.

And then he said, 'Anyway, what does any of it matter? Frankie was no great loss to anyone. Least of all you and Sarah. You did okay. You had all that money and Oaktree Estate. You were well sorted.'

The girl roars into life. She floods me with indignation that no one had protected me, no brother, no mother or friend had come to my aid. Cast adrift and left to survive because they all thought I had money – as if money would take care of me. Money was never my aim. A husband, a family, and a life as comfortable as Thora's. A normal, happy, family life. That was what I wanted. Matthew saw a woman surrounded by wealth yet clearly unhappy and failed to do the one thing that would help her. He has no interest in my welfare, and that's what was missing in our relationship. He failed to put my needs before his own. He strung me along keeping me from the truth. If he had loved me, he would have told me the truth to let me spend my dying days released from my torment and guilt. He had the power to make me happy, yet he denied me that.

My ears ring as he slumps to the floor. Blood spurts behind him, covering the wall and the floor. I waver, considering whether I should empty the second barrel into him. My shoulder is damaged, and my ears will suffer, but I step closer and do so anyway. To make sure. So it will be clear that I intended him dead. Not an accidental shot from tripping over my feet, or a tightening of the finger in rage: a mad moment head fit. Revenge served cold and efficient.

Chapter 73

Monday, 28 November 2016

It's taken me a lifetime to reach the oak tree where Sarah died. A lifetime since Frankie arrived and changed my life forever. A lifetime since my heart overruled my head about where my life should lead; a lifetime since Sarah said he was too old for me, and that she didn't like his long girly hair; a lifetime since I'd read that letter on my first visit to Oaktree House, the one that told Thora that Frankie knew he was her son.

At the edge of Dawnview Wood, the city spreads out below the hills, and I stand to enjoy one last reminiscence of that time long ago before I sit under the oak tree. The sky is clear, and the air is fresh with a swirling breeze from the south-west. It's another beautiful day here on earth.

Boxes of my tablets lie beside one of the giant roots supporting this magnificent tree. My choice of vodka instead of gin makes me chuckle in a manic guffaw. In my distress, I considered the effects of a hangover when choosing the liquor to help me leave this place. Failing to assemble truth and reality even this late in my life is further proof of my hopelessness. The ground is cold beneath my thin skirt. My clothes need to soak in cold water to remove Matthew's blood before washing. I'm good at some things, but not the important things.

My dad told me I was good at everything. I know he was wrong. Did he know that, too? Or did he die believing that I was his perfect little girl, his princess? His choice aches deep in my heart, but it was his choice. He's allowed that at least, for life was not kind to him; it had been tough for him to deal with the bad thoughts in his head.

Frankie is dead. Perry is dead. Matthew is dead.

It's a waste of time musing about how others will judge me,

and yet I do so. What astounds me most is that I looked down on Sarah. I was self-confident, outgoing and eager. I thought I knew everything. Indulged by my family, yet made to stand on my own two feet. Sarah was hesitant, with restricted thoughts, an unwillingness to go out into the world. Dogged by doctrine, she lived by the rules of others.

But I was not as independent as I thought. Sarah saw the world with all its faults. She had a grip on right and wrong. She was my best friend, and she never let our friendship diminish even though I rejected her and put her down. She saw through all the drama, the hormones and the mixed-up emotions. She rose with the truth when I drowned in it. She paid the price deemed necessary for her human fragility. She had honour where I had terror and cowardice.

Frankie's necklace creaks like a cranky chastity belt as I open the clasp. It slides from my neck. Its links chink down my breasts and land in my lap: a coil of little snakes, curling tightly shut in their death throes. If I had time, I'd bury it deep in the earth.

Vodka tastes weird without cola or lemonade and stings my throat. I press the tablets out of their little plastic cups into my lap. The internet search on my phone tells me the dosage. I'll take the lot to make sure. A couple of tramadols slide down to help the pain in my shoulder, marking the first step towards my end. The high-pitched buzzing in my ears retells of the explosive viciousness a curling finger can cause.

Hesitation illustrates the coward I am. Sarah did not flinch from her commitment to do what she thought was right. She knew she had to pay for her sins, and she delivered justice upon herself.

Her bare legs sway softly above me, and her clear pale face pulls into an indignant scowl as I fail to do what I should. I'm not brave or determined. I have to make a choice, but I make bad choices. I dither and do nothing but drop the tablets back into my lap. They bounce and mix with the links of Frankie's necklace.

Some escape and roll out of reach.

The girl is quiet: shocked into silence by the violence of my actions. She is rarely satisfied when I act on her urges to do the unthinkable tasks that she demands. Those I undertake always seem to fall short of her idea of perfection. She knows I'm a coward who simpers with fear. Who reneges on all but the things I can justify to myself. Killing a spider, undercooking Perry's food, driving on prescription drugs that cause groggy eyesight and a slow brain.

Experience tells me that she won't be quiet for long. How long after I move into the new Oaktree House will she start to play up? She'll swirl around my new home with more notions about how unjust my life is, how I fail to live comfortably on the foundations of disaster and death.

A fox walks along the fence towards the wood. He approaches quickly from the south-west with the wind behind him. He's young, not much older than a cub. He disappears behind a bush. I assume he will turn to move around the edge and change direction to hide behind the vegetation. He must know not to spend too much time travelling with the breeze and risk a predator's attack. To the west of me, I try to judge when I'll catch a glimpse of him, if at all. He breaks through the bushes and stops dead fifteen feet from me, making me flinch with surprise. He is the defiant teenager pushing the boundaries of safety.

We sit, the pair of us, not daring to move or give any indication of fear. The twelve-bore is out of my reach. I have long since forgiven the fox who killed all the chickens and reduced Sarah and me to tears of anguish. He watches me for a moment then sniffs the air before running off. Sensing that he is strongest, he finds little to challenge him here.

His absence inflames a feeling of loneliness and I envy him his arrogance, abandoning me here in this peaceful wood, on this cold day, with the sun's weak rays glistening on the leaves. A gentle breeze plays through the grass. If only this day could be captured and kept inside me where it could flow free and flush out all the evil and anxiety. If only life could be simple, straightforward, with easy rules. If only we could feel the certainty of the mundane mixed with the safety of the familiar, instead of life consisting of people with their own agendas, who hurt and use others to shore up their self-esteem.

The task that *the girl* has set me remains unfinished. Death is not what I want even if she persuades me that it will solve all my problems. I want life, I've always wanted life. The feel of the sun on my face and the grass below my feet and all that is good in the world. The enduring beauty of the harvest, the seasons, the sunshine and the rain. Family life has passed me by, yet I have survived without it.

A thought that there is still a chance to accept the life I have enlivens me. Do I have the power to adopt it? Can I kill *the girl* who has stifled and restricted me with her unfounded ideas about how her life should be? Can I at the same time exonerate Sarah and release her from all guilt? Do I have any power to make a difference?

There is a chance to put things right – a chance to be honest and responsible. The words required are easy, so, as soon as I'm put through to the police, I say them out loud.

'I killed Matthew Burcher and Perry Cutler. And I killed Frankie Dewberry. I'm sitting under the beautiful oak tree above the estate, just off the new ring road, east of Oaktree Cleave village.'

There. I've said it. It wasn't so hard after all. *The girl* has fled, killed by truth and confession.

'I forgive you, Sarah. I hope you'll forgive me.'

Sarah's feet brush my cheek as she flies free from purgatory. Neither of us will burn in hell. I'm sure of it. Hell is not another place at all. Hell is where you invite it to be. For the first time since my dad died, I give in and cry.

Epilogue

Sarah's letter to Carol

Wednesday, 30 December 1970

Dear Carol

There's no point living any more. My life is over. Not that it was a good life. It was an awful life and I couldn't make sense of it. I won't miss it so I'm doing the right thing.

When you stood over him with the gun, I knew you'd suffered too much for too long. I can't bear your pain, and I can't bear my pain. He didn't deserve to walk God's earth. He ruined us. He lied to me, said you'd split up, that you were only looking after Thora, that you were a nurse and nothing more.

That day you phoned he'd just dumped me because Lisa gave birth to Izzy that week. That's why he went home, not because of his mother. He told me when I told him I was pregnant and had insisted that we tell everyone. He didn't want that because my baby was the third baby. It was like they were toys, not real human beings, not our children.

He wouldn't tell you he was with me. He cared nothing for our child. Married to Lisa all the time and just messing about with the two of us. How could he? Lying is such a sin. I hate myself for believing him when he lied about the pair of you. Why did I when I could have asked you? But he told me to keep away and that you were fragile. That Thora's dying and death had made you unstable. That I'd trip you over the edge if you knew about us. That you'd kill yourself.

After Alice left me, I thought maybe he was right. I just needed the right man to sort me out. He was so lovable and treated me

304

like a princess and promised me everlasting love. And he smelt of you, and that gave me comfort, that your arms had held him as I held him.

You should have killed him, and my heart broke as you struggled. Why couldn't you hate him enough? He destroyed us. He made you hate me. He made us hate each other.

I was brave for you. I had to be. He was unconscious, so he didn't suffer, so I hope that will comfort you. It's a blur, the axe was heavy, but I had to do it. God gave me the strength when I needed it, like George slaying the dragon.

So, I've killed him, he's gone, and we're free. I'll go to hell to pay for my sins.

You hate me, don't you? Please forgive me for taking him. Don't think I killed him because you loved him and abandoned me. I killed him because he will destroy you. If you can't forgive me, then please pray for me so I don't burn in hell for too long.

Tell Mum, and Dad, and Matthew, I'm sorry because I can't live with the shame. And I can't live knowing that I can never tell you I love you. And that we can never be together. Not in the way I want us to be together. Because this world is too cruel and life is too strange and I don't know how to live anymore.

I hope that you will find happiness.

Your friend forever

Sarah xx

THE END

Author's note

I hope that you enjoyed reading this novel as much as I enjoyed writing it. If you did, I would be very grateful if you let me know by posting a review on Amazon.

Many thanks and happy reading!

Elizabeth Hill

Contact me at wickedwritersite.wordpress.com

www.facebook.com/wickedwriteruk